ONLY IN DARKNESS

BRENDA STANLEY

"We have to dare to be ourselves, however frightening or strange that self may prove to be."

— May Sarton

Massacre Rocks, Idaho, 1972

Volcanic eruptions and lava flow from millions of years ago formed the vast caves, tunnels, and jagged cliffs that line the Snake River as well as the narrow corridor that early pioneers named Massacre Rocks. Legend has it the area was the site of a clash between Mormon settlers and Shoshone Indians in the late 1800s, but there is little in the way of verifiable records of any event to constitute a massacre. Other names were given to the many cliffs and channels, including Devil's Gate and Death's Alley. In 1967, the area became a state park and a popular place for rock climbers.

Spelunkers came from all over the world to explore miles of caves and lava tubes hidden in the porous black terrain spread out for miles without anything else in sight. Most of these outdoor enthusiasts stayed near the scenic and well-traveled areas written about in the day's small number of outdoor magazines. Very few explorers ventured past the well-known cliffs with names such as Nailbiter and Sphincter.

Charlie Just and Martin Miller were looking for more than adventure. There were already incredible finds around southern Idaho, like the Minnetonka Cave and the Shoshone Ice Caves, which had brought fame and, in some cases, fortune to their discoverers. But the two scientists weren't searching for stalagmites and crystals like those found in the other caverns. What Charlie and Martin were searching for was something so odd and rare, the find would rival some of the most incredible treasures ever discovered. It wasn't just something that would bring them accolades in their field, but possibly change the course of history.

They had been out several times in search of the elusive cave. Still, after numerous discussions with past searchers and research into the accounts of what others claimed to have found, they felt confident they were at least within several miles of their life-changing find.

They searched for fossils found on a cliff's outcropping—a type of creature described as prehistoric. A steep descent from atop the volcanic rock cliffs above was the only access to where they had found the fossils.

The terrain was so brutal that even a small stumble resulted in bloody gashes if the rocks found their way around their leather gloves and thick canvas pants. The sweltering sun magnified the immense blackness surrounding them, making it impossible to be protected entirely without succumbing to the heat.

Martin threaded his rope into the descender of his harness, and then took up slack in the rope as he backed to the edge of the cliff. He clicked on the two-way radio attached to a strap on his shoulder, and Charlie did the same.

Charlie had secured the rope to a large boulder and had the safety line fed out and around to control Martin's descent speed. They gave each other a nod. Martin felt his stomach clench with excitement and wondered if it wasn't a sign that this one might be it. He could tell Charlie was thinking it, too. The research pointed to this spot, and now the time, climate, and preparation were all in their favor.

"On rappel," Martin said.

Charlie smiled. "Belay on," he said, giving the rope a tug for luck.

Martin took a deep breath and began the descent down the jagged face to the targeted outcropping below. It was there they hoped to find the rare and peculiar remains they sought.

It was almost one hundred and fifty years before pioneers crossing the Idaho desert plains came across the odd skeletal remains as they searched for passage across the mighty Snake River. A scout, scaling the rocky outcropping to see a narrower bend in the water, found the odd and mystifying skeleton. The bones were bleached white from the blistering heat of the sun and were lying as they had the moment they'd crashed to the solid rock surface—a skull, arms, hands, legs, feet, pelvis, ribs, spine—and something that protruded from its back in long, thin, web-like bands.

"Wings." It's what Orin Paul Jones, the scout who found the bones that day, had written in his journal.

His diary entry and rough sketch—along with similar writings of his brother Donald, whom he took to see it the following day—were the only recorded accounts of physical findings of the Winged Ones in North America. Martin was impressed with their detailed directions, descriptions of the landmarks and topography, and the geography's exact locations on their pragmatic maps.

Legends and folklore of the gorge's flying people had been that of ghost stories around campfires for decades in the small farming community of eastern Idaho. Tales of men leaping from the cliffs with large black wings exploding from their backs and demon-like eyes as they soared and swooped along the narrow canyons of the river at nightfall. Carvings of ancient native peoples in the many caves in the area known as Devil's Gate showed what some claimed to be the source of these folktales. The pictographs were crude and simple, brushed off as eagles and herons that filled the skies in the area. However, the writings of this young Mormon man were a recent discovery.

Lost in the attic of a relative, in a box marked Family History, the journals and three bone-like remains wrapped in cloth tucked away for decades were the first real evidence of something tangible. The remains were taken to the FBI forensic lab in New Mexico and tested. Two of the bones were human, a T-4 thoracic vertebra and a partial rib. The body of the bones was time-dated to have died around 1600 B.C. However, the third piece was indiscernible. It was bone-like with a leathery covering that was thick and hardened.

The report was inconclusive, not just in the type of bone or animal it came from, but its composition. The boney part of the structure was hollow like that of a bird, but found amongst the bones was an element unlike anything discovered before. It was a fine powder, but under the microscope, had a similar molecular structure to Cuben Fiber, one of the strongest materials on earth. What also made it unique is its thin and lightweight structure. While having long molecular chains and extra-strong intermolecular bonds like Cuben Fiber, this other material's discovery also had an additional element, making it unstable. When exposed to sunlight, the powder lost all its properties and simply turned to dust.

The scout's journal referenced the skeleton being sheltered from the wind and elements by an overhang and natural alcove that guarded it, and that he had left it with plans to return, but felt it shouldn't be disturbed. It was a sacred site. But then the journal took an awful and strange turn. It described his brother,

Donald's fascination with the discovery as competing with that of the Mormon prophet's unearthing of the golden plates.

His faith is faltering, and his countenance is turning toward that of one who rarely speaks and only grumbles when I discuss this with him. The other members are concerned, and the brethren feel he needs a blessing to bring him back, but I feel whatever is growing within him has already taken over his soul and can't be brought back. His eyes have darkened in a way that makes my own soul shudder when he looks at me.

Orin's entries continue to describe Donald's disenchantment with the church, and it isn't long when Donald's revolt turns from sour grumblings to violence.

One of the last entries in the journal describes Orin discovering Donald trying to steal the remains from the locked wooden chest he had placed there. The chest held some of the family's other prized possessions. In the first wagon closest to where the scouts rode was where Orin had put it for safekeeping.

When Orin caught him with the cloth-covered bones, Donald accused him of keeping the path of salvation from him and insisted on returning himself to retrieve the rest of the remains. When Orin threatened to expose his attempted theft, Donald furiously pummeled his younger brother so severely that Orin wrote his final journal entry months after the attack. Only then did he regain his sight. It told of the beating and the long recovery he had made and of Donald leaving before he could be caught and brought to justice.

I will close now and end this chapter of my life by putting away these bones and this tale and pray that no one else becomes so entranced by a prize that they lose sight of the path to our Lord Jesus Christ.

Genealogical records show that Orin Paul Jones, his wife, and four children reached the Oregon town his wagon train had set out for. Outside of Orin's journals, there are no mentions of Donald at all.

The journal and bones were found in the attic of his great-great-grandson's home, who died and then gave the house to a niece, who moved in and never cleaned out the attic until a family of raccoons made a nest and forced her to have the area cleared out.

Even then, it took a zealous neighbor to notice the box marked Family History and ask if she could read through the papers and journals. It was she who had discovered the bones and the connection to the writings.

Laura Holcomb never lived to see the result of her find. After the bones were sent away for testing, she demanded them back. When the family of Orin Paul Jones maintained their ownership of them, she threatened to find the skeleton's remaining pieces from what she had studied in the journals and maps. When a drift boat trolling the Snake River found her body in the brush near the cliffs' base the following year, everyone figured that was what she had set out to do.

It was a strange and forbidding pull the remains had on those who touched them.

The descent was smooth, but the sun was blinding as Martin pushed off the cliff walls about every few feet of the drop. There were few signs of life, except a bird spooked from its perch or a clinging bit of sage, but the view from the height of the gorge was breathtaking.

Martin figured he was three hundred feet down when the cliff tucked in and burrowed out into a small opening. It was just large enough to crawl into, and as he paused and looked into the shadowed hole, a chill blew and made him gasp.

He grabbed at the radio on his shoulder and pressed the call button. "I've found an opening. The air—it's bone-chilling," he said.

Atop the cliff, Charlie called out, "The colder the air, the deeper the cave. Is it the one?"

Martin looked below for the outcropping described in the journal. "I don't think so," he reported back. "It's too small. There's no ledge. I'm going to keep going, but it may be connected." He felt confident this wasn't it, but felt a bit disheartened, seeing how far he had dropped so far.

The valley floor wasn't far off, but the route the pioneers had taken to reach the ledge had been washed away by several years of heavy spring runoffs that pushed the river's flow into the base of the cliff, making it impossible to climb up.

Martin pushed against the jagged wall and continued his descent. His heart raced with the anticipation of it feeling real. His eyes scanned the face of the cliff, looking for signs of the telltale ledge. Then something small but solid hit his helmet and ricocheted into the canyon below. Martin looked up, and for a moment where the small cave had been, he saw a dark face looking down at him and then quickly pull back. At first glance, he thought it was Charlie, but then realized that was impossible. Even in the glare of the sun, the face wasn't the tanned-skinned and youthful bearded one of his friend and colleague. This one had the deathly glower of something Martin couldn't identify as human.

He grabbed his two-way and squeezed the button. "A face," he called into it. He blinked to try and clear his sight, but the thing was gone.

"Say again?" Charlie called back.

Martin began to squeeze the two-way again, but then wondered what he would say. Even he didn't know how to explain what he'd seen. He kept watching to see if it would reappear.

"Martin?" Charlie asked. "You there?"

"It's nothing," Martin assured him, but it was something. And he wondered if the heat was making him weak.

Then, as he was lost in thought, looking up at the ominous sight he had just witnessed, the outcropping he had been searching for came into view just a few yards from where he was hanging.

Martin paused, stunned at the way it had happened. He was still disturbed by the odd face in the crevice, and now this. For so many months, he had planned and researched this very moment. And in the acres of an unforgiving expanse of hardened lava, he was now at the needle of that immense haystack he had set out to explore.

He could hear his breathing inside his head.

This is really it, he thought. About twenty feet over, a discernible ledge was jutting from the face yet sheltered from the sun, wind, and rain. He grabbed onto the craggy cliff and moved like a clinging spider toward it.

Charlie must have felt the slack in the rope and called over the two-way, panicked. "Martin, what's happening?"

Martin didn't pause his crawl to answer. He continued until he reached the ledge and could stand freely on it. He took a deep breath and exhaled, smiling at his triumph. "I think I found it," he finally called to Charlie. "It's about twenty feet to your right. I'm standing on the ledge right now. It's about thirty feet across and maybe five feet out. The cave is pretty deep from what I can see and feel from here. I think this is really it!"

"Anything else?" Charlie asked, alluding to his hope that the treasure they both wanted to find still rested somewhere on that outcrop.

Martin was unhooking the carabiners from his halter and freeing himself of the ropes. He nodded in response to the anxious demands of the radio. Still, he didn't speak as he began to walk along the outcropping, studying the stony surface for any sign of the remains they hoped to find.

The journal had mentioned the bones being sheltered by an alcove on the outcropping. He looked specifically for an area that fit that description and saw a lip on the far side of the ledge that was curved and smooth, unlike the rest of the jagged surfaces. He started to walk to it, but as he passed by the cave's opening, something caught his eye, and he stopped.

In the darkness, he thought he saw eyes. Red and glowing orbs set back into the black cavern. Was it an animal? A marmot or a badger, perhaps. He stood staring back at the eyes watching him. A sick chill went through him as the thought of that face came back into his mind. Were these the eyes of that face? Of that creature? The eyes blinked, and Martin swallowed and took a step back.

"Well?" Charlie's voice crackled from the radio, shooting Martin's heart through his chest.

Martin grabbed for the radio at his shoulder and squeezed the call button. "I'm..." he looked up, and the eyes were gone. "I'm looking," he said absently. It took a moment to shake the jolt from his chest. Taking a few deep breaths, he continued to peer into the darkness, searching for the red flashes of light. When they didn't reappear, he brushed the incident aside and walked to the bowed-out edge for what he had intended to find. It was just as the journal had described; however, there were no immediate signs of bones.

He brushed the dust away from the floor of the concaved area, hoping maybe he had missed something. He searched the crevices and around the outside of the bowl-shaped area, but there was nothing to be found. He stood and took hold of the radio.

"I found the area, but there's nothing here," he called to

Martin. "I'm going to take some photos, and then check the cave."

"Nothing?" Charlie called back, sounding disappointed.

Martin rolled his eyes. It was as though Charlie was questioning his thoroughness. It was a constant irritation. Martin was well-aware he wasn't tenured like Charlie and had fewer years at the university, but his research was just as well-received, and his writings were far more extensive when it came to national publications. The only thing Charlie had on him was age, and that is why Martin was the one hanging from ropes and scaling cliffs while Charlie stood watching at the belay and finding fault whenever possible.

Charlie's original research partner hadn't even been able to hike the small path to the trailhead, let alone climb through the lava beds and granite walls to find their discoveries. Yet, when Martin and Charlie returned with whatever information they gathered, it would be Clinton Gregerson Charlie would call.

Professor Clinton Gregerson, the great archeologist who never discovered anything, but because of a journalist niece, was the subject of several sensational articles that placed him in the center of research and discoveries where Martin had done the majority of the legwork and actual unearthing, not to mention gaining a number of stitches and losing a tooth in the process.

Dr. Gregerson had always been gracious and, quite frankly, appreciative, both publicly and privately of the work Martin did. Still, Charlie's constant fawning served to wipe away any positive feelings Martin had for the professor.

Martin took his camera and snapped several photos of the wall, alcove, ledge, and the view to the top. He then clicked on the light of his helmet and hesitantly walked into the entry of the cave. Again, he scanned the area for the red-eyed animal— no need for a surprise encounter with a badger or cougar to ruin the outing and lay him up for days or weeks with another injury. He didn't carry a gun, but had a can of bear spray. Of course, using that within the small confines of a cave could be disastrous, making him wonder why he had it at all. He'd never had a bad encounter with anything other than a snake. That was a near-miss, but he was still always cautious. He knew that most critters would rather avoid humans, so he clapped his hands several times to scare off whatever belonged to those eyes.

The entrance of the cavern was wide and deeper than he expected. He was surprised there were no ledges or crevices along the walls because the eyes he saw weren't low to the ground but rather at eye level, and an animal would have had to be perched on something to be that height. He continued to look, convinced what he saw was simply one of the native creatures that inhabit the lava tubes, and nothing more.

The light bounced off the rough surfaces and then disappeared down a large black corridor. He paused a moment, and then noticed something out of the corner of his eye. In the light of his headlamp, he saw markings on the walls above him. He carefully made his way into the darkness and closer to the markings.

The light on his helmet picked up jutting crags and crevices as he went, guiding him on where to place a foot or hand. When he reached the area, he pointed the helmet light upward, and there the ceiling of the cavern opened up to show large carved drawings covering the walls and top of the cavern.

It was then he realized he was standing in a large domed room, and even with the minute amount of light from his headlamp, he could see that the carvings were detailed and massive. He stood awestruck as the light followed each area of the room and each section of the incredible sight. It was both beautiful and horrifying. Large winged creatures, swooping and soaring all over the walls of the cavern. Dark bodies with blood dripping from their teeth, claw-like hands, and evil-filled eyes.

Martin quivered. The eyes. Those eyes.

He took his camera and clicked on one of the light cubes, and snapped more photos using the flash. He decided to go back out and relay what he'd found to Charlie.

As he turned back toward the corridor, he spotted something in the corner of the room. He directed his headlamp at it. It was a tomb—a coffin-sized stone box tucked into a cavity along the wall.

A chill went over him. Was this the alcove mentioned in the journal? Had he read the entry wrong?

The tomb was settled securely in the carved recess of the rock. Its placement, along with the ancient pictographs, equated in his mind to something remarkable. This was big.

He walked to it and ran his hand across the stone surface. There were markings carved into the heavy lid, and he removed his headlamp and held it directly toward the marks to see what they were. In the dim light, and with the dust, he couldn't make them out, but they were apparently writings, which excited him.

He felt along the edge of the lid and pushed it, moving it slightly open. He placed the headlamp back on his head and used both hands to give the heavy cover a solid heave, and was able to push it open enough to see inside.

At first, he thought the tomb was empty, but then he noticed a shimmer. He reached in and tried to touch it. Filling the box was a sand-like powder so fine, it danced in the movement of Martin's hand. The small specks danced and glistened. He felt nothing, but could see it, and the sight was mesmerizing.

"Oh my," he whispered. His breath made the crystal dust waft up toward his face and out of the box. It made him almost giggle with delight, and then he heard a clamor behind him, and he turned.

The headlamp caught a dark form flash from the room, and he heard the sound of steps.

"Who's there?" he called, surprised.

Only silence. He stood up and let the headlamp search the room.

"Hello?" he called again. His heart began to pound. He tried to tell himself it was the animal he had seen before, but he knew the steps were no animal. He took the bear spray from its holster and walked toward the corridor, back to the cave entrance. The face in the crevice, the red glowing eyes, and now this. He had seen enough to know something wasn't right, and it wasn't just his imagination playing games. He needed to get out of that hole, that dark trap, and get free. Screw the finding; he would come back—with others and a gun.

He followed the path out with quick steps and felt his breathing release when the light from outside peaked through the rocks. Before even calling up to Charlie, he grabbed the rope, stepped into the harness, and latched the carabiner. He strapped himself in, took the radio, and made the call.

"Bring me up. I've found something amazing. It's this huge room. There are pictographs everywhere with..."

Martin stopped. Something was peering out from the darkness. The same red eyes.

"What?" Charlie prodded, anxious to hear.

Martin felt his stomach clench as he watched the eyes grow larger. They were coming toward him. He began to walk backward, pulled on the rope, and called frantically to Charlie, "Take up the slack! Take up the slack!"

He ran to the ledge and watched as eyes came out of the darkness. His entire body went weak at the sight of it. "Who are you?" he gasped into the radio before dropping it.

. . .

Charlie heard Martin's frantic words, but was still pulling up the slack. He then felt the rope quickly lose tension. He gave it a hard tug and felt it give. He grabbed the radio. "Martin, what is it?"

There was only silence.

He called again and waited. He tried a third time and still nothing. He tied off the rope, went to the edge of the cliff, and bent down to see anything that could explain the problem.

From the cliff above, he could see what appeared to be Martin lying on the ledge. He strained in the afternoon heat of the sun to see more, but the distance and brightness were too much. From his perch above, he could see his comrade wasn't moving, so he went back to where he had tied off the rope and began to pull.

It was carrying Martin, but it was not the weight he expected. He tugged furiously and brought him up a reasonable distance, tied the rope off again, and went back to where he had looked over before.

He could see the top of Martin's helmet, and while still strapped into the harness, he looked limp, arms hanging at his sides. Charlie went back and again frantically began to pull. He heaved until he could see Martin's head at the edge of the cliff.

He tied off the rope and went to him quickly. He bent down and placed his hands under Martin's arms and began to pull him onto the cliff ledge. That is when he realized the reason the weight was so light. When he lifted Martin onto the edge, Charlie reeled back in horror. There was nothing more to Martin than a head, shoulders, and chest. From his waist down, there was nothing but bloody tendrils and dripping fluids. Something had torn Martin's body off at the waist.

Charlie fell to the rocks and scooted back, screaming uncontrollably. The jagged rocks cut into his hands and legs, but he felt nothing. His chest heaved as he clasped a bloodied hand to his mouth, horrified and stunned at what he saw. He scrambled up and began to run, stumbling over crags and fissures in the black lava terrace.

As he ran, he searched for signs of their vehicle, parked at the base of where they had begun their hike. Whatever got Martin would surely have heard his screams and know he was there. Charlie pushed himself onward, frantic, half-mumbling and half-praying, into the empty dry heat of the wicked desert. The truck was his only chance for shelter and escape, and he kept his focus forward, begging under his breath it would soon come into view. When it did, a small gasp of relief escaped him.

The spires of the sun beat down on him, and when he grabbed the handle of the truck door, he flinched back as it burned his palm. He grabbed it again and flung the door open. Once inside, he closed the door quickly, locking it as well as the passenger side. He frantically searched for the key. It wasn't in the ignition. He rummaged through the cup holders, glove box, and center console. It was Martin's truck, and Charlie's hopes sank as he realized the keys were probably in Martin's pocket.

He let out a defeated cry. He looked under the dash. He'd seen the hot-wiring of cars in the movies and television, but he wasn't a "car guy" and knew almost nothing more than checking the oil.

He looked over the sparse and arid land leading back to where his dead friend still hung. His heart pounded as the gruesome sight of Martin's body filled his mind. He felt his stomach heave as Martin's last words rang in his head. *Who are you?*

"Who?" Charlie whispered to himself, horrified at what that could mean and knowing that whoever did it was still out there.

TWO

Massacre Rocks, Idaho 2017

They drove in darkness. It had to be dark. No moonlight, only the headlights of the car as they made their way to where the city disappeared from view, and so did everything else. That is until the fall when some unsuspecting hunter came upon the remains.

But that would take months.

There was still a week or two left before the snows came and hid things, at least what the animals didn't scavenge, and then what was left would show no signs of what happened.

Most of the time, they were never found, and no one seemed to notice or care. They were the bottom feeders of society. Sex offenders, mostly. They had served their time, usually, for a repeat offense—they always repeated—and unlike murder, their cases weren't high-profile. They were shuffled away both by the justice system and the families who bore the shame of sharing their name. So when they came up missing, it usually wasn't much of a concern but a relief.

The interstate off-ramp led through the Massacre Rocks

state park and toward Devil's Gate Pass, a fitting name for what, according to history, had happened there years ago. Lester Isom had begun referring to the area as "the garbage dump" when it became their routine place for what they had to do. It wasn't a description of how that stretch of Idaho wilderness looked, but rather what they did to it.

During the day, it was a rugged and awe-inspiring country —barren high desert with jutting basalt rock cliffs and sage-covered plains dotted with black lava boulders. At night, it was one of the darkest places in the world. Far from the ambient glow of a city and nestled in the large bowl of an ominous and isolated canyon.

"James Tinker." Richard read the police file as Lester drove. They always made the trips together. They hadn't officially worked as a team since Richard had retired years ago, but this was one assignment neither intended to quit on his own. It would have to be taken from them somehow by others who, by some unfortunate happenstance, ended up knowing the same ugly secrets they did—taken over because they would both be dead before what they must do was finished.

"His victims were a six-year-old and an eight-year-old. Little girls. He didn't even deny it." He closed the file and turned toward the backseat of the car. Their transport was still out cold.

Lester stared out at the road and slowed the car to make the turn. "Is he awake yet?"

"Nah," Richard replied. He slapped the back of the car seat a couple of times. "Wake up, Tinker!"

This startled Lester. "Jesus!" he snapped as he swerved the car and sat up straighter.

Richard turned back around and put a hand up. "Sorry. I'm just losing my patience. I'm getting too old for this shit."

Lester huffed. "Getting? We've been too old for years."

"Where am I?" a voice mumbled from the back seat.

Both Richard and Lester glanced back, noticing James Tinker was awake. They turned back around.

"Think he'll be a problem?" Lester asked.

Richard shrugged. "I've quit trying to guess."

It was Richard's duty that had brought them to the desolate and dark Idaho dessert. The past had Lester tied to it, but Richard had a commitment and an overwhelming stake in it. When he'd decided years ago, it was easy, but even though he had learned to dull his emotions and rationalize the task, he was fully aware of the vile depth of what they were doing.

"Where am I? Who are you?" Tinker asked.

Richard and Lester remained silent as Lester pulled the car into a gulley and away from the dirt road. The car heaved and bumped over the terrain. Headlights in the dark illuminated only quick glimpses of ragged trees and large craggy boulders.

Tinker was jostled about in the back and he complained with loud groans. "What the hell?" he mumbled when the path began to smooth.

It was then that Lester put the car in park.

"What's going on?" Tinker tried to sit forward, his hands cuffed behind him. "Am I going to jail again?"

Lester and Richard got out of the car, and Lester opened the backseat door. He reached in and pulled the large man out by his arm. James Tinker was forty-five and over six feet tall. He had never been married or had children of his own, but made his living as a choir director at a local youth center. That was where he'd stalked and groomed the numerous young children he befriended and eventually molested.

Tinker tried to look around in the cold dark expanse. "What are you going to do?" he asked. For his size, his voice was high-pitched.

Lester took keys from his pocket and unlocked the hand-cuffs on Tinker's wrists, but the man flinched away.

"Fine," Lester said. "You can keep them on."

"Tell me what you're going to do!" Tinker yelled.

"On or off?" Lester asked, unaffected.

Tinker turned to Richard, hoping for a better response. "Are you going to shoot me?"

Richard shook his head. "Nope. We're going to let you go."

Tinker looked around, his eyes wide. "Let me go. Out here? Why?"

"On or off?" Lester asked again.

"Fine. Off!" Tinker said frantically, and he turned and offered his hands to Lester.

When the cuffs were off, Tinker stood and rubbed his wrists. Lester folded the cuffs and put them in his pocket with the keys, and both he and Richard turned and started to get back into the car.

"You're just leaving me out here?" Tinker asked again, walking toward them.

Lester sighed. "Yep." He hesitated. "Oh, wait, I almost forgot." He leaned in and picked up something from the dash-board of the car.

Tinker flinched, but noticed in the glow of the headlights that the object was a small metallic whistle.

Lester put it to his mouth and blew, but there was no sound.

Tinker looked at him strangely. "What was that?"

Lester ignored his question and simply got in the car and closed the door. Richard began to do the same, but Tinker lunged toward him, grabbing at his arm. "You can't just leave me out here."

Richard turned and blocked him hard, knocking him to the ground. "I'd say you have less than a five-minute head start, and you'll waste it if you try that again."

Tinker scrambled back to standing, stunned at what he'd heard. "What does that mean?" he yelled.

Richard slammed the car door, and Tinker stood in the glare of the headlights, confused and irritated. As the car pulled away, he was soon alone in complete darkness. Soon, the sounds of his breathing were the only thing replacing the rustle of the tires on dirt.

For several minutes, Tinker stood shivering, wondering what Richard had meant by a head start. Were they coming back? Was someone else on the way? And what were they planning to do to him? He tried to listen, but heard nothing in the distance. They were gone.

"This is probably some stupid game they play with newly released inmates to make themselves feel like real men," he grumbled. "Take them out and leave them in the middle of nowhere for the night."

He huffed, then he sighed. Without any better ideas, he decided he would try to find his way back to the road.

He took a step, and as he did, he heard something like a scratch on a rock. Looking up to where the sound originated, he saw two glowing red eyes staring back at him from a distance.

He froze, not believing what he saw in the blackness. He blinked, trying to focus. Was it real, or just his mind playing games?

Then the eyes blinked, and a horrid chill rushed through him. His breath sucked in, and before he could let it out, the eyes disappeared. He swallowed, and the stillness of the night made it sound so loud, even his heart pounding sounded like thunder. So black. There wasn't a speck of light, and his eyes darted through the darkness, trying to find the red orbs again as his body stood frozen in place.

Another scratch from the side, and he jerked toward it. Frantically, he scanned the dark void—nothing. He waited—not breathing, not moving a muscle. Then he started to wonder if what he'd seen was just an owl or other creature of the night. He'd probably scared it away.

"This is silly," he said. "It's exactly what they want, to stick it to me." He let his shoulders relax, and he gave a small huff. Licking his lips, he took a deep breath, and then the anger began to set in.

"I did my time. Who are these cops to think they were better than me? Like they don't get their jollies off of young girls, too. They just never got caught. They probably kept my stash of photos for themselves, the self-righteous assholes. Jealous is what they are. Why else would they do this?

"Fine, I'll play your little game," Tinker said quietly to the darkness. He wrapped his arms around himself in preparation for a long cold night. "But I'll win."

"Not tonight," a low whisper came from behind him.

Tinker screamed and leaped up. He bolted forward, unsure where he was going, stumbling over sagebrush and rocks. He ran in the complete blackness, but a branch or stump tripped him and he fell. He rolled over and put his arms up, blocking his face. "Who's there?" he called out.

Silence.

He waited, gasping and frantic. When nothing happened, he slowly lowered his arms and tried to see something, anything, in the dark. "What are you doing? What do you want from me?" he called out. He kept looking as though something would materialize out of the blackness. Did those eyes belong to that voice?

Again, he paused and waited in the silence—nothing. The stillness was driving him mad. Swallow. So loud. The thing that was out there could surely hear him. Laying on his back with his belly exposed made him feel cold and vulnerable, so he rolled over and pushed himself up, hunched over and kneeling. He shivered. Cold? Or was it merely terror? It was undoubtedly dread.

"Take whatever you want." He reached into his back pocket for his wallet. "You can have it," he whimpered.

He waited. Still trying to see into the abyss, he whispered, "Just don't hurt me."

The red eyes appeared just above him. "You won't feel a thing."

Tinker screamed, but then the rip of flesh and gurgle of breath and blood filled the night, and then just as quickly, the silence returned.

CHAPTER

THREE

Milo

Massacre Rocks, Idaho 2017

I stand looking off the cliff at the raging river and jagged boulders below. I'm going to jump—or rather, let myself give in to it and just fall. That I know. What I don't know is what will happen next. There are two ways it will end, and the more I think about it, the more trouble I have deciding which result will be worse. Often, it's the not knowing that makes life hell. I've been in the dark and unaware for so many years. Now I know what I am. But it is the unknown of what that fate holds for me, should I survive, that makes me shudder.

I've lost my family, my friends, and everything I've ever known, and still, someone, or something, is out there hunting me down like an animal, trying to take what has completely altered my life. The only thing I do know is I'm going to take the leap. It will be a rush for a few seconds, and then I will hit the rocks and hopefully die instantly or—and this is what I can't fathom—if what they say is true, my back will explode, and I will transform into what my grandmother and the others of the tribe call the Winged Ones.

At that point, I will soar and begin a life of uncertainty, or I will be unable to work my new wings and crash to the ground, and all they will find is the evidence of what could be the last of my kind. It's a terrible fate, either way. I don't want to be alone. I don't want to live the rest of my life in isolation, afraid of who wants my curse and willing to kill me for it. I want to love, but they tell me there is no chance of that unless I follow those who have turned. I don't want to believe that, and the only way I will ever know the truth is if I take this first step.

My name is Emilio Chavez. I go by Milo. There was nothing special about my birth. My mother was alone from the beginning. She never talks about my father, so I'm not even sure if he's still alive. I have my mother's dark hair and eyes. My last name is hers, not his, so I don't even have that from him. I was a normal baby, and it wasn't until I was about three years old that the concerns began.

It was my mother who noticed it first. Or at least she was the first one to say anything.

She was drying me off after a bath and noticed the irregular ridges along my spine. The skin covering the bumps was dry and scaly. It wasn't a rash, but a distinct and hardened covering.

My grandmother looked at the patches, but stayed silent.

"Does it seem to hurt him?" my mother asked, her eyebrows knitted in concern.

My grandmother only shrugged.

That night, my mother showed my back to my grandfather. He saw the odd ridges and looked with forlorn eyes at my grandmother.

"What is it?" my mother asked, seeing their shared glance of concern.

My grandfather gave an apologetic smile and left the room. It seems that is when he began to retreat from our lives. I had always found my solace with him. My mother and grandmother argued continually. My grandfather was quiet and would whisk me away from their quarrels and outside where he'd find a nook or hollow near the lava rock cliffs near our house.

There, he taught me games with rocks and sticks or told me stories about other worlds. When he weaved his yarns, it was about strength and truth, and how being happy was important, but even more so, you should do what is right and stand up for that. Being so young, I didn't completely understand what it all meant. I just relished the colorful tales and my time with him.

As the ridges on my back became more prominent, my mother took it upon herself to douse me in lotions and creams, trying to soften the scaly patches, but nothing worked. She hesitated to call the doctor, hoping it was nothing more than a childhood ailment, but after several months, she finally insisted.

"I'm worried about him," my mother said as she fingered the ridges along my spine.

"Don't do it, Cassandra," my grandmother insisted when she learned about my appointment with the doctor. "They will only make it worse. It isn't something they will understand."

Confused, my mother took me from my grandmother's arms. "Understand?" she asked indignantly. "They will be able to help him. What if there's something wrong and he needs treatment? You want me to keep him from that?"

"Those doctors won't understand," she urged.

My mother rolled her eyes. She knew how my grandmother felt about doctors and hospitals, and she grew tired of the old ways and paranoia of anything associated with the modern world. They continued to argue until the day of my appointment.

My mother refused to listen, and she took me to the pediatrician. The doctor shuffled in, rarely looking up from his clipboard, ran a hand over my shoulder blades several times, gave a few befuddled hums, and wrote out directions on a small pad of paper.

I was diagnosed with a rash, and the doctor prescribed a thick cream that my mother applied to my back each night. It seemed like a simple fix, yet the wound between my mother and grandmother needed more than ointment.

As much as my mother hated to admit it, the ointment didn't work, and the growths on my back became even more prominent. This only intensified the tension in our house. I lost my grandfather on the eve of my eighth birthday. I had no idea what the connection was between the ridges on my back and the reason why he was gone.

My mother insisted on finding treatment from doctors, and that's when my grandmother did what she'd hoped she never had to do. She broke her silence and told her daughter about the curse my mother carried. A misery that was now mine.

"Your father came from the tribe of the Munzi in Nicaragua. He came here with others to escape. They were feared and hunted there. For a long time, they lived without problems. But then the others found out they were here and came after him. They'll come after Milo, too."

"Who will?"

"The same ones who came after your father. They'll know Milo has it. The men of the tribe pass something along to their sons. It is something only given to the boys. That is why you are free of it. We thought it was gone. That it was over."

My mother huffed in exasperation. "Are you saying my son is cursed?" she asked. "He has something on his back that needs treatment. Nothing more."

"It is a small thing now, but it will change as he grows. He will die if we don't take him to the colony. Only there will he be safe."

My mother's face turned red with anger. "Do you realize how crazy you sound? I don't want you around him if this is how you feel."

Esmeralda took my mother's hands. "I love him more than my own life. That is why I'm telling you this."

Her tone was so steadfast, it sat my mother into a chair. She fell silent. She blinked and just shook her head, confused.

"You need to know so you can protect him. Please, Cassandra, listen to what I say. It's what killed your father."

My mother scoffed. "I know what killed my father. Stop making up stories to try and erase what he did."

My grandmother sighed, defeated. "I know what you think, but I know what I'm saying is true. I saw it with my own eyes. Your father..." She paused a moment and brought his image into her mind. Her face went sad. "Your father was one of the last of their kind. He told me it only affected the boys, so we thought it was over when you were born. I didn't think about..."

She turned to me as I sat on the sofa watching my favorite cartoon, pretending to be oblivious to their discussion.

"Emilio." She said it in a tortured whisper.

"What is it?" my mother demanded. "Why can't the doctors help him?"

"It isn't something they understand. It's not of this world."

My mother stood up and put her hands to her face. "What? Not of this world?" she bellowed.

"Cassandra, please!" my grandmother pleaded. "If you don't listen, Milo could be hurt or worse."

"How?"

"The doctors don't understand what this is and think it is

cancer. They try to remove it, and that is when they either cripple them..." she searched for the words. "Or worse."

"So, if it isn't cancer, what is it?" my mother asked. Her tone was both demanding and accusatory.

My grandmother's face was pained. She dropped her eyes.

"Am I supposed to let him suffer? Do nothing?" my mother demanded.

My grandmother motioned to me. "He isn't suffering. It is part of him. When he's older, we can take him to the colony, and they will know what to do."

"What colony? He isn't some type of leper."

My grandmother shook her head slowly. "No, but he isn't like us and will need their guidance."

"I'm not handing my son over to anyone."

"Cassandra, this is bigger than you and me. He will need to be with those who can help him."

"He needs a doctor!" my mother exclaimed. "Handing my child over to a bunch of voodoo people isn't going to help him."

My grandmother lowered her head and spoke softly. "Cassandra, I know how you feel about what happened to your father, but the people who knew your father are the ones who know what Milo needs to survive. If we don't go to them, he will die."

"How can you say that?"

"I'm telling you this because I love Milo. I don't want to see him hurt." My grandmother turned and watched me as I stared at the television.

"If this is what happened to my father, then I want no part of it."

Esmeralda took an exhausted breath. "It's been years since I've seen any of the people of the colony. I wouldn't even suggest it, but Milo needs help."

"What is wrong with him? Tell me!"

"I'm trying. Please, Cassandra," she pleaded with my mother. "All I can tell you is I know what will happen if you don't."

FOUR

Milo

My grandmother, Esmeralda, was born in the middle of a sugar beet field. Her mother was so afraid of being caught and sent back to Mexico that she refused to go to the hospital. Her husband was a Mexican migrant worker, and neither had visas or any legal documentation.

They found work on the corn and potato fields in eastern Idaho, and Esmeralda grew up on the farms that employed her parents, learning only enough English to get by.

The family lived in a small house in an isolated migrant community on the outskirts of the small farming town of American Falls, Idaho. The small group of homes sat on a butte that lined the Snake River's lava rock cliffs. The homes were buffered from view with large juniper trees.

They stayed to themselves, and except for work, they stayed away from the outside world, finding what they needed within the community. As their numbers grew, their social ills grew, and with that often came the outside world. It wasn't long until the community disbanded and families went their separate ways. However, everyone in the community held a piece of that culture brought from their homeland in Mexico.

Years later, Esmeralda married my grandfather, Jorge Chavez, a Nicaraguan refugee who fled that country in 1973 during the Sandinista revolution. He lived for a short time in Arizona, but eventually moved to Idaho after finding work in the fields and then taking a job on the railroad. Jorge and Esmeralda met at a Catholic Church Christmas party in the city of American Falls, Idaho, which, after living in the tiny town of Aberdeen her entire life, was considered the big city for my grandmother.

After a very short courtship, they married, and Jorge convinced her to move to a small house across the reservoir at the base of the black lava rock cliffs that jutted from the Snake River. It was technically in the town of American Falls, but the closest home was over two miles away. At night, the sky was so dark, you could see the lights of an oncoming car for miles before it ever reached the home. My mother, Cassandra, their only child, was born two years later. Not surprisingly, it was a home birth. My grandmother's fear of doctors started early, and since the baby was healthy, she saw no reason to expose her to any unnecessary prodding.

For many years, I didn't notice or understand my grandparents' isolation and apprehension about the world. Even when I started to question their odd behavior, I had no idea just how horrific their reasons for hiding were.

My grandfather, at least, had his job at the railroad and his friend Richard Wilson. Those two things weren't connected, but Jorge clung to them as constants in his life, giving him some ability to communicate with the outside world.

My grandmother's refusal to learn English had her feeling

isolated and like an outcast. She doted on my mother to the point she'd wanted to home-school her. My grandfather practically had to pry his daughter from her fingers to get her on the school bus.

I don't remember my mother talking about it much. Still, I know she never brought friends to the house except for Mitchell Wilson, and that was only because Mitchell had been coming to the house since he was a baby and was already used to Esmeralda's "ways." Mitchell's father, Richard, was my grandfather's best friend. When I was young, before things changed, Richard would come by the house almost every Sunday afternoon to drink coffee on the porch and talk.

My mother and Mitchell stayed friends in high school, but Mitchell went to the Pocatello trade school and became a police officer in town after graduation. My mother took a job at a fertilizer plant and got an apartment in the city just north of that. She worked there for a year, but when she became pregnant with me, she couldn't afford daycare and rent, so she moved back in with her parents.

At first, Esmeralda was smug and often condescending about the circumstances surrounding my mother's situation. Still, when I was born, it was as if it gave Esmeralda a new purpose, and the mood of the house lightened.

I redirected her focus away from my mother and squarely onto me. She doted on me constantly, and when given a chance, wanted to take over just about everything. Surprisingly, this didn't upset my mother as much as you'd think, mainly because she got some much-needed respite from her demanding newborn. It was as though I was the panacea of harmony for the two of them. As a child, I spent so much time with Esmeralda, I can still trace every line in her spindly hands and smell the Amami hair-setting lotion she used at night.

However, when my grandfather died, and it was just the

three of us, that dynamic changed and the household became an always simmering pot that, depending on the day, one or the other had their hand on the dial, just waiting to turn it to boil.

Soon, my grandmother's suggestions for anything that concerned me, regardless if they were about my back or not, were met with rolled eyes and resentment from my mother. My grandmother became quiet when my mother was around, which wasn't often. My mother's work schedule was demanding, which had Esmeralda at home alone with me. When my mother came home from work, my grandmother often stayed in her room or went for long walks amongst the solitary and dusty cliffs near our home. But when it was just the two of us, it was as if someone had flipped on a light, and her inner being was allowed to come out and enjoy the sun.

During the summer, this often happened because my mother went to work and had to rely on Esmeralda to watch me during the day. However, when I went to school, our time alone was limited, but from the moment I came home on the bus, and the three hours before my mother got home from work, my grandmother and I had hours to talk, and she wasted none of it.

She said she was preparing me for what she had tried to warn my mother about years before. Looking back, I'm surprised that what she told me at that age didn't frighten me. It may have been the animated and passionate way she told what my future held that made it seem almost like an honor rather than an ailment.

"You are one of the Camazotz, the great Winged Ones, who fly at night," she told me as I sat in the large cushioned chair in her room. "You will have a long life and no disease, but you have to obey the law of the Munzi, or evil thoughts will overtake and destroy you."

Sometimes, she sat on my bed; other times, she paced as she

spoke, always wearing one of her floral cotton dresses and dark lace-up shoes. My grandmother was nothing if not consistent in her daily routines. She was always bathed, dressed, and done with her chores before anyone was awake. As a child, I wondered if she ever slept, having never seen her in a night-gown or without her black and silver hair neatly pulled into a knot at the base of her neck.

She told me the ridges on my back would someday evolve into spectacular expansive wings that would let me soar through the skies and carry me away from the burdens and enigmas I faced on the ground. Those wings were not only a vehicle for me to rise, but they also were the source of freedom and well-being for others, too.

Her animated face was like watching and listening to a cartoon or comic book written about me and my future. Her green eyes sparkled, and she used her weathered hands to describe the exotic names and stirring images of what I could expect. I was enthralled by all of it. Every day, I looked forward to coming home from school and listening to the story of what I was to become. The imperfection on my back wasn't my burden, but my prize.

"There are things we are born with that other people don't understand and may look at us as strange or different, so we keep those things to ourselves. That doesn't mean those things are bad. Sometimes, those things that make us different are what makes us exceptional," she told me. But she always warned me about talking to anyone, especially my mother, about our discussions.

It was during these warnings that her face grew sad and cold. She said my grandfather had died because he hadn't obeyed and that I had to keep everything she told me a secret. She said people and evil creatures out there would be trying to find me once they knew about this special thing I was.

My life for those years was surprisingly simple. I don't remember anything being difficult regarding the growths on my back or any other treatments or problems that they caused. But it was sometime around my fourteenth birthday that all of that changed. It was then that the pain began.

CHAPTER

FIVE

Huna's story
Masaya, Nicaragua 120 B.C.

When Huna was only five years old, he knew what love was. Not the love he felt for his mother, but true love that burned into his chest and made his heart ache. He knew because that was what he felt for Daisel.

Daisel was from the village while Huna lived in the chief's palace. It was a large stone building with many rooms and an open courtyard surrounded by a canal. It sat high in the jungle above the mountain they called Masaya.

Huna's father had died before his birth, and his mother Akna was the chief's royal healer, so he was raised in the palace with the chief's only son, a boy his age named Xbalan.

The chief was kind to Huna and treated him like a son, which Xbalan resented. The two boys spent most of their time with Akna and rarely saw the chief, but each was eager to please and strained against the other for his attention when

39

they did. Xbalan may have been the heir to the throne, but Huna's agility and striking appearance gave him favor with the king. It frustrated Xbalan, and he grew to hate Huna.

Huna was unaware of the rift with Xbalan, having been consumed by his longing for Daisel. He rarely thought of anything or anyone but her. To see her, he had to travel through the brush and trees to where she worked in the fields. Together, they hiked the lush hills and lava tunnels that spread out from the watchful and volatile mountain that provided everything they needed in this life.

"This one is so dark," Daisel whispered as they crept with hands outstretched into the blackness of a cave.

"It's far enough," called Huna. It wasn't so much the dark that scared him, but what might live inside.

"The Winged Ones are below," Daisel reminded him. "They don't live in the caves above the lake."

"How do you know this?" he asked her. "Who taught you this?"

"We all know the stories of the Camazotz," she said matter-of-factly. "They are of the Munzi tribe. They live far beyond in the valley below Masaya. They fear the great god and stay away. Masaya protects us."

Daisel continued to rattle off the stories of her youth. Huna wasn't sure if she even believed the ancient legend, but it was a good argument to persuade him to go with her.

When Huna still seemed hesitant, she rolled her eyes and huffed. "Maybe I should bring Xbalan instead. He doesn't seem so scared."

It was no secret that Daisel also entranced Xbalan. Because of this, Huna made it a point to sneak out to see her without him knowing.

"I'm not scared," Huna snapped.

Daisel turned away from him and smiled. "Then why do you want to run home?"

"It will get dark soon, and they will send out sentries to find me."

She raised her hands to the sky. "The sun is still high. Go if you must. I'll continue on my own."

Her voice was steadfast, but he still hoped she would turn around. Stories of the Camazotz, or the Winged Devils, said they lived in the caves and flew at night. They lived on blood and had talons on their black wings that were so sharp, they could slice a large boar in two with one swipe. The tales of these flying killers were enough to keep all the children close to home when the sun began to set. Huna had never seen them, no one had, but tales of their deadly deeds were enough to give him angst.

Daisel, however, seemed to have no fear. She was brave and stubborn with eyes so green, her dark skin and hair made them stand out like fiery emeralds. When Huna took her hand in his, he marveled at how delicate and soft it was. His, by comparison, even as a young boy, seemed large and abrasive.

"The view from up top is so beautiful. Please, Huna," she begged him.

He sighed and followed her, but the closer they got to the caves, the more he felt the goading pull that was getting worse every time Daisel convinced him to go there. He didn't know if it was something in the trees or brush that surrounded the area. He wondered if it was their pollen that made him feel strange. Or was it the mist that hovered in the air and coated the rocks and plants that lined the path? Something made his ears ring and his heart race the closer he got to those cold dark caverns. They became more foreboding with each visit to the daunting place. He was unsure if it was his reaction to the flora or fear of getting caught.

The older the two children got, the more daring Daisel became, and when she finished her chores, she waited for Huna in a large buttress root of a tree as he came to the fields to meet her.

It delighted Huna to see her, but he always tried to change her mind when he learned her plan to explore the caves. The stories of the Winged Ones pressed on Huna's mind, and he felt the odd stirring whenever they got near the caves.

Xbalan would try to follow, but even though he was the same age as Huna, he was not as tall or strong, and Huna wouldn't wait for him. It made Xbalan feel dejected and angry, and he would sulk off only to return and sneak behind them—just out of sight—and watch as they explored the forbidden caverns. Sometimes, he tossed rocks to land nearby and startle them into thinking something was there in the brush. It pleased him to see Huna act cowardly in front of the girl. He hoped she would see his weakness and toss Huna aside for him.

By the time Daisel was fifteen and considered old enough to marry, she had become one of the most striking and beautiful girls in the entire Catzu tribe. Her waist-length black hair shined like the wings of ravens. And her once thin and gangly frame was now becoming round and supple. Huna was so drawn to her that he had never even considered marrying another, and when Xbalan declared that Daisel was to be his queen, Huna was furious.

Huna went to find him and confront him, and when he did, Xbalan was defensive and unrepentant.

"I will soon be king," Xbalan said smugly. "Would you deny her the role of a queen?"

"I'll never allow you to have her," spat Huna.

"You have no say in the matter. The arrangement and the marriage will go forward."

Huna lunged at him and took a swing, catching Xbalan off-guard and connecting with his jaw. The punch knocked him into a table and sent the dishes on it, clattering to the floor. Xbalan was stunned, and Huna pounced on him and continued to hit his face.

The noise brought several sentries and the chief into the room. Huna was pulled off, but continued to shout and flail.

"Stop this!" the chief ordered. "This is the law of Masaya. Xbalan will someday be king, and he made his choice and fulfilled his duty as the next in line. You will accept that, or you will leave."

Huna was still panting and furious, but his emotions turned from anger to overwhelming sorrow. He shook himself free of the sentries' grips and stormed from the room.

When Akna found him, he was out where the stream pooled and the trees bent to form an alcove to hide within. He was distraught, and when she tried to comfort him, he brushed her off.

"This is my fault," Akna said.

Huna shook his head. "How? How are you to blame?"

She began to cry.

"You're taking fault for Xbalan's deceit? Stop protecting him."

She continued to weep. "I've failed him, too. What I did to save you both will now be your defeat."

"I won't lose Daisel. I'll die first."

Akna closed her eyes, knowing he had already sealed his fate.

. . .

When Daisel heard the news, she was distraught. It was Huna she loved, not Xbalan, and when she refused, her mother slapped her for not appreciating what the god Masaya had given her.

"How can you deny your family and your village these riches? How can you refuse a future chief?" her mother scolded her. She continued to berate her unappreciative daughter until Daisel just sat despondently.

When Daisel was finally alone, she ran from their small adobe hut and toward the large tree where she and Huna always met. Soon, he was there, looking as frantic and dismayed as she was. They clung together and cried.

They felt helpless and angry, and even though they knew they couldn't run from their horrible fate, they went to the caves to find solace.

Maybe it was grief, maybe it was desire, but the warm and windless day and the darkness of the cave gave Huna the courage to cup Daisel's face in his hands and kiss her. After all these years, it was their first.

"Let's leave together. We can live somewhere else," Huna said.

"How?" Daisel asked, unconvinced. "We have nothing."

"I can gather what we need and take gold from the palace." She looked forlorn.

"Do you want to marry Xbalan?" he asked.

"No!"

"Then what choice do we have? We will have to leave."

She sat for a moment in thought and nodded. "Yes, we have to leave."

They had to go back and act as though they had accepted their fate until Huna could gather what they needed for their escape. They had to act soon, as the marriage was to happen the night of the blood moon.

Having made their decision, they simply held each other until emotional exhaustion overcame them, and soon, they were asleep. It wasn't what they'd planned, and when they awoke, the night had folded around them. They both knew the wrath they would endure if they were found alone together after dark, so they decided to have Daisel go back to the village first and Huna to leave later.

"We'll continue to meet at the tree. I will bring what I can, and we can store things in the cave until we have what we need," he said.

She agreed, and he kissed her again. Daisel looked afraid as she left him, turning back just before the moon's glow dipped behind the hillside.

Each day, they met and took their supplies to the cave. It was becoming more difficult for Daisel to get away, especially after announcing she was the future queen. The people of the tribe gave her family gifts, and everywhere they went, the people of the tribe treated them like the royalty she would soon become. Watching her parents' joy made her sad about what would happen to them once she escaped and left them to face the shame. However, the idea of marrying Xbalan and living her life without Huna was too much to bear.

It was almost dusk when they rushed back to the village after a day of bringing more supplies for their escape. They had decided they had enough to get them from their village to the tribe of the Munzi.

They would be able to hide with the Munzi, and with the gold Huna had taken, they could live until they were able to find a permanent place in the tribe. It wasn't common for migrants to come to a tribe seeking solace and a new life. And often, it was because of an unwanted marriage arrangement. However, it never was someone who would be the next queen.

They hurried along the path through the brush, holding

hands. Coming through the trees and along the cliff leading to their village, they were startled by sentries waiting for them. They had nowhere to run. The sheer drop of the cliff held them captive.

When the chief stepped through the group, his face was both disappointed and annoyed, and when Huna saw Xbalan standing just behind him looking smug, Huna started to make excuses. The chief simply put up his hand and shut him down.

"You've betrayed me after I allowed you to live in my home like a son," the chief announced.

Hearing his father speak of Huna in those terms enraged Xbalan, and he lunged at Huna with a Quebracho wood sword. The swift thrust hit Huna at the neck. A spray of blood shot into the dim light of the moon as Huna went over the side and disappeared into the black abyss.

Daisel was stunned, and when what she'd witnessed hit her, she cried out, "Huna!" She fell to the ground in a heap of sobs, shivering in the night air.

"Take her back to the palace," the chief ordered the sentries.

Xbalan stood defiant as he watched the sentries lift her to her feet.

Tears streamed down her face as they led Daisel down the path and up the hillside to the palace. There, she was placed in a solitary room.

Xbalan refused to be humiliated, but when he went to her to exploit her fear, she still rebuffed him. This only aggravated Xbalan more.

Masaya rumbled and spit. The people of the tribe saw the display in the distance, and Xbalan blamed Daisel's defiance for God's anger. To punish her for her rejection, he offered Daisel as a sacrifice to Masaya. This way, he could appease their god and avoid the shame of her rebuff.

When they told the members of Daisel's village that she

would be the bride of Masaya, they all danced and cheered at the announcement. Being the queen of the tribe was a great honor, but being the bride of their god was beyond imagination. A girl from their village, as the bride, meant prosperity and special protection from evil and the great Masaya's wrath.

CHAPTER

SIX

Huna's story
Masaya, Nicaragua, 120 B.C.

Deep in the lush and shadowed jungle, Huna hid. The slash across his throat and fall from the cliff wasn't enough to end his life. He wasn't sure why, as he lay bruised and bloodied at the bottom of the cliff, but something odd had happened, something miraculous, allowing him to survive what should have been a violent end.

He heard the news of Daisel's impending sacrifice as he hid in the outskirts of the jungle. He watched the other members of the village congratulate Daisel's family. They brought goats, woven blankets, and other gifts in hopes of being blessed by association.

As the great god continued to roil and throw flames into the air, the tribe became anxious as the day of the union grew closer. They were counting on this virgin bride to appease the god and bring calm to his fiery rage.

Huna didn't believe the stories the elders told about the girls tossed into the crater. The tales of them living forever and

49

watching the tribe from their mountain thrones was something he may have believed as a child, but that was no longer the case. And now that it was Daisel, it didn't matter what great gifts possibly awaited. The only care he had was to save her.

It was one of the darkest nights of the year when Huna quietly crept the distance from the cover of the jungle to the area of the palace where they were holding Daisel. As a child, he had explored the many tunnels and passageways of the palace. He knew all the secret places to hide and get around unnoticed. But in the dim light of the moon, when he crept closer to the palace wall, a familiar voice startled him. It was Akna.

"Come," she said, and directed him to a dark recess where they could talk.

"I knew you were alive," she said, cupping his face.

"You won't talk me out of this," he warned her.

"Please, Huna. She isn't the one for you," Akna said.

Huna looked at her with rage. "She's the only one."

"No. It can never be. Even if you were the heir and could choose her, it will never be. You can't marry outside of your tribe."

Huna was still indignant, but confused by what she said. He raised his shoulders in question. "She is my tribe."

Akna nodded. "No. I tried to save you. I thought what I was doing was right, but you'll always be one of them. Your being alive is proof of this. You need to join your true tribe."

"True tribe?" Huna asked. "We are Catzu."

Akna lowered her eyes. "No. You are the son of a Munzi."

She then explained the secret she had held for so many years. "Chief Cordoba was unable to father an heir. The tribe was becoming anxious and fearful that the great god Masaya looked unfavorably on their ruler. I was a healer and was in the jungle gathering plants when I came upon a young Munzi sentry with two infants. I hid in the brush and watched. He had drawn his sword, but he knelt by the babies, unable to fulfill his duty.

"Because they were twins, they were considered a curse, and it was the young sentry's duty to kill them both to rid the tribe of evil. But as the young man watched the babies squirm and squeak innocently, he could not do the deed, so instead, he abandoned the babies in the jungle. I breathed a sigh of relief, and as the cries of the young ones began to echo throughout the jungle, I saw it as a sign from the maker.

"I gathered them up, and knowing the chief's desperation for an heir, took one of the boys to the Catzu chief, claiming the great God had blessed him with a son. Chief Cordoba was so happy and relieved that he made me his new son's nursemaid and invited the other child and me, who I passed off as my own son, to live within the palace walls. The two boys grew up in the same house, never knowing they had shared a womb and their blood—Munzi blood. It was a secret only I knew, along with the dire results it could bring."

"That's a lie," Huna raged.

"It is true. It's the reason you stand here today," Akna said apologetically. "You should go and be with the Munzi. They are your true people."

"They are evil. That is why the chief has banned them to the land below. I am not like them."

"Evil is only what you allow. Please believe me, Huna. You must go."

He huffed. "I'll never allow them to kill Daisel."

"There is nothing you can do. If you try to stop it, they will simply kill you, too."

"They already think they have. They won't expect me." He paused and looked at his mother. "Unless you deceive me."

Akna was panicked. "I love you, Huna. I would never hurt you. That is why I'm begging you to leave. Go and be where you'll be safe."

Huna did leave, but not where Akna had hoped. Instead, he went back to his hiding place within the jungle to make his plans and wait for his chance.

Daisel was despondent as she sat alone in the small cold room in the palace. It was Huna's former home, and yet, she'd never been inside. If it weren't for her horrific state, she would have admired the opulent furnishings and smooth stone walls inside. In her chamber was a small window high above that let the sunlight tease her, and she could hear people walking by, making taunts and insults about how sullen and thankless she was. Daisel didn't care what they called her. She didn't care about anything anymore.

She had just begun to envision her life with Huna. It was disheartening to see that most of those who had captured them were from her own tribe—former friends and cousins. Even her father was amongst those hunting her down.

She'd been locked away in the palace for mere minutes when they brought the midwife to her room to determine if she was still a virgin. The examination was invasive and disturbing, but what should have had her feeling violated and disgusted only left her numb. Daisel was not surprised by the announcement that she was pure, but that didn't comfort her. All it meant was that she would again be offered as the virgin bride and dropped into the fiery depths of Masaya.

When the midwife was gone, Daisel stood and walked to the room's small opening and tried to peer out past the guards. The pain of her family's betrayal and what she soon faced fell over her like a cloud, but it was the loss of Huna that devastated her, and she wept. The vision of him lying dead on the ragged rocks below the cliff filled her mind. Nothing mattered now. She closed her eyes in sorrow and went back to her dreaded waiting.

The next morning began as a day of celebration to prepare her for her future as a goddess. She was bathed daily, blessed, and placed in the ceremonial robes of the chosen one. Seven days of feasts and festivals were planned, and then to thank the god for all he gave them, they would offer Daisel as his new bride.

The Catzu tribe lived in the villages above the mountain's large caldera. They built their homes into the hillside, and the chief's palace sat on the highest terrace, looking over the valley. The room where Daisel stayed wasn't visible from outside, but she could see the orange and yellow colors of the sunrises and sunsets from the thin, long window at the top of the room. This is how she counted days to when she would be carried on a throne to the top of the mountain and tossed into the fiery mouth of Masaya.

Her days were filled with silent meals with the chief and lessons from elderly women on sitting, holding her head, and not making eye contact with anyone. Each morning, she was bathed by the wives of Chief Cordoba and rubbed with scented oils.

Her hair was combed and plaited and tied up with vines and flowers. They lined her eyes with dark ash and stained her lips with berries from the Ometepe bush. Only then was she allowed to be outside her room, even if it was only the chief and the others of the household who saw her. Daisel had never been dressed or primped over and wasn't used to the touch of strangers. It all felt awkward and uncomfortable, and she cried at night when she was led back to her isolated room. She missed her old life, but mostly, she missed Huna.

Her mind turned to him often as she was being painted and brushed. She wondered if he would have found her alluring with her decorated face, scented body, and elaborate clothes.

During their night together, he had held her close, but that was all. He didn't touch her in the places only a lover seeks out, and she wondered why.

Her heart fluttered and her skin tingled when she thought of this. If only they had enjoyed more time together.

When she awoke from her daydreams and her pondering about Huna stopped, the reality of what she faced came back, and she cursed herself for being absurd and thinking of such things. Daisel saw her reflection. She touched her face and studied herself. She was an object, an ornament they would toss to her death in the hope it would bring prosperity to the tribe, and here she sat, wondering how Huna would have felt about how she looked.

At night, she thought about her mother's stabbing words and her father's triumphant expression at finding her. Didn't they care about what was about to happen to her? Or would their status and new affluence overshadow any love they had felt for her? They had to know the pain and anguish she would suffer. Do they so easily push those thoughts aside? This all added to her feelings of despair and loneliness. They all knew her fate, and yet, went on enjoying her lot and eagerly awaiting her doom.

When the day of the marriage came, they took Daisel from her room early in the morning. Instead of her regular bathing and dressing routine, she was covered in shawls and taken to the temple. Once inside, the elders blessed her and offered a gift of gold jewelry or precious gems she would wear on her special day. When it was time for the elder of her own village to present his gift, she looked at him with pleading eyes, hoping that his past connection with her would do something to change her fate. He looked into her eyes, and then looked to the floor as he handed her the jewels.

She felt his hands tremble as they transferred the gift, and this made Daisel begin to cry.

"Enough!" the chief shouted, upset that Daisel was showing emotion.

The women in the room huddled around her, wiping her tears as the ash streamed down in dark lines from her eyes. They hustled her away from the elders and did what was needed to bring her back to looking regal. They didn't comfort her and were firm in their warnings about bringing disrespect upon her tribe and village—the same way her mother had scolded her.

Daisel knew that even if she escaped death, she could never return to her old life. She would be an outcast and probably killed anyway for the scourge she would bring to her people. At least her death as the chosen one would have her hailed as a goddess and always loved.

When they placed the last of the gold and jeweled chains around her neck, she was barely able to sit up straight. She felt the weight on her shoulders, and she tried to stay upright and steady.

They dressed her in a heavy tunic woven with the finest silk and gold strands and braided long-stemmed flowers into her hair. Then they placed a tall gold and gem-studded crown on her head. Before being led from the temple, they smeared more of the red stain on her lips as a final touch.

Daisel was helped onto a large platform and seated in an ornate chair. Flowers covered everything, and their smell was overwhelming and made her nauseous. She had been offered food and wine, but had none of it. Now she wished she had.

The sentries, eight of the tribes' strongest men, filed through from the temple's side door. Dressed in white robes, with their faces painted in the ceremonial marks, they each took their position, then lifted the platform with large poles laid underneath. They wobbled enough to make Daisel grab the sides of the chair and give a loud gasp, but they soon had the poles on their shoulders and the platform level. She took a relieved breath only to feel the dread of what lay ahead.

CHAPTER

SEVEN

Huna's story
Masaya, Nicaragua, 120 B.C.

Huna was at the caldera, waiting with the crowd. It was dark, and he blended in, wearing a cloak that covered him. He kept his gaze low and gently squeezed his way to the closest point where he could to see Daisel brought out.

A large platform built for the ceremony jutted out over the caldera's rim. She would fall into the dark pit below. Only her horrified screams would be heard and then slowly shrink away until only silence remained.

Huna looked around at the different groups of the Catzu, knowing Daisel's family were surely attending the sacrifice. Having Daisel be the chosen one would make them proud. This thought disgusted Huna.

He didn't believe in this god of the volcano, but even if he did, he knew nothing measured up to his love for Daisel. No amount of harvest, or rainfall, or lack of disease was enough to make him feel it was worth losing her.

Their last day together destined what was to come. They were drawn to each other as children, but the previous year had them both sensing a change. Neither knew when the other had gone from childhood affection to passion, but it filled them both.

The early morning of their final day together, as they stored their final cache in the cave, they had slipped away, down into the streams that led to the Munzi tribe. They both knew it was forbidden to go near the village of the Winged Ones. But like his skepticism of the god Masaya, he also doubted the stories of the bloodthirsty men and the strange power they possessed.

Both Huna and Daisel must have felt the impending doom, and they pushed their fears aside to enjoy the beauty of the jungle, as they had for years as children. That budding physical urge kept nudging them, and as soon as they were away from the borders of their tribe, their bodies seemed to reach out for each other. When they found the first thermal pool, the pull was so strong that they were losing pieces of clothing and were tangled together in long kisses before they were even in the water.

Huna ached for her, but the heat of the water kept him from being able to enter her, and when they heard voices in the brush, they quickly found their clothes and hurried back to their village.

Had they been caught, it meant death for them both, and yet, neither cared, so the passionate embraces and lingering kisses continued before they left each other's arms forever.

It was that day, those caresses, and that last deep look into her dark green eyes that he would never be able to forget or forgive. He couldn't let this happen. His love for her was the only thing in this life, and if it meant losing everything, so be it.

But it was Daisel, and just the mention of her name sent throbbing jolts of pain through his entire body, so strong that his audible groans were uncontrollable and had those around him taking steps away with looks of disdain.

He stood at the edge of the caldera, watching as the ceremonial procession approached. The crowd's chatter went silent, and then came together with a low and loud gasp merely at the sight of her. Having been sequestered away from her family and tribe, they were surprised to see her transformation from a girl to a goddess. Her striking black hair glowed from the torches that lined the path to the platform, and her dark painted eyes scanned the crowd, mesmerizing all who looked upon her.

Huna struggled forward, wanting her to see him, but knowing the immense number of bodies and faces staring out from the torch-lit night overwhelmed any chance of her locating him in the crowd. And even if she did, she wouldn't believe it.

Just the sight of her made Huna push his way toward her. He had to stop this.

The crush of bodies was thick, but he heaved them away and moved closer. When he came to where he was in earshot of the large ceremonial platform at the rim of the cliff, he stopped and waited. Chief Cordoba was on a pedestal beside a large ramp leading to the caldera's edge. It was eternal darkness—a never-ending black void. Farther out, the hot lava bubbled and danced in the dark.

The chief had begun to praise Masaya when Huna broke free of the crowd and came up behind the platform. He raised the cloak from his head. That was when Daisel saw him.

Her eyes went wide. "Huna," she said, surprised.

The chief heard her voice and stopped, stunned that she had dared to speak. He looked at her and followed her gaze to the outcast standing staunchly in the middle of the crowd.

For a moment, he stood perplexed.

Xbalan came to his side, his face showing fear and angst.

"You. Back away," the chief ordered. He nodded to one of his men, and the large, muscled sentry came forward.

"Stop," Huna ordered. His eyes fixated on Daisel, and his voice was so sure, the sentry hesitated. "She is not pure!" Huna shouted.

The chief gathered his senses, and then scoffed at Huna's attempt to ruin the ritual.

"Huna?" Daisel was still shocked he was alive and now unsure of what he was trying to do.

"She is mine!" Huna yelled out to the masses. "I have had her!"

The chief puffed out his chest and turned toward the crowd. "I know this to be untrue," his voice boomed. "I have seen for myself that she has had no man. She is pure, and Masaya will be pleased with his new bride."

The sentry stepped toward Huna, who ran and stopped just at the edge of where the immense chasm dropped off.

"Masaya will see your lies and kill us all!" Huna motioned to the volcano. He made a swooping movement, not only to the chief, but also to the masses watching.

The crowd murmured and began to stir, throwing Daisel odd looks and whispering to one another. This angered the chief, and he turned to the sentry who was already going after Huna.

Huna avoided the sentry and ran through the people, who backed away from him as though he were diseased. The sentry followed, but Huna fled and tried to run closer to Daisel, but as he got nearer to the platform, a man from the crowd came forward to try and stop him. As Huna tried to avoid the man's grasp, he stepped to the side. The caldera's rocky edge crumbled, and his footing gave way, the ledge began to slip, and

Huna felt his fate. He looked at Daisel, and her eyes showed the horror of what was about to happen.

For a moment, he tried to catch his balance and his eyes begged for it to be so, but before she could breathe, the rocks began to fall, and along with them went Huna. She watched as his face disappeared into the darkness.

Daisel collapsed to her knees. She sobbed, "No!"

The crowd gave a horrified gasp. Some of the women put their faces in their hands; many people looked to the chief. They had expected to see the young girl fall to her death, but not a young man as well, and certainly not one who had professed to take the virginity of the girl who was to be the bride of their god. What did this mean?

Cordoba stood tall. "The great god Masaya knows what is true and right, and he saw fit to take the one who would cast doubts and lies. We bring Masaya this bride who is pure and good, and in return, we will all be blessed with a bounty."

Two of the sentries lifted Daisel to her feet and removed the large tunic. She was red-eyed and shaken as they walked her to the edge of the platform. It was there that a section was cut out and held up with a hook attached to a rope that would be pulled at the appropriate moment, dropping out and sending her to her death.

The sentries stood her upright and left her standing alone, shivering and broken with a sea of eyes upon her. It was not the regal and gratifying sight desired, but the chief carried on, despite what had happened.

Daisel stopped her tears and simply waited. At that point, the vast depths of the hole didn't frighten her. All fear or care had left her when Huna had fallen to his death. She had been able to stay strong before, even in the knowledge that she would soon go to that very place. It was odd, but even facing death, there was something in the knowledge that he would still be alive that kept her heart alight, and now that was gone.

"Oh great God, Masaya," Cordoba chanted with his arms outstretched. "Take this our most pure and beautiful one as your own and bless us in return." It was quick, but he needed to get it done and over with so nothing else could go wrong. With that, he nodded, and a sentry pulled the rope. The hook caught and the platform shook, but refused to release.

In a frustrated growl, Xbalan rushed forward, pulled his sword, and plunged the weapon into Daisel's chest. Her eyes went wide with shock, and she stumbled back. A gasp and then a series of shrieks and screams came from the crowd. Xbalan watched, still fuming as she vanished over the edge in a harrowing, tumbling drop. But as quickly as her fall began, it stopped with the flash of black and a loud crack.

From the depths of the fiery chasm, a dark-winged creature shot up and caught her mid-fall. Its immense, black wings stirred the cinders and fanned the fire, spreading a blast of hot, ash-filled air over the crowd.

Xbalan began to run from the platform, but before he could, the beast swooped down and, with a single swipe of his wing, flung Xbalan into the air and over the edge. His horrified scream echoed out, then faded as he dropped.

The villagers scattered, crying and running frantically from the caldera and into the cover of the jungle.

Watching as they panicked, the demon flew low over them, feeling the rapid pulse of their heartbeats and wanting to kill them all. But instead, the creature turned back toward the cliffs, and with Daisel held close, vanished into the black night, leaving the masses terrorized and wondering if he would return.

. . .

When the demon was gone and the shouts and cries diminished, an eerie silence fell over the valley. Soon, those who had witnessed the event began to return from the jungle, fearful but wanting to know if what they'd seen was real. They crept with wide eyes and mouths agape.

Chief Cordoba emerged from the trees with armed and ready sentries, their eyes scanning both the caldera and the sky. He had watched the beast rise up and take his only son. What other scourges would he face?

The stunned and panting people were riveted, waiting, and wondering if the winged creature was what they had always feared. After cautious watching, the faces then turned to the chief. He stood hunched, still shaken, but when he saw his subjects looking to him for guidance, he tried to pull himself back to a regal stance. His mind reeled, refusing to believe what he had seen. This couldn't be. The storied winged and murderous creatures had been part of their folklore for years, but no one had ever actually witnessed the beasts. But he had seen the demon. He had witnessed the menacing power, and his people had, too.

Cordoba stared into their horrified and confused faces, but stood tall. He knew he must remain strong and carry on as their leader. Even if his courage had vanished, a show of weakness would ruin his stature as chief. He ordered the sentries to move closer—a show of strength, with their swords and arrows. He turned to face his people, and in the quiet stillness was when the murmurs began. It started low and hushed, but then the name Cordoba dreaded began to surface, first in whispers, and then in audible unison. "Camazotz."

Cordoba put up a hand to stop the banter. But then, the low rumble of voices turned to a loud chant. "Camazotz. Camazotz. Camazotz." It was useless trying to stop them. He, too, had witnessed the horrifying sight. It had happened so quickly, but he'd seen the immense spread of wings and heard the deafening call. And he had also looked into its face.

As the chanting continued, realizing what the creature was, or rather who he was, settled in his mind, and the heart-wrenching dread of what this meant sent a shiver through him.

When Huna, the young man he had brought into his palace and treated like a son, fell into the crater, he didn't meet his death but instead had become one with it. He had become the Winged Devil. The Camazotz was real.

If what the legend said was true, the adrenaline-inducing fall exploded the buds forming in Huna's back, releasing strong, expansive wings to catch his fall and bestow upon him the miracle.

Cordoba began to rack his brain about the Camazotz. It had started with those called the Munzi. They had inhabited the valley and mountains surrounding Masaya for many years. Still, they were not like the other tribes, and horrifying tales of large, murderous, bat-like creatures began to slither through the villages' huts.

A group of men, fearful of the tales, went to the Munzi tribe with weapons, and when they didn't return, it fueled the beliefs of the menacing creatures the Munzi had become.

The other tribes banned together and forced the Munzi into the rocky cliffs below Masaya. There were threats of death and the destruction of their villages if they strayed outside that area. To make their point, they took a dozen young men and pushed them into the mouth of Masaya, both a sacrifice and a declaration.

Before this tragedy, so many generations had passed since anyone had come in contact with the Munzi tribe that most thought the stories of the Winged Ones and even the war as mere fables. Tales of the Camazotz were what parents told their children as warnings for misbehaving, and those children grew up doing the same with their children. They had never thought they were actually real.

The chief and elder members of the tribe were now faced with the grim reality that the imaginary demons that haunted their dreams as children were confirmed.

The people of the tribes would look to Chief Cordoba to save them. But he, too, was in fear of what this meant. He recalled what he had heard growing up. The Camazotz were the Winged Ones with a thirst for blood and strange and powerful magic that flowed through their veins. At the onset of manhood, these boys became flying killers. The stories were both provocative and frightening, and after witnessing the scene at the sacrifice, he knew they were real.

Chief Cordoba then thought of Akna. Huna was *her* child. She had come into his tribe, into his home, with the gift of a son. What curse had she brought along with her? Akna's story of finding Xbalan as a baby also filled his mind with worry. Did he, too, have a connection to the Munzi? Could his son, his heir, also have had the blood of the Camazotz? Even with Xbalan dead in the pit of Masaya, he might still face the blame for the curse. If his home had been breached with their kind, how many more of these young men hid amongst the tribe, carrying the blood of the Winged Devils?

Cordoba had to decide how to handle this threat and keep the finger from pointing his way. He gave his first order. "All boys of a certain age are to be taken from their homes and detained." He could feel the fear and agitation growing within his tribe, and along with the danger, he didn't need a rebellion.

Cordoba used their fears of the Winged Ones to justify what had happened and gain support from his people, playing upon what they had witnessed and reminding them of past tales of torn-off heads and ripped-out hearts of those who stepped out of line.

He placed his spiritual leaders at Masaya. "Pray for forgiveness in the loss of the virgin bride and watch for any sign of the Winged One," he said. "Shoot it down if it appears again." He then spoke to the crowd. "Go back to your separate villages and pray that Masaya will not retaliate against you." What he needed was unity against this new threat. It could be a powerful part of his reign, or it could lead to his fall if it got out of his control.

In the days that followed, Masaya played along with rumbles and spits of smoke and debris, which gave Cordoba the chance to shout that the god was angry at the tribes and expected full compliance with what the chief was commanding. But on the third night, the earth shook throughout the valley. At the volcano's mouth, the sentries witnessed shoots of fire from the crater, higher than they had ever seen. The glowing bursts landed closer each time, and the ground threatened to open and swallow them. It was so haunting and intense, the guards fled back into the jungle, hoping to hide.

It was the only warning received of what was to come, and it wasn't enough. The storm of fire and ash that rained upon a number of the tribes below Masaya was daunting and complete. No one living in those tribes survived, including the entire Munzi tribe.

When the fires had died, and the rains came, the people of the Catzu and Tobo tribes who had lived on a mountain above the volcano ventured down to survey the destruction and see what remained of the ones they once feared.

What they found was a charred graveyard. Most of the area was a wasteland, but in the hills surrounding the cliffs where the Munzi had lived, the ash was thick, and the people were covered, having died, frozen in the position of their last moments of life. Perfectly preserved formations of bodies cast in solid ashen tombs. Children huddled with mothers—lovers in a last embrace. People hiding, shielding themselves, trying to avoid the inevitable. And throughout the village was the sign of that tribe's hidden anomaly, the distinctive trait of the legendary creatures called the Camazotz: bodies lying with the bloom of wings from their backs.

EIGHT

Huna's story
Masaya, Nicaragua, 120 B.C.

Deep in the jungle, near the dark lava cliffs just outside of the Munzi tribe's decimated village, was where Huna found a place for Daisel and him to hide. No one would search for them there. It was one of the few places below the mountain that Masaya's massive torrent of lava and ash had spared.

Huna was convinced, even with the decimation of the Munzi, that the people of the Catzu and Tobo would be hunting him for taking their god's bride. He took a deep breath as he laid Daisel on the cool, wet vista. Seeing her bruised and soiled face made him cringe, but the rise and fall of her chest gave him hope she would live. He had saved her, brought her back, and now waited to see what that meant.

She was breathing, and he could feel the beat of her heart, and while she had drowsily opened her eyes several times, when the memories flooded back, it was too much, and she soon fell back into a weary stupor.

She had died that day. Even though he'd saved her from the fiery pit of Masaya, the sword that pierced her chest had stopped her heart. But the miraculous phenomenon that caused Huna to sprout wings had also produced something even more incredible to course through his veins. And now her life was his, completely.

Huna found shelter back in the cave—their cave.

It was near a small stream and pond, and he left her there until he could scan the area and secure its safety. He also needed to leave her. The desires to take her were strong, and the pains he felt leading up to the explosion of wings from his back had returned. But this time, the desire was for something more than her body.

He loved her dearly, but the urges weren't for the nakedness of her skin and throbbing in his loins. These desires were to rip her throat open and tear her flesh to shreds. It scared and confused him, but it was becoming so strong, he knew it would overtake him if he didn't leave her and eliminate the urge.

The desire wasn't there in the daytime, but at night, the pounding in his head and chest took over, and like a beast, he ran toward the cliff and launched himself from it into the night, allowing his wings to burst out and catch him, releasing some of the urges, but unfortunately not all.

In the blackness, he rose above the trees and felt the valley floor for movement. As he soared through the cool air, he could sense the heat of life below, and his body shifted and moved toward it. His heart pounded, knowing that what he needed was coursing through the veins and flesh of an animal, and it was getting close, so close.

As he searched with glowing eyes in the darkness, he came upon the prey just outside a thatch-roofed hut. The waft of Huna's wings startled the creature, and it looked up and began to run.

Without thought, Huna swooped sideways and, with his wing, took the beast's head from its body with one clean swipe. With a turn, he pounced, crashing to the ground as he landed. Then, he was at the severed neck, sucking ferociously. The blood not only gushed into his throat but out of his mouth and down his neck and chest.

After several minutes, he leaned back, caught his breath, and stared at the bright flush of the moon. He was satiated. The desire to kill was gone. The blood covering him was thick and still warm. He stood and looked at the mutilated, headless body. And then the comprehension set in. This was no animal. He hadn't killed a deer or a boar. This was a woman. Horrified, he felt his stomach's fullness and realized what it was, and he became sick. He fell to his knees, but his body held it in. He needed it. The desire was so strong; he had no control and no care for what or who he killed. This is what I've become, he thought. The uncontrolled urge to have it would come back. He knew it, but when? He thought about Daisel. How would he keep her safe from him? And what will she do and think of him now?

When he got to the cave, he didn't sense her there and became frantic that she was gone, but when she emerged from the dark lava hollow, he immediately felt her pulse beating, and his heart calmed. Her eyes grew large at the sight of him, and she stepped back and put her hand to her mouth in horror.

Huna felt the clotted blood covering him and cursed himself for not washing it off before coming to her. He went to the small pool of water and tried to remove it from his face and hands. Then he went to her. His wings had folded behind him, but he knew she could still see them as he stood looking down at her huddling in fear.

"You're right to be afraid. I am one of them. I'm a monster," he said. He knelt next to her.

She started to weep and put her face in her hands. "But you can't be. You're Catzu," she cried.

He reached to her and pulled her hands from her face. "Look at me," he said.

She couldn't do it and continued to cry and turn her face away. Then she noticed her own hands covered in blood. She wiped at her face and realized it covered her mouth. She looked to him with both fear and question.

"You're alive. It's all that matters now," he said.

She shook her head, unaware of what he meant. Through wet red eyes, she peered at him. "Am I? How can that be?"

He looked down and swallowed hard. "This is what I am, and we can never return," he said. He released her hands. "I will never hurt you. Do you understand?"

She took her hands back and wrapped her arms around herself, turning away.

"Do you understand?" he asked her again.

She gave him a cautious look, and with tears still falling, she nodded.

He didn't push for more that night and left her alone by the tree. Huna laid a mat and other items he had taken from the village close by and then made himself a place to sleep where he could watch the area, and her.

Daisel was tired, but now that he was asleep, she could study him in the moonlight, and that was all she wanted to do. She remembered her fall, and then seeing his face in the glow of the molten lava below in the caldera. How had she survived? She saw cuts and bruises all over her body, but no pain. She felt nothing more than tired.

The horror of seeing the person she loved transformed into a demon and then plummeting into the volcano, she still wondered if it was just a dream or if the blow from the fall had knocked her senseless. And if this was real, Daisel wasn't sure if she wanted to be alive.

She watched as his breathing became loud, and his face relaxed. In the white light of the moon, she studied the shape of his nose, jawline, and curve of his mouth. It was him, but so much had changed. His chest was bare—the scar of the sword's swipe still visible at his neck, and shiny streaks of blood mixed with the dirt and sweat of the night. He was no longer the village boy or even the young man she had kissed in the pools. In just a matter of days, Huna's back had not only grown large wings, but the once supple and thin form also seemed to have aged and hardened.

The blood on him wasn't what scared her, but rather, it was the fury in his eyes just before he'd left her. The look wasn't one of passion but of predator, and it gave her such a sense of dread, she knew her life was in danger, and to see it gone when he returned covered in blood, she knew what he must have done, and it was only a matter of time before it was her blood covering his face.

As she watched him sleep, she wondered what strange creature he had become and what that meant for her. He had rescued her, but was she truly saved? The other tribes would see her as a curse, so they would never allow her back, and she had no idea what was in the jungle past the small hikes she and Huna had taken when they were young. They were on their own and facing a life of isolation, if not a life of constantly being stalked and hunted. The worries and wonders clouded her mind, and soon, the haze of confusion lulled her to sleep.

In the morning, Huna awoke, afraid that Daisel was gone, but when he bolted up, he found her still huddled by the tree, asleep. She started to stir, and then the happenings of the night before must have returned to her mind, and she shot from her dreams to find him staring at her. She drew her legs in closer, and Huna felt his heart sink.

He was hungry, but not for blood. It made him wonder when the frantic urges would return and how long he would have to stay with Daisel and try to bring her back to him. She was distant and scared, and he wanted her to look at him like she did before.

Later that afternoon, after he had made the shelter stronger with limbs and thatch to protect against the rains, he knew they needed more than just the berries and bugs he had been able to gather that morning.

"I'll go get food," he said. He looked down and saw the blood splattered on him and went to the stream to wash more completely. He removed his clothes, and Daisel watched both intrigued and terrified of the large wings protruding from the center of his back. They folded behind him, and the skin covering them was black and thick.

Huna felt her gaze. He looked over to see her watching and felt awkward. He turned back and finished, and then pulled on his clothes and sandals. His black hair was still wet when he returned to her, and he combed it back from his face with his fingers.

"Stay here," he ordered, then he walked into the brush.

Daisel watched until she could no longer see him and wondered why if he had wings to fly, he didn't use them. She wondered how long he would be gone and what he would bring in return. She remembered the bloody sight she'd witnessed the night before, and again, she began to worry for her safety. Maybe she should try to escape and take her chances that the people of the tribes would take her back. They had to know it wasn't her who had caused Masaya's reign of terror. She didn't choose what Huna had done. He had caused this.

She started to wonder if she could escape him and blame all this horror on him. After all, he was the devil with wings. If she escaped him, surely they would see her as a goddess rather than a curse. Being spared, they would feel gratitude for being alive. She felt her heart lift at the thought, and then she started to run.

Through the lush green and thick vines, she ran toward the villages of her family. She was unsure of the route, but followed the immense mountain she knew was nearby. When she reached a peak that looked over the entire valley, that was when she saw the still-smoldering caldera of Masaya in the distance, and the realization of what had occurred returned to her mind. The horror of seeing Huna fall to his death, and to save her, flashed back, and her heart broke again at the thought of losing him forever. He hadn't chosen to become the Camazotz. It was his fate, but it wasn't his plan. The stories she'd heard about the Winged Ones made her shiver, but with him and what he carried had saved her. Without his blood now running through her veins, she would be dead in the depths of the volcano. The thought of what he was now still scared her. She felt who he was before still lived inside him. She fell to her knees, exhausted and broken. What had she done? Alone on the top of the mountain, she turned back, hoping she could return before Huna knew what she'd tried to do.

As Huna set out to find fruit, roots, or possibly quail, something made him stop and place his hands to his ears as a high-pitched noise echoed in his head. He went to a tree and leaned on it for balance until the sound let up, and he could focus again. The noise was so strong, he felt it throughout his body, and along with his hunger, his stomach felt sick. He waited until the queasiness passed and then started his quest again, but soon, another of the debilitating blares came again, and he went down on one knee in pain. When the blares ceased, he climbed to one of the hill's high points and tried to see. As he waited and watched, smaller, less powerful echoes filled his head, and he could feel them coming from the northern side of the valley. It was the area close to the villages of the Tobo tribe, and he wondered what was causing the odd, deafening sounds. It was as if something was calling him, beckoning him to come that way, and yet, he heard no words, just noise.

Huna knew there was a risk in returning to any of the villages, but the echoes' pull was so strong that he had to know what they were. He decided to return at night and see what he could find under the cover of darkness. He had been stealthy enough to find his prey in the village the night before, so he hoped he would have the same luck again.

It had been a long day of hunting, and the sun was just starting to set as he returned to the shelter with an armful of bananas, two doves, and a small fish. He was proud of his success and anticipated Daisel's response to his hunt, but she was gone. At first, just a tingle of worry went through him when she wasn't right where he'd left her. He thought maybe she was at the stream or was gathering sticks for a fire, but the more he searched, the more the dread set in, and soon, he knew she had escaped.

He dropped the food to the ground and let out a roar so ferocious, it made the birds in the trees clatter into the sky. His eyes glowed with anger, and he felt the throbbing begin to pulsate in his back. Why did he love her so when this pain was what she caused him?

He ran to the rocky edge of the cliff, and as the brilliant

orange blaze of the sun left the horizon, he pushed off from the edge and hurled himself down the steep wall. It was almost too late, but his wings unfurled and caught his fall, propelling him up and crashing him through the tops of the trees. He'd find her and show her the pain she had inflicted on him.

In the darkness, he skimmed the tops of the trees, searching for her distinctive pulse and scent. He sensed other life, but it wasn't her, and then before he felt her, he heard her. It was a horrifying scream for help. The sound took him directly to where she was. He came to land through the broad palm leaves, and there he found her lying on the ground, shielding her face with her arm. Hovering over her was a dark creature with wings spread wide.

Huna thrust himself forward, knocking the beast away. The thrust spun the creature, turning it over. In the dim light of the moon, he saw it was another of his kind. But this one was just a boy. With eyes glowing red and blood covering his face and chest, the young one pushed himself up to standing, his dark wings hunched around him.

Huna, seeing the blood, looked to Daisel in fear. She was terrified but alive. She scrambled to her feet and ran to a tree for cover.

Huna stepped around to shield her.

When the creature saw it was Huna, his face turned to shock, and he dropped to his knees at Huna's feet. "I didn't know she was yours," he cried. "I didn't touch her. Please spare me, Great One."

Huna studied the boy. He was wiry and young, but his body and wings were strong.

"I've been searching for you for days," cried the boy. "My name is Hagan."

Huna stepped back. "Why? What do you want from me?"

Hagan swallowed. His eyes were weary. "The chief has

ordered the killing of us all," Hagan said soberly. "They are hunting for you. That is why I am here."

"Who are you?" Huna asked.

"I am Munzi, and the chief is burning us all."

Huna shook his head, confused. "The Munzi were killed by Masaya. I've seen the ruins. There are no others."

Hagen took a deep breath. "There are others. When the fire takes them, the wings come. That is why they are burning them. The chief and others know about the ash."

Seeing Huna's perplexed face, the boy continued. "The fire releases the wings, but it's the ash they are after." Hagan took a labored breath. "They call it the miracle."

CHAPTER

NINE

Huna's story
Masaya, Nicaragua, 120 B.C.

Huna sequestered Daisel inside the cave. It was the only place where he didn't feel the pull of her presence. He had allowed Hagan to live, but was now questioning that decision. He was a threat, but not the only danger Huna faced. If what Hagan had said was right, he would face being hunted and set on fire if captured.

The act of burning the bodies for the ash lacked reason. Huna understood why they would want to kill him after the wrath at the caldera, but what benefit was this precious Camazotz ash Hagan spoke of?

For days, Huna stayed near the cave. He gathered food from the jungle and woods just below, keeping Daisel shielded from anyone or anything that might be close.

On the eighth day, Huna could no longer be still. His need to roam was strong, and his curiosity of what had taken place after Masaya's destructive reign overtook him.

He woke Daisel and said, "I'm leaving to hunt. Stay inside the cave until I return." Even after her thwarted attempt to escape the week before, he was confident she would remain but still warned her, "Those like me will also be out looking for prey."

He had spent most of the night before thinking about what Hagan had said about the others' fate, the miracle ash and the chief burning them alive. As he lay awake thinking about the other young men and the curse they also carried, it was the first time he had thought about what he had become. He had heard the tales as a child, but had never believed the stories of the Camazotz and certainly never imagined he was one of them. Even with his transformation and ability to fly, he was still unconvinced he was what they called a Winged Devil. He stretched out one of the appendages at his back and touched the thick but malleable skin. The pain of their bursting from his back had been immense and oddly soothing. The adrenaline rush from the fall and the intense heat from inside Masaya was what had seemed to trigger the transformation. The talon at the tip of the outermost span was like glass, and still had his first kill remnants. He then extended both wings, took a deep breath, and stood tall. He waved them back and forth. They were part of him now. Like an arm or foot, he felt the sensations of cold, heat, and touch throughout the skin and bones of his wings. He controlled them, and yet, the desire to kill was connected but out of his control. Would he spend the rest of his life searching for blood and hiding from those who would hunt him down?

Before the sun rose, Huna went to the decimated fields and former village of the Munzi tribe. When he reached the valley, the hardened, ash-covered village's silence was deafening. Not even the birds had returned. As Huna walked around the dust and cinder tombs, he saw several shapes that reminded him of what life was like before the devastating shower of fire and soot brought that life to a sudden and horrifying end. He felt an overwhelming need for the comfort of his mother and of the life he'd had before. Those days now seemed fabled. They were happy, carefree times that had always included Daisel. He felt buoyed by the fact that he still had her, at least physically.

By the light of the moon, he stepped around the lifeless formations, trying to decipher what they were. He saw shapes of livestock, burned-out houses, and those of people. The form of what looked like a child and parent made Huna's heart ache. He again thought about Akna. Even though she had kept the truth of who he was for all those years, he still loved the woman he had known as his mother. And now he also knew the truth about Xbalan. Not only was he a brother but a twin to him. Huna wondered if his bitter feelings for Xbalan would be different had they been raised as brothers, yet, he had no misgivings about his brother's fall into the caldera. He deserved his violent end for his betrayal and what he'd done to Daisel.

He found the sun beginning to peek above the mountains, and he shaded his eyes, surprised that he had already spent so much time walking the ruined site of his supposed birthplace. He continued to search around the homes and streets, and finally came upon what he had come for, a solid cast showing the outline of a body. It lay with one leg bent, an arm over the face, and with a bloom of wings.

The cast was solid, so he extended the talon on his wing and used it to chip away at the slag covering the body of what would have been another Camazotz. When the sharp claw finally punctured through the cast, he could see into the dark, hollow cavity that something was shimmering. At closer study, he saw what looked to be crystals. The boy Hagan had told of miracle ash. Could this be it? He then thought of what it actually was—the cremated bodies of the Winged Ones. Just like the chief burning the boys, these people faced the same fiery death.

Huna reached in, and when he pulled his hand into the sunlight, the glistening dust turned to drab dirt. He rubbed the powder to stimulate the shimmering he had seen, but it was nothing but dull, dark-colored sand. He reached in, and again when the shimmering crystals hit the light, the brilliance was gone. The next time, he wrapped his black wings around the ashen tomb, enclosing himself and blocking out all the light. Inside his small cocoon, he dipped his hand in and pulled out a handful of the shimmering powder. In the darkness, the colors swirled in his hands. Not only did they radiate light, but they floated and danced as if each speck was alive. He was mesmerized, then he looked at the back of his hand. The luminescent dust covered a scar from a careless boyhood cut caused by a knife. When he brushed the ash away, the area that was once a raised jagged line was now smooth and unblemished.

He gasped. He placed the crystals back in the dark hole, opened his wings, and in the amber light of dawn, rubbed the back of his hand to see if the scar was really gone. It was. Could it be true? Could the ash of these people—his people—heal and cure? What he had just witnessed wasn't the same thing as the elixirs of plants or the salves made of muds that Akna used on the sick and diseased people of the tribes. Those took days or weeks to work, and often didn't.

So much had shaken his world in those last few days, he questioned his own ability to decipher what he'd found. Hagan's words and some pretty dancing dust didn't mean it was a miracle, did it? He looked at the back of his hand again, and a sense of dread came over him. Had he just found the reason the others wanted to take his life? Like cannibals, would they feed off what his body could produce? He took the small pouch he had brought and, enclosing himself again into darkness, gathered some of the dust into it. He carefully tucked it away to keep it from the light.

Huna folded back his wings and stood to leave. It was then that he felt his head begin to spin. He knelt and waited for it to pass. His entire body felt weak, and he was shaking. It had happened before, and each time, it was when he had used his wings when the sun was bright. He sat, resting, and began to think about his body's reaction and the similarities to the dust crystals in his pouch. Their response to the light when he'd lifted them from their dark tomb was as if they had died. If the ash was part of his people, his lineage, then maybe the light had a harmful effect on him as well.

Huna knew that his desire to fly was never there during the day and heightened at night. When he did expose his wings to the sun, the effect it had on his body afterward was detrimental. What was worse was that the urges increased, and his need for human prey always occurred on the nights after those exposures to the light. The more he processed this, the tighter he tucked his wings into him and away from the sun.

As he hiked along the jungle trails back to Daisel and their shelter, he continued to think about the comparisons between the ash, the crystals, the light, and his own body and wings. The legends of the Winged Ones—the Camazotz—were common throughout the tribes, but so were tales of snake-headed men, talking cats, and ghost women who kidnap spoiled children. Huna had always viewed the stories as ways to control his behavior.

He'd found them scary and gripping as a young boy, but had never believed they were real.

The stories of the Camazotz were that of a hideous enormous bat with a long forked tongue and pointed ears. Fur covered the body, and the feet and hands had claws. Huna looked at his own hands as he thought about this. He may not look like the Camazotz they'd described to him as a child, but the stories must have come from somewhere.

There must have been people like him before. A chill went through him as he wondered how many other of these extraordinary and outlandish creatures told in tales were real.

By the time he got back to Daisel, it was night, and she had built a fire. She smiled at him, and it gave him comfort as he was still unsure of her feelings and her willingness to stay with him.

"I've found something," he said, pulling the pouch from the fold of his wing. "It is the ash that the boy, Hagan, spoke of. There is something about it that cures."

Daisel looked at the pouch, and then at Huna.

Huna put out his hand. "Remember when I cut my hand with my mother's knife when I was a boy?"

She nodded, and then looked down at his hand. Seeing no scar, she looked back at him with a furrowed brow.

"It took the scar away. Right before my eyes," he said.

"What did?" she asked.

"The ash in this bag," he said, lifting it toward her.

He directed her to a place they could sit away from the glow of the fire, and he carefully untied the pouch and took some of the dust from it. It sparkled and fluttered all over his hand.

Daisel's eyes were wide. "What is this?"

Huna hesitated, watching the sparkling dust covering his hand. A sorrow fell over him as he imagined the charred bodies that made up the mesmerizing crystals. He sighed. "It's the ash of the Camazotz who died from Masaya."

She shook her head, confused.

Huna continued. "Those who were killed by the fire and ash that covered the Munzi village. The ones I could see that had the wings. I dug into where they lay, and this is their ash," he said, motioning to the glistening dust.

They both sat watching in awe as the crystals shimmered and spun.

"This is them?" she asked.

Huna nodded.

"You said this healed you. How?"

Huna held up his hand. "It was on me where the knife had cut me. The scar that had been there since I was a boy just vanished. Look. It's gone."

She took his hand and examined it.

The feel of her touch was something he had missed for so long that Huna closed his eyes for a moment, remembering the days before all the horror that had torn them apart. They were in love once, so in love that the fear of death didn't keep them from being with each other, and yet now, she looked at him differently.

When he opened his eyes, she was still watching the iridescent show. Her face was soft but awestruck, and Huna realized it was the first time he had seen her smile since the upheaval of their world. It sent warmth through him, and playfully, he bent closer to the glistening dust and lightly blew them toward her.

They swirled up quickly into her face, and she inhaled in surprise. Huna sat back, worried he may have scared her and ruined the moment, but then her face went from lively interest to something much more intense. She sat still, looking at the crystals and taking several deep breaths as though something had made her unsteady. Daisel then looked up at him, and with continued deep breaths, her eyes scanned his face, chest, arms, and back to his eyes.

Huna sat confused, wondering what it was she was feeling

and thinking. Then her smile turned. She didn't look angry, but wanton, and she moved toward him. She put a hand to his face and stroked his cheek.

"What is it?" he asked.

She didn't answer, but sighed, contented.

Huna felt his body tense. What had he done that she now looked at him with longing? He watched the shimmering powder still dancing in his outstretched hand. Daisel bent down and let the dust drift up and onto her face. Again, she breathed it in. She smiled and raised an eyebrow. Then she leaned into him and, with both hands, pulled his face to hers. The kiss was warm and wet, and Huna's enduring desire for her made him reach out and pull her into him. Her hands went for him, too, caressing his chest and stomach. Huna felt his body begin to throb, and then the pounding ache started in his back and the desire to have her turned, and he knew it had to end, and quickly.

"No," he said breathlessly, pulling away.

"Yes," she said, pulling him back.

Huna's eyes began to blur, and his head buzzed as the growing urge compounded his desires for her. He pushed her away, shaking his head, and staggered to standing.

"Why?" she asked, her voice beginning to sober.

"I can't," he muttered, and then he quickly left her.

Huna ran aimlessly. He could feel the blood pulsing in her as he crashed through the tangle of vines and leaves until he found the cliffs. He was already frantic for it, and when he jumped, his first instinct was to turn and go back for her. She was easy prey, and her warm, fresh blood was already in his focus. It took everything he could muster to find the few pieces of lucidity still in his mind to keep him from taking her, ripping open her flesh, and devouring the pulsing blood he so badly craved.

Huna pushed himself toward the village, and soon, the

other beating hearts and pulsating vessels registered and filled his senses. He quickly found one alone, separate from the others near a stream. The scent of blood and the heat radiating from the body drew him to his target with precision. The kill was easy, for this one was old. The man never saw him, and when Huna finished, he stood and surveyed the bloody slaughter. Unlike before, he felt no remorse, no disgust, just completion and relief. He could now return to Daisel without worry. That was what it had become. It filled his need so he could safely be with her.

When he returned through the brush into the clearing of their shelter, the fire's embers were still aglow. Daisel was lying on a layered mat and surrounded by soft hides Huna had scavenged from his nights of pillage. She was still awake, and when she saw him, she didn't flinch at the sight of his blood-covered body, but instead, lay back and opened herself to him.

Huna hesitated, confused by the change of her feelings for him.

She said nothing but nodded, and with her eyes, told him she wanted nothing more than to be with him completely.

He came to her and knelt at her side. She put a hand to his face and pulled him to her like before. She kissed him and moved her hands over his chest and down his stomach.

Huna's heart began to pound with her touch, and he lay her back and pressed his body on top of hers. Daisel's moans were low, and her legs were wrapped around his waist, pulling him to her, but when she hugged his back and touched his folded wings, he tensed and pulled away.

Their eyes met, and both were breathing hard. Huna swallowed, and his face was full of fear.

Daisel's eyes remained on him. She blinked slowly, and then tipped her head back. This show of trust and lack of inhibition gave Huna the answer he desired. He let out a deep breath and sank into her. His entire body, flush with excitement and his desire for her, built as he found her mouth and kissed her so deeply his yearning to devour her was as strong as it had ever been. When she opened to him, and he came into her, the explosion was not only through his loins, but his back as his wings thrust out the moment he erupted into her.

TEN

Huna's story
Masaya, Nicaragua, 120 B.C.

It was at night, as Huna laid in Daisel's arms and the sky was at its darkest, that he could hear the cries. The noise was blaring in his head, a high-pitched screeching that made his ears throb and his stomach turn. It began slowly, and then reached a pitch so sharp that blood often dripped from his ears.

Most of those nights, he waited it out, cringing and moaning until the noise left him. He then fell back asleep, even more exhausted than before. However, at night, the need to hunt grew along with the noise and his need for blood. He stood and felt the sound beginning, along with an enormous pulling sensation.

Daisel was asleep amongst the hides, and watching her, he knew he needed to leave, so he set out in the darkness and flew over the valley and toward the blaring cries.

At the crest of the mountain, he paused and noticed that the noise came directly from the direction of his old home—the

Catzu tribe. Huna's need for blood was urgent, and he knew the risk of hunting near the Catzu was high, but the call was so clear and powerful, he continued toward it.

Hiding in the top of a Quebracho tree, he peered down to where a large group of people had formed. They were standing around half a dozen piles of brush lined in a row. Several of the mounds at the beginning were scorched and had smoldering flames. Huna was still a distance away, but even in the dark, he could see that one of the men was Chief Cordoba. In seeing the evil leader, his desire for blood increased. The pull to fly down and kill was strong, but as one of the piles went up in flame, the loud noise began and soon intensified. The blaring squeal came to a peak to where Huna could hardly maintain his balance. He braced himself against the tree and cringed, trying to hold his ears and head.

The pain was intense, but then within seconds, the noise quit. He opened his eyes, and at the center of the fire, he watched as enormous black wings grew out of the flames. They extended like a flower blooming, but then the fire overtook them. The smoke started black, but then a glistening light sparkled from the flecks of ash that floated from the fire.

Huna watched, mesmerized. He leaped from the tree and swooped down to another closer to where he could get a clearer view. He watched as the shimmering lights from the burning wings kept rising into the dark. At the sight of this, the people cried in awe. Huna sat up in his perch and felt incredible wonder as he examined the burning pile, but then he saw the body. His stomach sank when he realized what they were doing. Just as Hagan had said, they were burning those who were like him. They were killing the boys who might become Camazotz.

The chief ordered some men to start gathering the ash from the piles that were no longer ablaze. The ash was obviously precious, and they hurriedly scooped what they could into baskets and tarps, covering them quickly as they went. Some people tried to get close to the sparkling dust, but were pushed away by the sentries. The chief ordered them to stay back and kept his men busy at their work.

When Huna arose from the depths of their great god Masaya and stole the sacrifice they were offering, he not only confirmed their belief in the winged creature of death but their certainty that angering the gods would cause their destruction. His treacherous act against their divine savior was what they believed caused the destruction of most of their people and the land of the tribes. Those who were like him were now considered demons and destroyed. Not only was he marked for death, but so many others were now facing that same fate. Even the young men who hadn't come of age were being tortured and killed to expose what they were and rid the land of the curse they brought. The fire released their wings and sent that blaring call he had heard at night. But what was this mystical dust coming from their demise? It danced and shimmered in the dark.

When the fire had consumed most of the brush and the first bodies, the group moved on to the next pile, and there tied to a stake in the center was a young man. He was not much older than a boy. Thin and angular, he writhed and cried and tried to free himself from the ropes. The chief motioned to the heavens. The ceremony was apparently used to keep the god's anger away and the people of the tribe's faith entrenched in fear. He put the fire to the brush, and within seconds, the pile and the young man were ablaze. Huna was shocked by how quickly the flames consumed the boy's body.

The noise began again. It wasn't the sound of the young man's cries, but it came from him somewhere, and Huna doubled over as the noise grew. Like before, within seconds, it was over, and as he looked up, another set of large wings emerged from the orange glow of the fire. Again, there were cheers, and when the wings and body of the young man were charred and gone, they harvested the ash and moved to the next pile.

There another young man struggled and cried out, knowing his fate. Huna felt sick inside as he sat and watched the fire take over, but this time the fire wasn't as fierce, and the poor boy suffered and wailed until Huna had to look away. He waited for the screeching blare to begin, and when it didn't, he sat in the tree, wondering why. When he looked again, that was when he saw it. Unlike the others, which had bloomed the massive spread of wings during the roar of the flames, this fire produced nothing. The boy simply burned to death. He wasn't one of them.

The chief and others looked disappointed, and with this being the last pile in the row, they began to wander around, surveying the destruction they had caused and their incredible success at ridding themselves of the Winged Devils. There were six piles in all. From his perch, Huna could see that four had produced the coveted wings they had desired. And it was there that the gathering of the ash had taken place. They had killed off four of his kind, but he wondered how many more they had burned as he had laid awake all those nights with the blaring noise in his head. And how many more still faced this horrendous fate.

Huna, wrought with angst after what he had watched, also had the urgent and undeniable need for blood that he had pushed off for far too long.

Desperate, he lifted his head and breathed in the night air. He felt the pulsating pull of prey in the jungle below. The target's heart vibrated in his head, and the urge to slash and bring the body down burned in his chest. He pushed off and was airborne with one brush of his wings as he flew over, tracking his game.

The panting and thrashing through the brush and vines made it easy for Huna to follow, and soon, he was upon his victim. He swiped but missed the head, and then used his weight to pound the body to the ground. He was angry by his miss and bit into the neck to draw the blood. When the warmth reached his mouth, a terrible taste made him reel back, and he pushed the body away. Huna tasted the blood, and an intense flush went through him, unlike his other kills. This one was different. He took a step back, and his mind began to clear. Looking down at his kill, he realized the body was that of a young man, not much more than a boy. And when he studied it closer, he saw the small black folds beginning to emerge from bloody gaps in the boy's back. He had killed one of his own.

Huna knelt and touched the wing, taking it between his thumb and forefinger and gently pulling it until it released. The wing didn't expand and explode out in the fervor as Huna's had, but instead lay limp on the jungle floor's wet grass. The terror of being stalked had triggered the boy's fledge, and Huna had ended it before it was complete. This boy had escaped Chief Cordoba's capture only to be hunted and killed by what he would eventually become.

Huna rose, but continued to examine the dead winged tangle of blood and body. Then he sighed. He knelt and brought the boy up to him. The small body was frail, and Huna looked at the lifeless face and limp arms. He touched the wound on his neck and again felt the strange and unappealing taste in his mouth. And then, just as he had done with Daisel, bit into the boy and brought him back. He wasn't sure why, but with this boy, he felt the need to save him, and by doing that, the boy was bound to him forever.

The kills had now changed. No longer did he feel the guilt or remorse of the first slaughters. Huna now reveled in his power to control not only life and death, but the very soul of the being. He affected their death and whether they had a life after. And those he did bring back to life became like him. Along with Hagan, those who lived in darkness were loyal to their savior.

The most devoted of his followers was the first boy Huna saved. Huna gave him the name Vida. Through his many kills, Vida became a large and fearsome hunter. His eternity would be spent following his master and living with those who also found prey in the night.

For Huna, the pride in his colony of followers allowed him to push aside his past life and bask in what he had created. The kills were no longer dreaded; in fact, he had now come to enjoy them. His body and very soul not only survived, but thrived on the blood of man.

It was his destiny when he took that leap to save Daisel, and becoming the murderous creature of the night was how he was able to have her forever. He had always felt he would do anything to save her, to be with her, and standing awash in the blood of others, he knew that nothing in his life was ever more true.

ELEVEN

Huna's story
Masaya, Nicaragua, 120 B.C.

It was a night without a moon, and Huna was hunting alone. Although his need for blood had been satisfied the night before, his desire for prey had him restless.

As he neared the village, he could feel the pulse of life even before he saw the small fires burning outside the huts.

A rumor had spread that the Winged Devils feared fire, that it rendered them powerless. This, of course, wasn't true and allowed Huna to prey upon their gullibility.

He perched high and waited. Soon, a woman left one of the huts and began wandering into the palm-covered area near the edge of the clustered dwellings.

He spread out his wings and expanded his back and chest. He dove from the branches into a free fall, swooping toward the dark area he had seen the woman go. His hunting had become both perfected and precise. The use of his flight and the stealth of his wings made for a clean and efficient kill. He usually sought out those who were away from the village, and he avoided areas where he might be spotted or his kills traced. But that night, the pull of his desire was so strong, the mere need for blood wasn't enough. It was the kill he wanted. The feel of ripping flesh and draining a body of life was what he desired.

The sensation of her blood pulsating drew him down. She was squatting in the brush and never heard or saw him. The kill was quick and quiet. It was the warmth that flowed into him that usually satisfied his body's need; however, something was missing this time. The blood lacked the normally potent high that the others possessed. The desire was unquenched. He needed the pulsating rush that fear released into the blood. His prey had to know they were doomed.

With a face covered in blood, he heard a voice call out. He wrenched back—he'd been spotted. Then he felt the rush of an arrow pass by him and knew it was time to flee. As large and proficient a killer he had become, there was still a risk of being wounded, captured, and burned. The daylight would be coming soon, and with that, he would lose his ability to fly, becoming vulnerable.

Into the darkness, he rose. The beats of his wings brought him high into the black sky and out of sight. He would return another night to satisfy his hunger and remind those of his reign.

As the day began to creep above the mountain peaks, Huna made his way back to Daisel. With the light, he closed his wings tightly to his body and hiked back through the shaded paths that followed the stream leading to their refuge.

As he walked, he spent some time cleaning the blood from his face and chest, hoping to rid the signs of his deadly night. He knew she was aware of what he did, but he still felt the need to keep the things that made her cringe away, hidden.

The dust is what brought her back to him. He saw the change in her face, the lust in her eyes when she inhaled the glistening sparkles. She didn't seem to let anything keep her from pulling him close and taking him in. And yet, Huna still felt the need to keep his murderous acts from her, so he scrubbed the blood away and rinsed the death from his skin and hair before making his way to the cave.

When he walked into their small shelter, she sat in the morning sun looking guilty and despondent. In her hands was the pouch containing the mystical dust, opened and empty.

"I don't know what happened to it," she said softly.

He had kept the dust in the dark and offered it to her at night when he longed for her. He had never told her to stay out of it or had hidden it away from her. His reason to keep it in a small dark corner of the cave was its fragility to the light. He hadn't explained that to her. Huna hadn't talked to Daisel about the dust because part of him didn't want to admit her desire for him was disingenuous.

"You opened it in the light," he said. "Now it's gone."

The look on her face was so disappointed, he felt his entire being wilt. It was as if her will for life had left along with the powder.

"I'll get more," he blurted out desperately. He knelt next to her, and when she winced away from him, he knew that without the shimmering dust, her feelings for him would be as fragile and fleeting as the powder that had ignited them.

The entire day, she stayed distant, and when night came, she huddled by the fire. Huna didn't press her and took a seat across from the flames. She looked up at him with those brilliant green eyes he had loved since they were children, but at that moment, they glowed with an intensity that made Huna gasp.

"Why do I want it so badly?" she asked, disturbed. "It is all I think about."

"I will go and bring back more," Huna assured her.

She nodded, but closed her eyes in despair. "Why do I feel like I'll die without it? What is it? What did you find that has such power over me? What do you plan to do to me?"

Huna's heart sank. "I saved you."

Tears filled Daisel's eyes. "Saved me?" she asked. "From what?"

"From Masaya. If I hadn't, you'd be dead."

Daisel sat back stone-faced as tears rolled down her cheeks. "I am dead."

When Daisel fell asleep that night, Huna flew to the tombs of the Winged Ones. He had to bring her back and knew the only way was with the crystals. When she wanted him and was happy again, he could talk to her and make things right. She had smiled at him and stayed with him before he'd found the powder, and he knew her desire for him was deep inside her somewhere. The glistening dust was just an aid at a time of such upheaval and angst in their lives. He knew this was a desperate attempt to keep her, but he had nothing without her, so he continued the rationalization in his mind as he went to attain the miracle dust.

When he arrived at the dark and silent graveyard of the Munzi, he searched for a tomb that showed the apparent bloom of wings. Using the same method as before, he punctured the cast with his talon and reached inside to gather the dust. The shimmering spectacle lifted his spirits and gave him hope that what Daisel had said was just momentary sadness. He could bring her back. He would be able to make her want him again.

He placed as much of the dust as he could into the pouch, secured it, then went to the next tomb and did the same. As he went from one ashen grave to the next, he noticed that many had already been pillaged. It was something he hadn't seen before, and he wondered if it was something he had overlooked or if the damage was more recent. How many of the Winged

Ones were there? If others knew of the power of the glistening dust, the supply would surely not last long. His stomach seized with the thought of running out. What then? How long would he be able to keep Daisel happy and want to remain with him without it?

Before dawn, he flew back to her, and when he arrived at the clearing, he went to the nest of hides where they slept. Hearing his footsteps, she rolled and leaned up.

"Do you have it?" she asked. Her eyes searched him for any sign of success.

Huna nodded and presented the pouch.

Daisel all but pounced at it.

He pulled it back, and she looked up at him with surprise that soon turned to a glare.

"We must be careful," Huna explained. "It is scarce. I'll give you what you need, but we can't lose it like before."

She held her glare and dropped her shoulders in a sign of indignation. "You'll make me beg, will you?"

"No," Huna defended. "But it is precious, and it must last." He not only meant the dust but the effect it had on her.

She let her face soften and took a long and tired breath. Through long lashes, she looked up at him. "Just a little then?" She gave a small smile.

Huna nodded, and Daisel gently took his hand and led him down onto the soft fur-lined bed. When she inhaled the small sparkles and snuggled into his chest, Huna thought he actually heard her purr.

In the early morning hours, as he lay awake wondering how long the precious ash would last, his thoughts turned to the young boys burned at the stake. The supply of the miracle dust was finite. For Huna to keep Daisel with him forever, he would have to hunt for more than just blood.

TWELVE

Pocatello, Idaho, 2017

The sun had just crested the peaks of Scout Mountain and the light glistened on the wet grass of the old cemetery. It was early September, and a slight breeze made the morning crisp enough for long sleeves.

Jennifer Berchtold was a runner and her favorite place to stretch out and go each morning was the quiet and empty paths of the Mountain View Cemetery and the trails of the hills that snaked through and connected to it.

The large craggy cottonwood trees were probably as old as the first graves dug in the late 1800s. They gave shade and framed small dirt pathways throughout the acres of grass and tombstones.

Her friends often chided her about her creepy choice of jogging route, but for her, the silence, lack of cars, dogs, and people made it the perfect place to renew her body and soul. With earphones playing her favorite playlist on Pandora, she escaped for that hour in the morning before her day as the Bannock County Assessor began. She could forget the stream of complaints about tax payments and increased valuations as she kept a steady pace for those three miles.

On that morning, her breath was visible, and as she pulled her sunglasses down from the top of her head, the sky was just starting to brighten. She took the hidden path that led from the oldest part of the cemetery to where the new grave sites began and up a small crest that was shaded and secluded. She rounded a clump of dogwood brush and came upon a smoky haze. As she ran through it, it started to clear just enough for her to see a large, dark figure in the distance. It was hunched on the ground, hovering over what was burning.

She slowed and came to a cautious stop. Whatever it was, it hadn't noticed her. It was moving, up and down, heaving in the early morning dimness amidst the haze.

A black vinyl-like covering rose and fell, almost billowing. Then she saw feet protruding from under it. They were pale and upside down in the dirt and grass. The sight alarmed her. She tried to get a better look in the low light and removed her sunglasses.

As she pushed them up on her forehead, they toppled and fell to the ground. The noise was enough to alert the creature, and the figure rose and turned.

The large black covering lowered at its sides and revealed a monstrous face. Jennifer's body went cold and her chest heaved. It was a man, but he looked inhuman. His skin was discolored and taut, and his upper body oddly large, the dark covering folded back into wings that protruded from his back. He glared at her and then stepped away. She looked down and saw a body lying face down on the grass, its back torn open.

Jennifer put her hand to her mouth in horror. The creature's mouth opened, and she wasn't sure if it was a breath or a hiss, but an icy tingle shot over her, and she gasped and stepped backward. She started to speak, to try to explain, apologize—

beg. His eyes were sunken but fierce. He stepped toward her, and she turned and bolted away.

The dogwood scratched her face and legs as she crashed through it. She forced a breathless scream as she ran frantically. No one could hear her until she reached the entrance by the road.

But she continued to try and yell. Her gasping was loud, and she pushed herself, unable to look back. Dodging trees and praying the thing wasn't chasing her, her earbuds fell to the road, and a high pitch grind pierced the morning silence. A red-hot fire struck her legs, and she hit the ground so hard her nose crunched, and her teeth broke into her mouth. The sting of the asphalt scrape of her face and hands was the harsh reminder this wasn't a dream. She pushed herself up and tried to crawl forward, but she was weighted and stunned. She tried to drag herself, but the pain in her legs was throbbing. Then she turned back to realize her legs were gone, literally severed from her body.

An icy burn pulsated as she saw blood oozing from the gashes. Her head began to spin, and her stomach seized as she watched the pool of red pouring from her on the path. Her breathing faltered as she panicked and scanned the area, looking for the monster that was surely stalking her. As her vision and mind began to sway and fade, she saw the dark figure in the distance coming toward her. She used what strength she had to pull and drag her body away from it. But when she turned back, it was only darkness.

Jennifer's torso, legs, and head were found in the dry creek bed, covered with brush, just a few yards from where the killer had struck.

But the pool of blood was so small, considering the degree

of violence that had taken place, the cemetery workers had almost overlooked it. It wasn't until several hours later that they followed the thin trail of blood to the body and called the police.

Investigators scoured the cemetery for evidence and found the disturbed grave of James Lopez, a sixty-seven-year-old migrant worker who had died two days earlier. He had died alone. They found the body when someone reported a stench coming from the isolated house outside of town. There was no funeral. Someone had dug up his unmarked grave, torn his body apart, and then hastily reburied it. There was no motive for why someone would be stalking a graveyard, digging up the dead, and killing those who may have stumbled upon those acts.

Police had a deranged murderer on the loose in their city, yet they were hesitant to release the information because it was so horrific, it was sure to cause panic. They had no idea what could have caused such precise and deadly wounds, yet left almost no blood. And what motive could this killer have to dig up an elderly man's body, remove parts of it, and then rebury it?

After interviewing those closest to Jennifer, investigators assumed she had stumbled across the killer as he was mutilating the corpse and was simply in the wrong place at the wrong time. The medical examiner determined a single slice, mid-stride, caused her death. The blade had to be huge. There was no hacking, no sawing—just one single swipe. And there were no other wounds except the scratches and bruises from the fall.

"The blade cut through bone. Femur. Both of them. And she was beheaded with one swipe. Clean cuts." Dr. Fred Angeli had been the Bannock County Medical Examiner for two decades and had seen a number of murders, but this was something he knew was beyond his knowledge.

"We need to bring someone else in on this," he said. "I can't even imagine what could have caused this type of wound, especially out in that area. It would have had to be massive."

Derek Bloxam had only been a detective for a year and knew he was green, but even he thought this was a case he'd never see the likes of again. His partner, Lester Isom, was less than a year from retirement, and he stood against the wall of the morgue and sighed loudly in annoyance, not only for the amount of work this murder would add to his final caseload, but also for the call he would have to make. A call that would dredge up a past he thought he would finally be able to bury.

"Farm equipment?" Derek asked the doctor.

"I can't figure anything else large enough to do this." Dr. Angeli shrugged. "And almost no blood."

"My dad went to school with her," Derek said.

The doctor nodded noncommittally as he read his notes. Pocatello was a small town. Many people had grown up there and never left.

"What about the corpse? What was done to it?" Lester asked. "They said it was hacked up, too." He knew what he was looking for, but didn't want to raise suspicions by being too specific.

Dr. Angeli folded several papers back over the clipboard. "Yes, cut up, but also burned," he read. "However, the slices on the corpse weren't near as clean or as large. Two pieces of burnt flesh from the sides of the spine on the upper back are carved out and missing."

Lester groaned, hearing exactly what he expected.

"About the size of a brick on each side," the doctor explained. He tried to use his hands and the clipboard to show the dimensions. He looked at Lester, who simply nodded, uninterested.

Derek lifted his shoulders in question.

"Anything missing from her?" he asked, motioning to the covered body.

The doctor shook his head. "Just blood. And nothing burned. Nothing makes sense."

For Lester, it made far too much sense. The kills were almost identical to what he'd seen as a young officer all those years ago. And it was then that he felt the crushing weight of knowing the people of the county would be looking to him to keep whoever was doing this from doing it again. And if the pattern followed that of the past, the horror wouldn't stop with just this one.

"The state investigators will be here in the morning. The sheriff and county commissioners want to wait to hold a news conference, but the word is already out," the coroner said.

"Goddamned city cops," Lester grumbled.

The cemetery was technically in the county, but the city employed the cemetery workers. The city police were the first ones called.

Lester had been a county deputy for thirty years and had seen the city police department grow from less than a dozen officers to almost a hundred, and yet, the county saw its numbers and impact shrink.

It irritated him to see the city officers get the cases he'd used to. He spent most of his time on farm and property issues, or problems on the reservation.

He was looking forward to getting out of it and away from the frustrations. However, this case would only add to it all. It was complicated, and would involve experts from other agencies. That meant young hotshots ordering him around and treating him like the small-town cop he was. He took a deep breath and let it out slowly. Why was this coming back to haunt him now?

"Come on," he ordered Derek. He'd have him do the reports.

At least having a rookie as a partner was a benefit of his last year on the job. He could shove off the paperwork and other crap jobs on him, and this case would have a truckload. Right now, he had a phone call to make, and it was one both he and the man on the receiving end were both going to dread.

THIRTEEN

Pocatello, Idaho, 2017

It was the phone call Richard Wilson had feared for thirty years. He had hoped and often even prayed it had been long enough that the nightmare had ended, but the moment he heard the name, he knew it was beginning all over again. His stomach sank with the first utterance. A voice he hadn't heard in years, but one he knew well. The person on the other end of the phone was Dr. Luis Davila.

"There are three killings so far—two young men, then a woman. It happened yesterday morning," he said. It was the same tone he had used decades ago when this same horrific event killed dozens of young men and threatened an epidemic across the country.

Nonchalant and unshakable, the doctor did his job and discussed the plan as though it was as routine as scheduling a dental cleaning.

"Are you sure he isn't straying?" Davila asked at one point.

Richard began to object fiercely, but then took a step back. Could he really be sure? "Why would he? We were just out there a couple of nights ago. We've never missed a drop-off. Are you sure this is the same?"

"Yes, and there have been biopsies done on about a dozen boys. They have the markers," Davila said sadly. "He's back, and there could be others."

Richard felt his shoulders sink. "How can this be? I thought he was the last."

"We hoped he was the last."

Richard took a deep breath, trying to let his weathered body adjust to this news. "Why do you think it's him?"

"None of us were sure he was gone," Davila said. "And we knew the others who escaped might turn. We all made the decision to let them live."

"We all thought they were past the point of turning. None of us thought they were a risk." Richard shook his head, refusing to feel guilty about not killing children. "So, you think these killings and new cases are because of the ones who escaped? Not new ones coming in?"

"I believe so. All the tests have come from boys living in southern Idaho."

Richard sighed. "Do you think these boys are descendants?"

"Most likely," Davila said. "And the murders are clustered within a five-mile radius."

Cluster was an appropriate word, thought Richard, especially if this was a repeat of the horror before. For Richard, it was the part of his life he wished he could close the door to and forget. "What type of killings? You said there was a woman. She obviously isn't one of them."

"I think the woman was just collateral. She was killed in the cemetery, and they found a grave disturbed. I think the deceased was one of our original four who escaped. He was the same age, and the autopsy shows his back had been cut out and burned. The name doesn't match, but I'm sure those who escaped did what they could to hide. I'm surprised they stayed around here."

"And the boys who were killed?" Richard asked.

"Yes. Both had the signs. Their tests haven't come back, but they were killed for the drug. One of the boys was found along the river bottoms south of town, and the other was up near Red Hill."

"It sounds like there could be more than just one," Richard said wearily. "Who else knows?"

"It was Lester who called me. He'll be working the cases like before."

"Lester? I was just with him on Friday when we were out there..." he trailed off, knowing that Dr. Davila was aware of what they were tasked to do. "He didn't mention a thing. He was still talking about retirement."

"He didn't know the killings were related to all this until yesterday. The two boys were found in different counties. We need to get to the boys who have the markers and get them to the colony. I can get the list from the CDC."

Richard shook his head. Having been retired for over ten years, he had just assumed that terrible horror in 1973 was long over, and besides his once-a-month unpleasant reminder, he was enjoying sleeping in late and casting a line while forgetting what day of the week it was.

"Other investigators are being brought in from the state. Unfortunately, the word has already spread. Even the news media is aware."

"How aware?" Richard asked.

"Not enough to compromise things...yet. But our situation is different now. The amount of technology compared to back then is what could change things. We certainly won't be able to get away with what we did before. But so far, no one has witnessed anything. We have no sightings like before."

"And you're sure it's the same?" Richard asked again, but he already knew the answer. The reason he asked was to give himself one last grasp at the hope it might not be. He desperately hoped they had misread the signs and were being overly sensitive to clues that these were just terrible murders, not the work of the one who had changed all their lives and kept them wondering for decades if they had really rid the world of the devil himself.

"Yes, I'm sure," Davila spoke with the measured monotone he always had. "We have the same type of killing along with the same blood and tumors as before."

"I thought it was over," Richard said with regret.

It was in that unforgettable year, they had done the unthinkable and controlled it, eliminated the risk of it returning —or at least they thought they had. It was unconventional, unthinkable what they did, but sometimes sacrificing a few to save many is what must be done. Since the public was unaware, they could carry out their assignment without the typical chain of command.

And now, Richard sat wondering what was going to happen as they all sat in the same room together again and he had the chance he knew he would one day get, but had never wanted, and that was to say, "I told you so."

Richard Wilson always knew he wanted to be a cop.

His dad and grandfather were both with the Seattle police department, and Richard wanted nothing else but to join them.

When he made sergeant at age twenty-seven, he had already been on the force for six years. He was encouraged to stay on and work toward the promotion of lieutenant, but he'd had other plans.

The newly formed Drug Enforcement Agency was hiring

new agents, and he knew that was where he wanted to be. However, with a year of college left before finishing his degree, he was facing stiff competition to get in. He hoped his years on the force and rank would help his chances.

In 1972, he left the only city he had ever lived in and flew to Washington, D.C., for ten weeks of training. If he completed the course, he would become one of the first DEA agents in the country and work undercover to fight against the illegal drug trade. It was a dream come true, and he passed the course easily and flew home to his not-so-supportive wife. The thought of him running with the most dangerous drug dealers in the country frightened and confused her. Even though she was an educated and liberated young woman for that era, she couldn't understand his desire to put his life, and possibly theirs, at risk. She didn't feel the rush he did when he made the arrests or completed a successful buy.

For Richard, it was like being an actor in a movie, playing the role of a dealer. He only wished they had awards for under-cover acting because he was good at it. No, he was great at it.

His first assignment was Yuma, Arizona.

Heroin was the drug of choice, and he immediately found the informants and dealers he needed to get into the right circles. His partner had graduated the class before him and had already spent a year at the Albuquerque bureau before being assigned to Yuma.

His name was Mike Pritchett, and he was a Mormon from Utah. Straight from the middle of the non-drinking, non-smoking, non-swearing capital of the country, and now he was dealing drugs and talking shit to the point Richard wondered how he was able to pull it off. Mike was also married, but unlike Richard, he had four children. Richard was surprised that someone with a family would put himself in some of the most harrowing situations imaginable.

"What does your wife think about this job?" Mike asked as they drove to a trailer in the middle of a dusty Arizona mesa.

Richard paused for a moment, and then raised his eyebrows and shrugged. "I don't talk about it much. She has her work, and when we're at home, we talk about other things." He turned to Mike. "Why? What does your wife think?"

Mike took a deep breath. "She isn't happy about it. She thinks I should have taken a job on the farm like my father. She says it would be a lot safer, but I think she mainly misses her family," he said. "I used to tell her about what I did to include her in my work, but that backfired. Now I hardly say anything. She's got her church assignments and the kids, and if she knew what I was doing, she would worry and make me crazy."

"The late nights used to have Michelle crazy, too. We don't talk about it anymore," Richard said. In fact, he and his wife hardly spoke at all.

"There is a lot of divorce in this job," Mike said. "I can see why a woman would get sick of being alone and raising kids, not knowing when or if her husband will come home."

"Not to mention looking like a drug dealer even when I do clean up," Richard said, motioning to his shaggy hair and long mustache.

Mike laughed. "I went to a daddy and daughter event at our church, and I realized my daughter was walking in front of me and acting like she was with another father. I guess it isn't too cool to have a dad whose hair is longer than yours."

Richard laughed. It was something he hadn't thought about because he and Michelle had decided years ago they didn't want children, but then again, he had put blinders on when he went after this job, and it probably wouldn't have mattered anyway. It made him feel selfish, but he rationalized it wasn't something he could change now.

For almost a year, Richard and Mike worked the case of a

Mexican drug cartel who had found a consistent and reliable channel to bring in heroin to the southwestern part of the United States. The drug was so addictive, it convinced Richard there was nothing more potent or evil, which made the work even more relevant in his mind. He was in with the group, portraying himself as a small dealer. He was under the radar, but still able to gather information through the trust he had built. Mike was his distributor and worked even more closely with the group's leaders.

Richard watched closely and was always amazed by Mike's knowledge of the business and the use of linguistics and terminology. His Spanish was fluent, and while Richard could get by with his broken grammar and jargon, Mike's was spot-on and flawless.

"I spent two years in Brazil on a church mission," Mike explained. "I felt like my calling to go to Brazil was God's way of telling me this was the path I should take in life."

Richard wasn't into religion, so he didn't say much. It didn't make sense to him, but much of what Mike said about his faith didn't. Richard did have some curiosities about the strange customs and notorious history of the Mormons. Still, he felt opening that subject would offend Mike or give him the impression that Richard was ripe for proselytizing.

Several broken-down cars and trucks were parked at odd angles when they arrived at the trailer. The wind whipped dust and debris around them as they gingerly walked to the front door. Richard knocked and listened, waiting to hear the code they would respond to and allow them in for a buy. Nothing.

Silence except for the blustery bits of dirt hitting the sides of the trailer.

Mike tried to peek through the tattered aluminum blinds on the front window and saw movement. He knocked again.

"Gordo, it's us. Open up!" he shouted, blinking away the sand from his eyes.

The door cracked and a large Hispanic man stood in the gap. "We've got nothing today, man," he said quickly. His eyes darted, and he was sweating.

Richard tried to look past him. "What do you mean you got nothing? We drove two fucking hours. You said you had the stuff."

Gordo was yanked back from the door. Richard caught a glance of a tall, darkly dressed man who ducked out of view, but then the door slammed.

"Gordo?" Richard yelled out.

Mike stepped back, sensing danger.

They stood for a moment, wondering if they should continue to call out or retreat. After a few stunned and confusing moments, they decided on the latter.

As they cautiously walked back to their car in silence, a horrid scream pierced the air, and both men turned back toward the trailer—the sound of crashing and commotion, and then a loud, piercing shriek. With guns drawn, they ducked behind their car.

"What the hell was that?" whispered Mike in a panic. "We need back-up."

Richard agreed, but their surveillance team was far enough out that it would take at least a half-hour for them to get there. Usually, they could watch from a distance, hidden by other cars and houses, but this trailer was in the deep desert, and there was nowhere to hide.

They slid into the car and, while still ducking down, started the ignition and quickly pulled away. When they were at a distance, they radioed the men waiting and told them what had happened. When they reached the truck where the others were parked, they radioed back to the bureau and explained what they had heard.

To their disappointment, their supervisor told them to return to the office to plan for what to do next.

"It was fucked up," Richard explained to the others. "I don't know what that noise was or who else was in there, but it's bad news, even in Gordo's circles."

"Why would someone bother with Gordo?" Mike wondered. "He's a street dealer."

Richard huffed. "He's a dealer, and who knows what these users will do to get their stuff."

When they returned the next morning, they surrounded the trailer with a half-dozen other agents. Richard called with a bull horn for Gordo to come out, but there was no response.

One of the officers shot a smoke bomb through the front window, and within seconds, the entire trailer billowed with a white haze. Still, nothing happened. When the smoke had dissipated, they stormed the trailer.

Inside was stilled chaos. Torn drapes, overturned furniture, and the body of Gordo, his head sliced off so precisely, it was as if a surgeon had done the work. And yet, the only signs of blood were a few splatters up the walls and on the floor.

"Do you think someone came in and cleaned things up?" one of the younger agents asked.

"And leave the body? That makes no sense," Richard snapped back.

"What could have done this?" Mike asked as he studied the severed head of his best dealer.

Richard thought back to the horrified look on Gordo's face when they'd left and felt his insides clench. Gordo was a drug dealer, and yet, Richard felt pity for the man.

The thought of anyone enduring this type of torture was

terrible, but he saw in Gordo's eyes the horrific knowledge of what was about to happen, and that made Richard shiver.

"Heroin dealer?" the lead investigator asked.

"Yes, but this buy was that new drug, the Milagro," Richard answered.

"He had it?" the investigator asked, skeptical that a lowlife such as Gordo would have access to something so rare.

Richard nodded. "He had ties deep in. We had been working it for months."

The investigator looked back at the rest of his crew skeptically. "We've been working that drug out of Yuma through the Espinoza cartel, and we've seen nothing. Why do you think this was the real thing?"

The investigator's sardonic tone made Richard stand up straighter. He felt anger rise in his chest, and that's when Mike stepped forward.

"It was *our* sample they tested," Mike said. "Remember the meeting where we all discussed the sample that was found? That's how we know."

Richard lifted his chin to emphasize Mike's point, and the investigator nodded defeat.

Richard started to speak, but then a soft knocking came from the other room, and they all put their hands to their guns and paused. Eyes darting, they all listened. The dull thudding came again.

The lead investigator motioned to Mike, who was closest to the room.

With breath held, Mike padded toward the noise, and the others followed. He bent down cautiously to where he had zeroed in on the thumping. He slid a metal-framed twin-sized bed away from the wall and pulled up a ragged woven rug.

There was a metal ring attached to a floorboard. He looked

up at the others to show what he'd found, and then with one hand, while the others aimed their guns, he pulled up the board, revealing a shallow hole. He stepped closer, and there in the darkness, a squinty-eyed face peered up.

"Hands up!" Mike yelled. *"Manos Arriba!"* he repeated in Spanish.

It was a boy. He flinched back, but slowly put his hands by his head.

Richard walked over and bent down, and he and Mike pulled the young man from the small crawl space. As they did this, he cringed in pain. He was thin and weak, and his eyes were vacant. Mike led him to the bed and sat him on the edge as Richard and another officer cautiously looked into the hole with flashlights for any others.

Mike bent and studied the boy. Dirt and sweat covered him, and though his body was small and sickly, he looked to be in his teens. A tiny wisp of stubble lined his lip.

Another officer handed him water, and the boy drank like a starved animal, choking as he gulped the water down. When he stopped, Mike stood and then backed away.

"Watch out," he warned the others. The boy heaved and vomited the water onto the floor. His body exhausted and his will depleted, he curled into the bed and began to cry. Mike found an old T-shirt, handed it to him to wipe his face, and sat on a chair facing him. "You're safe now. We're going to get you help."

The boy looked over at him with both fear and disgust.

"I promise. No one else is going to hurt you," Mike said, handing him the water again. "Small sips this time."

The young man took it and nodded.

"How long were you down there?" Mike asked.

The young man shrugged and shook his head.

"What's your name?"

The boy peered up. "Jorge," he answered.

"Who put you down there? Was it Gordo?"

The boy swallowed and swayed, dehydrated and waning. He shook his head.

"Then who?" he pressed.

"Gordo was hiding me," the young man said in a hoarse whisper.

"From who?"

Jorge waited a minute, and then his body shuddered. He mumbled through dry, cracked lips, "Diablo."

Mike and Richard both shot each other a glance.

It was a name they had heard before, and one they dreaded.

In the early part of summer, the head of the Yuma bureau gathered the agents to discuss a new drug recently discovered coming from Mexico. Richard took a seat near the back, and Mike slid into the seat next to him.

Fourteen young men dead. All were tortured, either thrown off buildings or cliffs or burned alive, and many of the bodies had been mutilated. The photos were graphic and horrifying, and Richard could hardly identify the burned victims as human. It was too disturbing. Their skin was charred black, and their faces were non-existent except for a gaping hole that must have been a mouth, screaming out in pain.

"All between fourteen and sixteen years of age. Not one had been reported missing. Our agents found them out of Guadalajara." The director paused and looked at the floor for a moment. "This is what we see with this new drug. They found another group of boys six months ago near this area.

"They were partially burned, and one had parts of his spine

removed. Large chunks just carved out of his back. It was done postmortem. We see this at all the murder scenes, but with only some of the bodies. Our informants tell us the murders are connected to a man they call Diablo. He's the primary source of the drug." He paused as all the agents scribbled down the name. "We're assuming these boys are street runners who stole from him, but we've never had contact or even a description—just a name. We're not sure if these killings are to prove a point or keep them quiet, and we have no idea about the holes that are carved out of their backs. We've had no press, and don't want any. We have no information about what this is and don't need the public frantic. What I do need is a source to tell us where this drug is coming from and where to find this Diablo."

The meeting and name replayed in Richard's mind as he and Mike shuffled the boy past the severed and blood-splattered body of Gordo toward the police car. Richard was sure that if they hadn't shown up yesterday, the boy would have ended up burned alive or thrown to his death like the other boys who seemed to follow this new mystery drug. He wondered what lure it had that caused such horrific acts of gore and violence in the quest to attain it.

He had witnessed the wrath of heroin within the communities he served. Even some of the officers he'd worked with had personal stories involving their kids or other family members robbing them, striking out when they were loaded—all desperate acts to get their fix, but nothing he saw compared to this.

He knew the high must be so incomparably addictive, the thought of being without it drove these murderous acts.

What he didn't understand was how the burning and mutilation connected with attaining the drug. Was it to hide some-thing or to threaten others not to defy the cartel? Whoever Diablo was, he was now in the crosshairs of the DEA, and Richard wondered how many more burned boys they would find before they could stop this drug dealer with the devil's name.

CHAPTER

FOURTEEN

Yuma, Arizona, 1972

The high experienced by those addicted to Milagro was something that eluded investigators for months. What was it that made this drug so appealing? Attaining the drug and the gruesome and murderous acts were well-documented, but how the drug affected those using it wasn't transparent.

The bureau's forensic chemists had briefed the agents about Milagro and its chemical properties, but no one had ever discussed the signs of an addict or the sensations the drug brought on for those who used it. The lure was still a mystery to the agents who witnessed the devastation in its path, which made investigating it a frustrating enigma.

It was especially true for Richard, having seen firsthand the bloody corpse of his informant and the devastated young boy they had saved from an almost certain tortuous death. It wore on him the way it did when he was a young detective investigating a murder and not knowing a motive. The "why" wasn't just crucial to solving a crime; for him, it gave perspective on the mind of who he was after and gave him some idea of what he faced.

Kidnapping and torturing young boys were not what he had seen even within the most dangerous drug gangs, so he knew this drug was unlike anything he had ever worked with.

It was a mandatory meeting, and both Mike and Richard took their usual seats at the back of the room. When the expert brought in by the DEA began to explain in detail what he had seen the drug do, Richard moved closer.

"We've been able to isolate a specific protein that seems to be what makes this drug so powerful. This protein in the drug, when introduced into the blood system, is shown, at least in our early studies, to repair damaged cells in the body," the man said. "Our studies are still very new, but we've seen it destroy viruses and eliminate and repair cancer cells."

The small group of agents all paused in thought, and most sat up, leaned forward, and found pens to take notes in anticipation of what more he had to say.

He wasn't the typical DEA scientist. Most of them were harried and disheveled-looking. This man was tall, with immaculate clothes and black hair combed neatly into place. His skin was dark, and he spoke with a slight Spanish accent. But what didn't fit with his impeccable and astute appearance was a pronounced limp that required the use of an ornately carved cane.

His name was Luis Davila. He was a neuroscientist and pharmacological researcher at Stanford University.

"So, what's the high?" Richard asked. "And if this is something medically beneficial, why aren't companies trying to produce it legally?"

"Who's not to say that they won't?" Davila pointed out. "As I said, this is very early. It is something we've never worked with before, so there is still much more study needed before we know it is safe and that it is what we think it is."

Richard and the others nodded, thinking about what the doctor had explained.

"But what about the high?" Richard asked again. He was now standing. "Drug addicts and dealers don't kill people for medicine no one knows about. They rob and kill for money and the high."

Dr. Davila nodded and took a deep breath. "There is a euphoric high. We've seen and been told that the person has the sensation of lightness, of contentment. They feel like they are invincible. Like they can fly."

This statement hit both Richard and Mike like a slap. For months now, they had seen the photos and investigated the remains of numerous young boys found at the bottom of desolate desert cliffs. They had assumed they'd been pushed, tortured for information, or punished for not complying with a dealer's demands, but now with this new information, they sat back and wondered if these boys hadn't jumped.

"What's the drug made out of?" one of the other agents asked. "Where does it come from?"

Davila raised his eyebrows. "Good question," he said. "Right now, all we know is that the protein is derived from an iron-rich substance, like blood."

"This drug is made from blood?" Mike asked, looking disgusted.

Davila nodded. "We believe it's from blood, but that is where it gets complicated. We know that all the samples tested are the same type of blood. However, it's a blood type that we've never seen before in humans or animals—that is, until recently—and the samples we've received are from a very small group of patients, who are all fighting the same rare disease."

"The blood comes from people who are sick?" asked another agent.

"As I told you before, it all needs more study," the doctor replied. "This is really all I have for you at this time."

When the meeting was over, Mike, Richard, and several other agents stayed in the room and discussed the information.

"A drug made from the blood of sick people that makes you feel like you can fly and cures disease?" Richard pondered aloud. "It's even more fucked up than I thought."

Mike laughed. His Mormon upbringing usually kept him from using the crass language that was commonplace around the bureau, but he couldn't help agreeing with the sentiment.

As the weeks passed, Richard and Mike watched and waited for another opportunity to find an informant with ties to Milagro. With Gordo gone, they were hesitant to call on his contacts immediately and raise suspicion. Soon, it looked to be the only way they would get any traction on a drug that was difficult to find, but kept leaving gruesome reminders that it was flourishing. There was no pattern or noticeable group of addicts or even users, but the trail of young bodies smashed at the bottom of cliffs or burned alive continued to grow. This made the need to infiltrate the drug's line into the country even more vital.

It was less than two weeks later when Dr. Davila came back to update the group. A strange and deadly occurrence had happened at an isolated place along the jagged cliffs and prehistoric lava beds along the Snake River in southeastern Idaho. Hundreds of miles from the Mexican border where the drug seemed to be clustered, the Milagro was found covering the hands of a cave explorer found dead at the bottom of a cavern.

"His climbing partner is hospitalized and unable to talk

about what happened," Davila explained. "The killing looks to be animal-related."

Richard's brows furrowed, wondering what possible connection that incident could have with the drug.

What made the find even more crucial and interesting were patients in that same area with a rare congenital abnormality that, when biopsied, had the same blood type as the protein found in Milagro.

"The blood in their veins had slight traces, but the blood in their tumors is where the blood type was concentrated." Davila paused to allow them time to consider the odd discovery.

"What in the hell?" Richard said, thinking what the rest of the small group was also contemplating. He turned to the large paper map on the wall. "The Milagro comes up from the border. Have we found it anywhere else?" he asked. He knew the answer, just like everyone else. It was no, and he shook his head. He turned to Davila. "Have there been any other cases of this abnormality outside of that area of Idaho?"

"No. However, there was a cluster of similar cases in Central America in 1945," Davila said. "But most of the people who had the condition have died or were killed during the surgery to remove the tumors, so I don't know if it's the same condition. I've contacted their health ministries to find out what I can."

"You said the protein is concentrated in a tumor in people that have this blood type, and that you find this blood type in patients with this birth defect. What is this disease?" Richard asked.

Davila thought for a moment, and then, steadying himself with the cane, reached over his shoulder with his other arm and pointed to his back. "It's a growth that forms on the sides of the spine by the shoulder blades. The tumor intertwines with the spine."

Richard felt his stomach drop.

Mike looked at their supervisor, Jim Greaves. "Do we know if any of the murdered boys had this defect? Isn't that where they had those chunks cut out of them?"

Greaves nodded. "I believe so. I can put in some calls. It's worth a try."

Davila looked surprised. "What boys?"

Richard briefly explained the murdered boys they had seen in connection to their investigations of Milagro.

The look on Davila's face was both telling and somber.

"You don't think they're killing these kids for their..." Richard's question faded, but it was apparent that the entire group was thinking it. "Can we go to Idaho and talk to these people? What about the guy who was found murdered? Can we talk to investigators up there?"

The supervisor took a labored breath. "I know this is important, but we've got heroin, cocaine, and opium dealers I'm still trying to work here. Make some calls first. If you leave, I'm left with ten agents for the entire state of Arizona."

"Get the state narcs to pitch in," Mike said. "They're always griping about us taking their glory anyway."

"And we should put out a notice to hospitals and doctors to be on the lookout for this defect, this tumor. It could be our link to the source of this drug," Richard said. "This guy Diablo is probably out there hunting them down already. These people could be in danger when they're looking for medical help." He took a deeper breath. "We could have a mole in the system who is alerting him to when these tumors are tested and come back positive." Then he turned to Davila. "Do you think that could happen?"

"Anything is possible," Davila said.

Mike broke in. "But none of the murdered boys was even reported missing. These were street kids from Mexico, not children whose parents were getting them medical care."

"We're getting way ahead of ourselves," Greaves said. "We don't even know for certain if this drug is really related to this blood thing. Right, doc?"

Davila stammered. "There are still lots of tests to be done, but..."

"See," Greaves said. "Make some calls, and let's meet again when we can outline what we have that is concrete." He dismissed the meeting and left the room.

Davila looked perplexed as he gathered his notes, so Richard went to him and thanked him for his information.

"I'm sure this feels like a battle you're never going to win," Davila said as he shook Richard's hand.

"Like President Nixon said, 'This is a war,'" Richard said as he walked Davila to the door. "It's not something I expect to see an end in my lifetime."

Davila started to say something, but stopped. When they reached the door, he gave Richard a small smile. It felt like he wanted to talk, but instead, he said goodbye and left quickly.

When Richard walked back to the office, Mike was standing at his desk, putting papers in a briefcase.

"There are too many similarities not to be connected," Richard said.

Mike nodded. "Quite frankly, this whole thing makes me sick. The idea of blood and tumors and using the bodies of people to make this stuff is kind of like cannibalism."

Richard reeled back. He hadn't made that comparison at all and was surprised at his colleague's reaction, having seen his grittiness in so many other more repugnant situations. "I hadn't thought of it that way, but Diablo doesn't seem to be above anything."

Mike continued aimlessly shoving papers into the case. "I have to go home and help Sheila with the kids. She's not feeling well again."

"Having four rug rats can do that to you," Richard said thoughtlessly.

Mike looked up, his face drained. "Yeah, but it doesn't help when I've got all my stuff to do as well."

"I can do this," Richard said, reaching for the papers. "Let me help."

"No," Mike said, putting his hand on the papers. "I'm good. Just tired. And hearing all this crap about dead kids and weird drugs made from people's tumor blood doesn't help." He closed the briefcase. "I don't see how you do it without a belief in something higher. Without my faith in God, I don't know what I'd do." He put his head down. "I'm sorry," he said. "I shouldn't have..."

Richard put a hand up. "It's okay. I'm good," he said. "This stuff gets to me too. We all have our ways of coping. Go home and take care of Sheila and the kids. I'll see you in the morning."

Mike took a deep breath and gathered the last of the papers. "Thank you," he said before leaving.

When Mike was gone, Richard sat at his desk and wondered how long Mike would last as an agent. He had seen officers burn out before, and heard story after story from his father about cops who let the stress end their careers. He didn't know why the job didn't seem to faze him. He never let the angst or horror of what he saw affect him to the point of losing sleep. He figured it was because he was raised in it, and when it came to his relationship with Michelle, he knew there was more to their problems than just his job.

His devotion to the work had led to the loss of commitment to his marriage. As he sat and thought, he wondered why he wasn't unhappy about that realization, but after a while, he shrugged, and his thoughts turned back to Davila. Soon, hours had passed, and he forced himself to push away from his desk and make his way home.

· · ·

Richard's phone was ringing when he opened the office door that morning. He answered it, and then sat stunned by what he heard. He leaned back in his chair and let out an exhausted huff when he hung up. He stared ahead, but the icy chill that ran through him had his mind completely blown. It can't be, he thought. It's too coincidental.

"What's with you?" Mike asked. The drop of the phone startled him as he sat, mindlessly filling out reports. When he saw Richard sitting stunned, he leaned forward and asked again.

"He's got family in Idaho," Richard mumbled.

"Who does?"

"That kid." Richard looked up. "That kid from the trailer. They're sending him to southeast Idaho. He's got an uncle there. That's where he was going when they grabbed him."

Mike listened, but then he sat up and shook his head. "Southeast Idaho is where the cluster of people lived who had the tumors that produced the drug. The blood drug."

"He wasn't just some street urchin, kidnapped with the rest. That kid was a target," Richard said.

"Do you think he has the disease?" Mike asked.

Richard looked over at him. His eyes became wide with the realization of it. "We need to find out."

"Call Davila?" Mike asked.

Richard nodded and quickly picked up the phone.

They met at Davila's hotel. He had already checked out, but hadn't left for the airport. The three sat in the hotel diner, sipping coffee—though Mike had water—and contemplated the outlandish but likely situation.

"If this kid does have that disease, what will happen to him?" Mike asked. "We've heard what the blood is used for, but what about the person who has the disease? Does it eventually kill them?"

Davila looked surprised by the question. "We've never identified anyone who has lived long enough to say. They may be out there, but we only know of the ones we've found recently."

"All in Idaho?" asked Richard.

Davila nodded.

Richard looked at Mike. "We have to go out there. I don't care what Greaves says. This proves there's a connection, and we have to go."

"Shouldn't we have the kid tested first?" Mike asked. "We need to make sure."

"Where is the boy?" Davila asked.

Richard felt a sickening chill shoot through him. If Diablo had killed Gordo in his quest to find this boy for his blood, he would still be out there waiting and watching for his chance to strike again.

"He's with a foster family, but the social workers were planning to send him to Idaho to his uncle," Richard answered. "They just told me this morning."

"You don't think he's already gone?" Mike asked.

Richard turned to Davila. "Can you stay? Just until we find out if the kid is still here and whether or not we can get the test done?"

Davila nodded.

It took Richard an hour to track down the social worker who had called and informed him of the boy's relocation, but he was relieved to learn he was still in the system, and they had two days to get the tests started.

"The results could take weeks," Davila warned when he heard the boy would be leaving the next day.

Richard paced and sighed loudly. "Why can't they see he's in danger? We can't just let him go without protection. Do they honestly think Diablo will let him run off into the sunset and live happily after all this? I'm surprised he's still alive."

"He's not going to strike when the kid's in state custody," Mike said.

Richard paused. "How long, really?" he asked Davila. "Before the tests come back?"

Davila shrugged. "I'd say at least a week, but probably longer. This isn't a common test, and they only do it at a specific lab. And it's not something we want getting out."

Richard paced more, then he stopped. "We've got to hold him here."

Mike sighed. "On what? We can't keep him from his family."

"But he's in danger," Richard said.

"Greaves doesn't see it that way," Mike argued.

"Then I'm going with him." Richard crossed his arms defiantly. "I have to. If we lose him, we've lost this entire case."

Mike cocked his head. "Do you really think Greaves is going to approve you giving some kid around-the-clock protection in another state? We don't even have proof this is connected yet."

"Of course we do," Richard countered. "The source of the drug comes from that area. That kid said he was hiding from Diablo. That guy who was there with Gordo was Diablo. He's the one who killed him. It's all connected. He's after that kid. And as weird and crazy as this all is, that kid is what that drug lord is after, and we have to protect him. If it were a hundred pounds of that drug being shipped out, they would be doing everything in their power to go after it." He stood and waited for a response.

Mike scratched his head and took a long, labored breath. "I'm not going to disagree with you, but I don't see how you're going to convince Greaves."

"If we don't, that kid's a goner. We all know it. That evil

bastard's out there, and I have a feeling he already knows those tests will come back positive."

Mike nodded. "You're right, but we've got hundreds of other cases, and this is just one kid."

Richard centered his stance. "Well, if that one kid is going to Idaho. I'm going with him."

CHAPTER

FIFTEEN

Milo

My grandmother's talks diminished as I got older. I started finding television and my friends more entertaining than her stories. I began to forget about her tales of my impending lot in life and had written off her outlandish ideas, much as my mother had. I saw her stories as a sad and lonely attempt to gain my attention.

My mother was still distracted and cold to her, and my grandmother was now even more isolated and alone without me to entertain. She walked for hours in the lava and sage-covered canyon, and to my surprise, she never invited me to join her. It was her solace away from the sad and lonely life with the only family she still had.

But when my back started to ache, her stories came back to me in great detail. She had explained that when I came of age, along with the other changes in my body, the ridges on my back would expand and begin to burn and throb. Sometimes, my skin would even become so tender and irritated, it would split and bleed.

Up until that point, the ridges and rash were nothing more than odd, scaly patches along each side of my spine. I lived in Idaho and the weather was often cold, which meant I spent very little time without a shirt. When I had to undress around anyone other than my family, I did what most kids do who are dealing with a physical imperfection: I became stealthy at hiding it. Other than that, it didn't bother me.

That all changed one night after a high school dance. I had never been to a dance or even considered going to one until that night, and especially not one that was in a different town, but something pulled me there.

The week leading up to it, I woke several times in the night with thoughts of the dance and an odd desire to go. I had no idea how I even knew it was taking place, but I found out and planned to be there.

I went with my best friend, Don. He was baffled I wanted to go, but agreed to tag along. I think he was curious about what we'd see and why I felt the need to be there. It wasn't as though I didn't show any interest in girls, but I just never did much to pursue them. Neither of us had girlfriends, and since we were in tenth grade, we didn't carry much importance in the hierarchy of teenage status.

I kept a close eye on my few dark hairs above my lip and the increasing size of my chest and arms, but I still wasn't much compared to the bulging shoulders and hairy groins of the boys just a few years older. Don had it worse. He was short with a shock of red hair. The older boys taunted him, saying, "He's got red hair, even down there."

We were the bottom feeders, so why we even bothered to go to a dance made no sense. I wasn't looking to dance. I'm not sure what I was expecting, but when I stood with my back to the wall of the gym, staring at the others swaying together like awkward tangled trees, even in the dimly lit crush of bodies, she seemed to glow.

That was when I knew why.

I knew her. But I hadn't noticed the shape of her face or the soft way her dark hair fell in large curls around her neck and shoulders. It was the same girl I'd walked to the convenience store for candy during the summer of our fifth grade, the one I got in trouble with for picking the freshly bloomed roses of her neighbor, and the one up until that moment I never thought I'd see again.

It was Clara. My childhood friend. But now, a warm shiver went through me, and I felt something I'd never even considered before. I put my hand in my pocket to hide my new feeling. It had happened many times before, but not in such a significant and potentially socially lethal place.

Don looked over and realized what had happened and let a small burst of laughter escape. I hit him with my free hand and looked over to what had caused my condition.

Don followed my gaze. "She's hot. Too hot for you," he chided. "Who is she?"

I stood and watched her. She smiled and laughed with a small group of girls. "Clara," I said, in a trance.

"Wait," Don said. He turned from me to Clara. "So, that's why we're here. You knew she'd be here."

"No. I didn't know."

"Whatever," he said with an eye roll.

"No, really. I didn't know," I insisted. And it was true. I had no idea what had pulled me there that night.

He watched her for a moment. "Are you going to talk to her? How long has it been?" He stopped, remembering the small bit I had told him of our somber past and how it intertwined our families.

I didn't respond. He knew what I was thinking and wondering. Would she treat me differently now? Would she even act like she knew me?

"Go ask her to dance," he said, nudging me. "But you'll need both hands."

I shrugged him off and walked away. I found a darker part of the gym and stood focusing my mind on dead puppies and my grandmother's feet to alleviate my inconvenient setback.

I kept my eyes off her, and then I felt a hand on my arm. I turned, and there she was, large green eyes so vivid even in the dimly lit gym, lips shiny and full. The sight of her made me weak, and yet, she struck me as strange. It was her, and I was so glad to be near her again, but something was odd.

"Hey," she said with a smile. "I can't believe it's you. What are you doing here?"

"Hey," I said back and shrugged, trying not to be overzealous.

"My dad said you moved away. Did you move back?"

I cleared my throat and tried to act like I was bored. "No. Same old house by the lava caves..." I stopped, wondering why I had begun to bring up the past. "The one out by the reservoir."

She looked stunned. "Really? All these years you've been there?"

I nodded.

She looked deflated, and her smile dissolved.

I was surprised to see her look disappointed, so I blurted out, "I should have called. I wanted to. I don't have your number."

Clara sighed, and a small smile crept back. "It was a long time ago. And I didn't have a cell phone back then."

I tried to look at her, but my heart was racing and a pang shot up my back. I took a deep breath, hoping to calm myself.

She pulled out her phone. "What's your number?"

I grabbed my phone, and when we finished putting in our

numbers, she looked up and smiled. "It's weird, but I had a feeling I'd be seeing you."

I nodded, unsure if I should tell her I'd had the same overwhelming pull to be there.

"I remember all the fun we used to have," she said softly. "We should hang out sometime." She said it hesitantly, as if she was unsure I'd want to, then she beamed at me. "Like we used to."

My heart and stomach flipped. I nodded. I couldn't imagine anything being like it used to be, but the thought of spending time with her was something I had thought about often over the years. I stood smiling. I was still admiring her skin, the way her shirt hugged her tiny waist, and her supple curves.

Then someone violently slammed into me. The shove was so unexpected, it knocked me to the ground. It was not so much from the force of the push, but the shock of it.

When I looked up, I realized the crowd around me was snickering. Standing above me were three guys dressed entirely in black. In the dim light of the school gym, I could see they were older and bigger than me.

"Victor," Clara huffed. Her breathing seemed labored as she coughed and brushed by them, coming to my aid.

"What?" the largest of the three asked flippantly. "I didn't see him. I was looking for you."

"Yes, you did see him. Why are you even here?" She was by my side, helping me up, but this embarrassed me even more.

Victor had black hair and wore a long trench coat with a hood. The others were dressed similarly, and all three wore dark glasses. It was odd, considering it was night and we were in a dark gym. Even with his glasses, I could see him glaring at me. The other two stood to his side. Their faces were vacant.

He turned to Clara. "Let's go. Your cough is getting worse. We need to get your meds."

"You don't know what I need," Clara snapped at him. She turned back. "Are you okay?"

I got to my feet, and when I saw Victor looking smug, my anger took over. I felt my stomach begin to heave, and a shot of pain burned up my back. I gave a yelp that startled Clara.

Victor snickered.

"Shut up," I growled. I was so horrified, and with every ounce of effort I could muster, I tried to stand upright, but an odd stirring in my head made my eyes blur, and my head began to buzz.

Victor stepped in front of Clara, and he towered over me. I felt the pain increase in my back, making me wince and take a step back.

He scoffed as I backed down.

"Quit following me," she spat at them.

Victor took a deep breath, then motioned for the others to back away.

Clara came to my side. She put her hand on my back. "I'm sorry. Are you sure you're okay?"

My stomach seized with her touch. "I'm fine," I said, brushing her off, embarrassed. "Who is that?" I asked, looking to where they stood.

"It's just Victor, my stepbrother," she said, annoyed. She looked over her shoulder at the three who stood off to the side, watching us.

"Stepbrother?" I asked, surprised. "Did your parents get divorced?"

She stared at me, confused, and let out a knowing huff. "I forgot you haven't been around all these years." She shook her and sighed. "A lot has happened. And yes, my parents aren't together any longer."

I felt my heart sink. "I'm sorry."

She shrugged. "It's been a long time." Then she covered her mouth with her elbow and coughed.

"Clara," Victor called. "I'm sure your little friend is fine. Let's go."

She flashed him a glare, and when she turned back to me, I saw pity in her eyes.

The ache in my back was now constant, and that, along with my anger and humiliation, made my upper lip begin to sweat in that terrible way it does when you're about to vomit. I began to shake, and I knew I had to leave quickly.

"I have to go," was all I said, and I practically pushed her aside as I ran for the door.

"Milo, wait!" Clara called.

I didn't answer and practically ran to the exit. When I pushed the bar to open the door, I turned back to see her watching me with Victor now holding her by the arm. She looked annoyed, also disappointed, but I couldn't stay.

I was grateful that she didn't come after me. I turned back and bolted through the door. When the cool air of the night hit my face, I took a deep breath, trying to keep the impending rupture at bay, but the pain was still there, and I lunged for a large metal trash can and retched as others snickered and made comments about my inability to hold my beer.

At that point, what usually would have horrified and embarrassed me hardly fazed me, as the pain was the only thing filling my mind. Along with the burn came fear. What was wrong with me? The throbbing was the exact area of the bulging patches along my spine. Once benign, although annoying, the site now throbbed so intensely that had I been able to reach back, I would have clawed it out with my bare hands.

"Milo, you okay?" Don asked, now at my side.

I looked up at him with a face that must have spoken for me as his brow lowered and his eyes grew large.

"Get me home," I blurted.

The drive was a blur. I remember throwing up into an empty McDonald's bag in Don's car and apologizing for it, but the rest was a muddle of pain and streetlights. Most of the way, I sat crumpled in agony in the seat next to him.

When we arrived at my house, he helped me to the door and into the house. When my mom entered the living room, she looked scared and confused. I heard Don trying to explain what had happened as I made my way to the bathroom and sprawled myself at the base of the toilet. Moments later, both she and my grandmother were in the doorway of the bathroom.

"Were you drinking?" my mother asked. She sounded more perplexed than accusatory.

"No," I mustered. "Is Don still here?" I wasn't sure why, but something told me what I was feeling wasn't something to be shared, even with my best friend. When my mother said he had left, I broke down in tears and told her of the excruciating pain between my shoulders.

My mother brought me a wet washcloth to wipe straggling vomit from my face, and then she helped me to my room. As we passed my grandmother's room, I glanced in just long enough to see her sitting, watching me with tortured eyes. She was usually prone to drama, so I let the pain and exhaustion keep me from lingering on it.

My mother settled me onto my bed. I moaned, feeling as though a truck had hit me. Every muscle felt sore.

"The flu?" my mother asked.

"It's my back. Those things on my back." That was all I could muster.

"Let's take off your shirt and look," my mother said.

"No," I said, wanting to be left alone. "Let me just lay here."

"Should I call the doctor?" she asked.

"No!" I said forcefully. I sat taking measured, deep breaths, and eventually, the pain eased. When I could look up and speak to her without cringing, I convinced her I was fine and just needed sleep. She was not eager to leave my room, but I insisted. When I tried to lie down, my back felt like it was on fire, so I slept on my stomach without covers.

My dreams were vivid, and I was restless, and I heard the door to my room open several times in the night. My grandmother's stories continued to play over in my mind, making me wonder if there was merit to the bizarre tales and foreboding.

Could it all be true?

SIXTEEN

Milo

Surprisingly, by morning I felt much better. My back was still tender when my shirt brushed over it, but I came to breakfast and refused to let anyone see I was sore. My grandmother gave me odd glances, and my mother pushed her and told her to stop it.

"Are you sure you're well enough to go to school?" my mother asked.

"I'm fine," I said. And when I began to drive off, I could see them both standing in the doorway, watching my truck leave.

At school, Don was all questions. "What the hell happened to you?" he asked in the hall. "Those guys were jerks, but what made you so sick? It took me all Sunday to get the smell out of my car."

I gave an exasperated groan. "I know. I'm sorry." I didn't know what to tell him. He was my best friend. I had known him for years, and yet, even what was happening to me was too bizarre to reveal. "I was sick all weekend," I lied.

"Clara's been calling, worried about you," he said.

I felt my chest tighten. "She did?"

He held up my phone. "You left it in my car. I finally answered it."

"I've been looking everywhere for that. What'd she say?" I asked, taking it from him.

"She thought you were trying to get away from her or something. I can't believe she even cares. I told her you were gay."

I stopped mid-step and turned to him, shocked.

He looked at me, and a huge smile spread across his face.

I punched his arm and huffed. "Asshole," I said.

Don gave his goofy snort, the way he always did when he thought he'd gotten away with something. He stopped before we went to our separate classes.

"So, what did happen?" he asked.

I paused for a moment, and then shrugged.

He shook his head and squinted his eyes, unsatisfied. "There's something weird. Are you sick?"

"No. I told you—"

"I know, but it's not just what happened the other night. It's..." He paused and cocked his head. "You look...different."

I looked down at myself. "What do you mean?"

"I don't know, but something is different."

I shrugged. We walked a bit more, but then I stopped and made sure we were out of earshot. Don raised his brows.

"Did you notice his eyes?" I asked.

Don thought a moment, his face pinched. "Whose eyes? They all had on sunglasses, remember? It was weird. It was night, and they were in the dark gym. The whole thing was nuts."

I nodded, remembering, yet realizing I still saw the red glow. "I know it was dark and all, but his eyes were red. You didn't see it?"

He thought a moment, then shook his head. "No. They were

probably all high on drugs. All I saw was what jerks they were. You sure you feel okay?"

"Yes," I assured him.

From his expression, I could see that he didn't believe me, and he kept looking at me oddly. I felt my forehead begin to sweat. Did Don see what was happening to me? Was he suspecting the abnormal and alarming changes I was experiencing? I wondered if I should tell him, trust him with what my body was doing.

Then the bell rang, sparing me that decision.

Don gave me an annoyed huff as we parted, obviously unhappy with what he saw as my avoidance. It wasn't what I was trying to do, but I didn't know how much I should say or even what was really going on.

In class, I was useless. The rest of the day, all I did was think about Clara. After the fourth-period class break, I was in my truck and heading for her school. I didn't know where the courage came from, but I had to see her. I could have just called, but even after almost an hour's drive, my desire and nerve hadn't waned.

When the bell rang at her school, I stood by my truck at the edge of the parking lot, watching the school's doors and searching for a glimpse of her long dark curls.

I wondered if Victor would be there as well, but whatever spurred me to skip my last two hours of class and make that drive had emboldened me against him.

As I thought about that night at the dance, I pictured Victor's eyes and wondered why they were so unsettling. I didn't like him, but it was more than just his hovering over Clara. There was a disturbing, dreadful sense that filled me even when I simply thought about him. I was discouraged and surprised that he was part of Clara's life. He annoyed her, and it bothered me the way he held onto her as if she was his.

My thoughts went back to Clara's parents. I was surprised to hear they had divorced, and felt sad that I was so out of touch with her life that I had no idea. And now she had a stepbrother who was bent on keeping me away from her. It was as though he was part of the reason we'd been torn apart before. I knew that wasn't the case, but I was frustrated with having yet another barrier. Victor was older and bigger, but what I felt for her and the past we shared had me ready to do whatever it took to be with her.

As I waited by my truck, searching for her, I felt eyes on me. When I turned, I saw a man standing in the shade across the street, watching me. He was covered in dark clothes and wore sunglasses as though trying to be stealthy. He quickly tried to act as though he was looking somewhere else. He was far enough away that I couldn't make out the details of his face, but even at a distance, he was oddly familiar. I could tell he was old by how his body hunched over at an angle, and his dark skin looked weathered. I'd seen him before somewhere, I knew it.

He looked again and realized I was still watching him. He turned and took several hobbled steps toward a car parked nearby.

A chill went over me as he ducked into the car and closed the door. "Esmi," I whispered. It was my grandmother's nickname. I've heard only two people call her Esmi—my grandpa and another man my grandma had taken me to see years ago. My grandfather was dead, and I hardly remembered anything about the weird meeting in the desert when I was a child. And yet, as I walked toward the car, all I could see was the vision I'd had of that man from when I was young.

He didn't look back as he pulled away. And then, the blare of a horn shocked me, and I realized I was standing in the middle of the street with a small blue Toyota at my knees.

I apologized to the woman at the wheel and hurried back to

my truck, but watched as the old man's car disappeared in the distance. So strange. Who was he, and why would he leave so suddenly?

Soon, there was noise and the sound of chatter and laughter. There were people all over the parking lot, and I began to worry. I had missed Clara leaving the school while distracted by the old man. I scanned the area, looking for her. I began to feel foolish, thinking I would find her amongst the hundreds of others who were making their way out of the school and on their way home or to after-school jobs.

Just as I was about to pack it up and head back home, I heard her voice.

"It is you."

I turned, and her face was bright in the afternoon sun. I loved her dark curls, and the red streaks in them flickered in the light. It was then I realized I wasn't near my car, but had somehow made my way to the school.

"What are you doing here?" she asked.

"I felt bad about running out on you." I had no idea what had drawn me there, but it sounded good.

"Are you okay? I tried to call you last night. Don said you were pretty rough."

I nodded and gave her a sheepish smile. "I'm fine."

She stood for a moment, then cocked her head and studied me. This made me feel awkward, and I looked down at myself, wondering what it was she saw.

"You look different," she said. "It's weird."

I laughed. "I look weird?"

"No!" she said, putting a hand on my arm. "I mean, you seriously look taller or bigger or..."

I raised my eyebrows and gave another laugh. "Well, it has been a while since we've hung out. We were just kids."

She shook her head. "No, I mean since last night. I know it

was dark in the gym and all, but you seem different." Different. She was the second person that day to tell me that. Then she sighed, shrugged, and gave me her perfect smile. Her blue eyes looked at me. They were just like I remembered, but then I paused. I thought back to the night in the gym. Her eyes had been a vibrant green then. At the time, it hadn't clicked, and while something had struck me as strange, I hadn't realized what it was.

I had always been aware of Clara's light blue eyes. That had changed. And what was it about Victor and the red glow I'd seen in his? It must have been the lights, or lack of them in the gym, that made them look that way. That was all I could surmise.

"Do you want to do something this weekend?" I asked. I heard the words and couldn't believe I had mustered the courage to say them. "Or does Victor have other plans?" I said it to save face if she turned me down and gauge what control he had over her life.

She rolled her eyes. "He keeps treating me like I'm a kid. Ever since..." She stopped. Her gaze centered on something behind me, and she rolled her eyes in frustration.

I turned, and there he was. He stood at the far edge of the parking lot, the same dark glasses and black coat billowing in the breeze. He didn't move, but simply watched us.

I turned back to Clara. "What's with him?"

"He's always been like this. Even before my dad married Eva," she whispered as though he could hear us from that distance. "He acts like I need his protection. And it's getting worse—he follows me everywhere. He's run off a lot of my friends and any boy I talk to."

I took her by the arm and turned her away from him. "He's not running me off," I said. I guided her through the parked cars in the lot and toward my truck. "Why doesn't your dad do something?" I asked as we walked.

She looked down. "My dad thinks Victor's being a protective older brother, and besides, he doesn't want to get Eva upset."

"Is Eva your stepmom?" I asked.

She shivered. "Yes, but she's no mom. She hardly speaks to me. But she sure has my dad wrapped around her finger. My mother left when I was only nine, and soon after, my father met and married Eva. Her son Victor never lived with us—he stays with his father, who lives in a city just west of Pocatello. At first, I enjoyed the idea of having a brother, especially being an only child, but now Victor is like a constant shadow. The older I get, the more possessive he's become."

I turned back, and Victor was gone. I stopped and scanned the area, sure that he was still lurking, but he was nowhere to be seen. "He left," I told her.

"He'll be back," she said, disheartened. "I can never seem to shake him."

"What grade is he in?" I asked, knowing he was older.

She huffed. "He's not even in school."

The surprise on my face was evident. "How old is he?"

She shrugged. "I think he's twenty or twenty-one."

"Does he have a job? Or a girlfriend?" My questions were direct, but I was even more disturbed by what I heard.

She thought a moment, then looked at me, surprised. "I don't know."

"It's screwed up," I said. "He can't keep harassing you."

She nodded, but then sighed in defeat. "What can I do?"

"Isn't your dad a cop?" I asked. I remembered seeing him as a child and admiring his dark uniform, shiny badge, and a large holstered gun.

"Yes, but..."

I shook my head. "But what? You need to tell him so he can make it stop."

She looked at me with a face full of angst.

I shook my head in frustration, but I was afraid if I pressed her to do more, it would just push her away.

We walked for a moment in silence, then she stopped. "So, do you still want to do something this weekend?" she asked softly.

My disappointment fell away, and I felt my heart rise along with my smile. "Of course."

"What do you want to do?"

I smiled. "Just hang out. Anywhere. Without Victor."

She laughed and nodded.

"Maybe a movie?" I didn't care. I would have stayed there in the parking lot all weekend just to be with her.

She smiled, and we agreed on a date and time.

"Can I give you a ride home?" I asked, motioning to my truck.

"No," she said, and I felt my heart drop again.

My disappointment must have been obvious because she laughed. "I would, but then I would have to figure out a way to come back and get my car."

I gave a relieved smile. She hugged me and left me standing, feeling like my world was entirely right.

I took a deep breath and felt the button on my shirt pull. I looked down and saw the gaps between each button. I wondered when that shirt had become too small. Then I remembered the difficulty I'd had that morning pulling on my jeans. I then realized that Clara's comments about my looking taller and bigger didn't seem so weird after all.

I put my hands on my chest and did a bit of a survey of my body, and then realized I was still standing in the middle of a place filled with my peers. It would be a bad thing to be caught feeling myself up.

As I drove home, I kept looking at my legs and checking my face in the rearview mirror. Something *was* different. Don saw it, and so did Clara. When I got home and found the privacy of my bathroom, I stripped off my clothes and stood staring at my expanded chest, defined stomach, and enlarged arms. Other times, I had mulled over the shape and size of the parts that mattered as a man. I realized that whatever happened the night before had not only changed the size and sensation of the growths on my back, it also affected every other part of my body. But in a matter of hours? It baffled and unsettled me.

I looked toward my grandmother's room. Her stories began shooting back into my mind, like mini-movies of the visions I'd created in my head while hearing them when I was young. Or was this simply that? Was my mind playing with the fears of my ailment and concocting dreams to help me deal with what I may be facing? I lived with a constant pull—my mother's beliefs that I would eventually need medical help and my grandmother's tales of my back, not as a disorder but almost as a path to divinity.

In the mirror, I studied myself and wondered what the only person who mattered to me at that moment would see. Just the thought of Clara sent warmth through me. That simple sensation should have done nothing more than rush my heart, but instead, it started the throbbing in my back, making me cringe and take a seat on the edge of the tub until I could relax enough and wait out the pain.

I was annoyed and frustrated. If nothing more than thinking about her would set me off, I began to fear the thought of being alone and close to her that weekend. Horrific thoughts of my back throbbing, my body aching, and vomiting because of the pain kept haunting me. What if that happened with her?

The thought was so humiliating and terrible, it had me on the verge of calling her and canceling everything.

I was quiet throughout dinner, but did my best not to raise questions with my mother by forcing small talk about the weather and homework, excusing myself to my room to study.

I awoke that night to Esmeralda sitting in a chair by my bed.

"It's started, hasn't it?" she asked.

Her face was somber, and although there was little light in my room, I could see her eyes. I was tired and still not feeling well, and the sight of her was disturbing.

"Leave me alone," I huffed.

"I can't," she said. She was facing forward in a daze.

My eyes began to see more in the dimness of the night, and I could make out her hunched-over form, rocking slowly. "Go back to your room," I told her.

"I can never go back. *You* can never go back."

She was wringing her hands. Her voice was the same tone I had heard her use for so many years with my mother. The days of her whimsical and lighthearted fables were gone. Her words and mood now felt heavy and ominous.

"It's when you can't take it any longer that the fall will release you," she said, her voice increasing in urgency. "The pain will be gone. It's the only thing that will take it away. But only in darkness."

I rolled over with my back to her. I was tired and not in the mood for her drama. All I wanted was to sleep.

"Yes, Grandma," I mumbled, trying to brush her off. "I remember the stories."

"Do you remember what I showed you?" she asked. "Do you remember the Cliffs of the Dead and what I told you? Only the fall will take the pain away."

I imagined myself at the cliff's edge. The same black porous rock that we went to when I was young. The rim was sharp;

there was no gradual descent—it was absolute. The height was dizzying. The river below was thin, and I took a deep breath before taking two steps back and leaped from the perch. The weight of my grandmother's discourse dissipated as quickly as I fell. The squeeze in my stomach I'd expected wasn't there, and instead, a billowing softness filled me. The fall turned to a float, and I was gently lulled down to the canyon floor.

I don't remember when she left my room or when she stopped talking to me that night. The next morning, the pains in my back were gone, and I felt more rested than I had in weeks. When I came into the kitchen for breakfast, my mother looked at me oddly.

"You look happy," she said, almost sounding annoyed.

I shrugged and looked toward my grandmother's door. It was closed. I felt a pang of guilt for ignoring her the night before and drifting off to sleep, but her nightly visits soon became disturbing omens that woke me at odd hours and kept me awake with haunting predictions and somber loathing that stayed with me throughout the day.

In class, in my truck, or whenever I found myself alone with my thoughts, I heard her voice in my head. The same phrase I'd been told as a child, whether I was sitting in my room or playing amongst the lizards and sagebrush-dotted cliffs, was drilled deep into my bones. It pulsated along with the throbbing pains in my back.

"Only in darkness."

CHAPTER

SEVENTEEN

Milo

As I pulled into the school parking lot that morning, I was already late. My mom's car was dead when she'd tried to leave for work, so I had to pull my truck around at an odd angle in our narrow gravel laneway to connect the jumper cables.

"Good thing I have a man around," she said, squeezing my arm as she got into her car.

I wasn't positive that she meant her comment to be cutting, but it was a reminder that both my father and grandfather were absent. Regardless of whether she'd wanted to hit me with her anger at them being gone, it was tiresome how she continually made it clear that her being our sole support was what made our life difficult.

I was well aware that my grandfather had left after the tragedy that had torn my family and Clara's apart, but I've never known why my father was missing. He was never there, so it wasn't near as big a hole in my life as when my grandfather was taken. Maybe it's because I've always felt it was, in some

157

way, my fault. Even though I've been told you can't blame a ten-year-old boy for something like that, I'd seen the way they all acted. I heard the way they'd yelled at me and demanded to know why I'd left her.

I saw the pain in my grandpa's face when Clara's father had ripped her wet and bloody body from him. And yet, even though they'd all seemed relieved to find her alive, it was my grandpa who I discovered weeping the night before he left us, the night Clara's grandpa came to our house, and I overheard him ask in a hushed and urgent voice, "What did you do?"

It was the last time we saw Richard, and it was the last time I saw Clara.

My family became even more sequestered to the little house along the basalt cliffs of the Snake River. And like every other part of my life, I watched the people I loved either leave or fade into the shadows.

I stood on the gravel driveway and watched as she drove off to work. I wanted to feel sorry for her. Instead, I was annoyed at what I'd lost and for what I didn't know. I was even more irritated when I saw the time as I reached my truck. But when I checked my phone, I saw Clara had sent a message, which eliminated any thoughts except for her.

It was Friday, and I had asked to see her that weekend. I wondered if Friday night would seem too soon and too eager for our date. It was a rare weeknight when I didn't have to work at my job cutting grass, painting, or cleaning public restrooms for the city's recreation department. I texted her back and asked if she had to work or had plans for that night. I sat in my truck, waiting for her reply before I could even put the key in the ignition.

"Parents are gone to Utah for the weekend. Movies at my house?" was her reply.

My entire body prickled with the idea of being alone with

her, but then Victor came to mind. I wondered if he would try to interfere.

I pushed the thought away. I smiled and texted a smile to her.

I pondered how much things had changed for us in such a short time. We were friends when we were little kids, and even then, I had a crush on her, but now it was different. I had been with her just twice and for only minutes, and yet, I was so drawn to her. She looked at me differently, touched me purposely, made me want more than just the friendship we'd had in her backyard during family barbecues when I was young. That seemed so long ago. For Clara and me, it was over a lifetime. And after what had happened, I was surprised she felt comfortable inviting me to her home.

After the night of the incident, when we were children, the family get-togethers ended. They didn't charge my grandfather because he was gone, but the insinuations and speculations lingered, and it seemed like my family's downfall was contagious. The rumors drifted through the small town like a dirty haze that would settle on them if they came near us. No one wanted to be tied to any of it, so many of our neighbors and friends became awkward or simply vanished. Even being so young, I knew what shame was, and I became keen at recognizing the looks of disdain directed at us.

The isolation felt like being sent to another state. It took years for those feelings to fade, but they never really went away.

I lost touch with Clara, but I never stopped thinking about her. Even with my vague memories, I still felt a sense of guilt and confusion I never completely understood.

"Come over at 7?" Her text buzzed in my hands and jolted me from my stupor, making the phone and my heart jump.

I spelled out several replies, deleting them and starting over until I had one that sounded like I wasn't too anxious, then sent it. I took a deep breath. It would be torture having to sit through hours of classes waiting to see her, not to mention a long drive.

I sat debating if I should go home first. Just the thought of my mom and grandmother's questioning and worry about how my being around Clara would play out made the day drag on. I decided to keep my plans to myself and tell them I was going to Don's. By the time the last bell rang, I was exhausted with both planning and anticipation.

I was focused on getting to the parking lot and took the back hall through the chorus rooms and behind the auditorium, and that was when I heard it. The sound was so high and pure that my chest warmed from the vibration, and I stopped and let the waves of the melody run over me.

My breath caught, and I gasped when the music ended. I stood feeling weak but exhilarated and wanting more. I took a few steps, and it started again, slowly and climbing until, without awareness, I was walking toward it.

Around the shadowy corridors of the backstage halls and down the stairs, I found a door. It was slightly cracked, and in the darkness, a small stream of light spilled out along with the writhing melody. I paused a moment and just listened. I had heard the sound of a violin, but this wasn't just music; it was hypnotic in its effect on me. It wasn't just what I was hearing, but what I felt throughout my entire being and everything—my body and mind were directed toward it.

I reached for the door, and when it started to open, it made a slight creak, and the music stopped. I pushed the door wide and found a woman with olive skin and the greenest eyes I'd ever seen. She was dressed in a long black gown, staring toward me. Her black hair was long and tied back loosely with a gold ribbon. She lowered the violin slowly when I stepped into the room and didn't seem surprised to see me there.

"I didn't mean to interrupt you," I said.

She didn't answer, but simply looked me up and down. She wasn't a student because she was far older than any high school girl, yet she wasn't old. Her beauty was something I'd seen in old photos, the ones without color, yet her skin was radiant, the type of glowing that comes from a fire.

"You play really well," I said, feeling like I should turn and leave. Yet, I felt drawn into the room.

"Why are you here?" she asked. Her voice was low and austere.

"I heard the music and wanted to see where it was coming from."

Her gown was ornate, and I wondered why she was dressed so formally during the afternoon, alone in the high school's orchestra practice room.

"Where are you from?" she asked.

"Here," I answered. "I was born in Idaho."

"No," she answered sternly, her eyes seeming to flare.

I flinched, surprised by her harshness.

"Where does your family come from? What are you?"

I shrugged, worried I would answer wrongly again.

Then I heard the sounds of others in the hallways. She heard them, too, and looked agitated.

"My mom was born here, but my grandparents came from Mexico and Nicaragua," I answered. "Why?"

Her face softened. "Come forward, Huna," she ordered and held out the violin's bow for me to take.

I had no idea what she wanted or why, but I stepped forward and, without hesitation, reached for it. When my hand was open and extended, she took the bow and, without force or aggression, touched the sharp end to my wrist, drawing blood.

I recoiled in pain and looked at the small cut. I looked up at her with shock. "What the hell?"

She looked past me toward the door as the sound of footsteps came behind me. I turned, and an older man in coveralls came through, pushing a garbage can on wheels. A light came on, and he was startled when he saw me.

"What are you doing here in the dark?" he asked.

I stood there surprised as my eyes squinted in the brightness. The dark? I quickly turned back toward the young woman, but she was gone. I looked around the entire room, and it was empty. I looked at my wrist, and the blood had streamed down and was dripping onto the floor.

"Are you okay," he asked. "What did you do?" He was looking at me as the bloody stream made a line across my wrist and through my fingers.

"Nothing," I said, pushing past him.

"Wait," he called after me. "Are you sure you're all right?"

I ran to my truck, wondering what had just happened and what it all meant. The dreams I'd been having were disturbing enough, but this was no dream, and the blood on my hand was real. Whoever that woman in the black dress was, I knew she wasn't a student. I wondered if she was real or an apparition intent on finding me, to warn me of what was to come.

As I drove home, I thought about my grandmother and contemplated telling her what I saw. I knew it'd bring on the tirade of ominous warnings and whip her into a frenzy that would surely start another argument with my mother. But she was also the only one I could talk to about this, and at the moment, I felt I had to tell someone what had happened. Even if it was Esmeralda, I needed someone to confirm what I'd seen was real, and that it wasn't just my mind spinning out of control.

As I drove, I replayed the whole scene in my mind—the light from the door, the music, the deep green of her eyes, and the sigh of her voice. It all came back so clearly, I felt the pierce of the bow as it stabbed my hand and the warmth of my blood again as it ran down my arm. Within minutes, the sky went from bright blue to azure to a golden orange, then turned dark, and then I was home. I don't remember the drive home—turns, stop signs—it was all a blur.

When I pulled into our house's gravel driveway, I realized my mother's car was already home. I turned off the ignition, but sat in the cab, still debating what to do. With my mother now home, it was impossible to speak to my grandmother without causing a problem.

My cell phone went off in my lap and made my heart jump. I grabbed the phone and looked at the screen. It was a text from Clara.

"Where are you?" it read.

I squinted at it, confused, and then I looked at the time. It was 6:35 pm. School ended at 3:40 pm, and I was usually home just after 4:00 pm. I had lost over two hours and had no idea how.

"Sorry. My mom is having car trouble. Be there soon." I typed back. It wasn't exactly a lie, as I'd spent time that morning jump-starting her car. I was frantic as I dashed into the house to find both my mother and grandmother with looks of concern.

"Where've you been?" my mother asked.

"I had some stuff I had to do after school," I mumbled as I brushed by them on my way to my room.

I dropped my backpack on my bed and then went toward the bathroom. I needed to clean up and get to Clara's house quickly. As I came around the corner, Esmeralda gave me a questioning look, then saw the blood on my arm.

I shook my head at her, hoping she wouldn't alarm my mother.

She took a deep breath and kept quiet as I ducked into the

bathroom. I washed the blood from my hand and arm, but the cut refused to let up. I found a bandage in the medicine cabinet and tried to paste it over the wound. For a moment, it seemed to work, so I went on trying to clean myself up and look the best I could for Clara.

When I finished, I found Esmeralda waiting for me in my room. She stood, wringing her hands and studying my wrist. "You talked of blood in your dream the other night, and now this," she whispered.

"It's nothing," I said, changing my shirt. "It's just a scratch."

"The dreams are more often now. You need to tell me what you're feeling and if the changes I told you about are happening."

"Where are you going?" My mother asked from the doorway of my room.

It surprised us both, and Esmeralda and I jumped.

"What's going on?" my mother asked, seeing the apparent guilt on our faces.

"Nothing," I answered quickly. "I'm going to Clara's." I cringed, letting it slip.

They both looked at me, surprised.

"Clara, who?" my mother asked, as though there was more than one in my life.

I cocked my head at her, annoyed. "You know who."

She lifted her eyebrows and looked at my grandmother.

I gave a huff and rolled my eyes, annoyed. "Just because you all aren't friends anymore doesn't mean we aren't," I said, pushing past them to the door.

"I didn't say that," my mother called after me.

"You didn't have to," I snapped back.

"Milo, wait," she called as I opened the door to leave.

I paused and looked back at her.

"The girl is evil," my grandmother said from inside the house.

"Mother!" my mother yelled, turning toward my grandmother. She turned back to me apologetically.

I glared at Esmeralda and shook my head, disgusted. "No wonder people think we're freaks," I said as I walked out.

A gust of wind hit me as I slammed the door. I stopped and took a breath before continuing to my truck. For so many years, I had pushed the pain and aggravation of what had happened and how I had lost Clara from my life that having those memories and realization come back was daunting.

I walked to the truck, half-expecting my mother to follow me, and when she didn't, I was relieved. As I pulled out of the driveway, I made a point of not looking back at the house.

I drove to Clara's house, remembering the route as though I was seven years old again, watching the houses and fields from the back seat of my grandfather's car. The streets and skyline hadn't changed much in the nine years since I'd been there. When I pulled up along the curb of her house, a twinge of sorrow fell over me as I felt the loss of our younger, happier childhood.

In my panic of being late, I hadn't let the anxiety of being with her hit me. But as I realized I would be alone with her for the first time in years, I worried about how I looked and what I would say. I stood at the door and second-guessed if I had used deodorant when I felt the wetness of my underarms and beads of sweat form at my neck. I took a deep breath as I pushed the doorbell.

My fears of being awkward and goofy left me at the sight of her. Large blue eyes and a mess of dark curls, she grabbed my arm and pulled me in before I could say a word or realize her eyes had changed yet again. Her exuberance in seeing me had my chest swelling, and I couldn't stop smiling.

Her house was a lot like I remembered. From appearances, her life hadn't changed like mine. There were photos of her smiling happily as a child scattered on thin, polished tables in the entryway, and even her dog, a black lab, now with a completely gray muzzle, still met me at the door.

"Gordon!" I said, petting his head.

"You mean Gordo," she corrected me with a smile.

"That's right," I said. "I can't believe he's still around."

"I know," she cooed at him, patting his graying face. "He's getting pretty old."

She directed me downstairs to the family room, where a large flat-screen television hung on the wall, and covered in blankets was a wraparound sofa. It was the same room where we'd watched Disney movies on VHS as kids, but the TV and furnishings had changed.

"Look good?" she asked.

I was about to answer when she cuddled into my chest and hugged me. "Or we can make a blanket fort under the kitchen table like we used to?" she teased.

I laughed, and she led me to the sofa, and we fell onto it. For a moment, we just sat there still hugging each other, and she leaned up. "I still can't believe this is you and me," she said. "Can you?"

I just stared at her. She was the most beautiful thing I had ever seen. The cool basement room and the soft leather couch had me wrapped into her with both my arms and my eyes. I wanted to lean down and kiss her, but before I could, she pulled back.

"I'm going upstairs to get some food," she said.

My face must have spoken volumes because she gave a small laugh and hugged me again.

"I'll be right back. I promise," she said. She stood up and

went upstairs, leaving me with a burgeoning ache in my back and an old dog staring me down.

When I heard the creak of the back basement door, I shot up to standing. We were supposed to be alone, and I was sure it was Victor, trying to keep that from happening. I crept toward the door, and when it opened, I stepped in front of it and was ready.

Instead of surprising Victor, I spooked Clara's grandfather, Richard, a man I'd known since I was born but hadn't seen in years.

He gasped, but I immediately put up my hands and apologized when I recognized who he was. "Mr. Wilson," I said, "I didn't expect you to be around still."

He was carrying a large bucket with water that sloshed, and when he saw me, he smiled as he sat it on the floor. He scratched the back of his neck. "I'm old, but I'm still around, Milo."

"Oh, I didn't mean..." I was flustered. He remembered me, and I wondered how he felt having me there.

He laughed. "I'm messing with you. And I'm not going to be in your way. I just got back from fishing over at Chesterfield Reservoir. I'm going to clean and put these fish in the freezer here. Mine's not big enough. Then I'll be heading back to my place."

"Can I help you carry that?" I asked, seeing him struggle as he went to pick up the bucket again.

"Sure," he said, setting it back down and putting his hand on his lower back. "The washroom sink is where I was planning on cleaning them." He pointed to a door down the hall.

I came around the sofa, reached down, and grabbed the bucket handle. I then realized the blood had soaked through my bandage and was dripping down my arm. Richard noticed it as well.

"You're leaking," he chided me.

"Yeah, I cut myself on something at school today," I said, setting the bucket down and trying to wipe my arm with my other hand. Several drops of blood fell into the water, where four limp and lifeless fish bobbed.

He handed me a rumpled cloth handkerchief he pulled from his back pocket. "It's one I use to wipe sweat, not snot," he said.

I took it and gave him an uncomfortable laugh as I wrapped it around my wrist. I then carried the bucket into the washroom and sat it on the linoleum floor near the large sink.

He thanked me, and we stood awkwardly, both feeling the weight of the years that had passed.

I heard a muffled cough, and when Clara came into the room, I was so relieved, my shoulders sank.

"I told Grandpa he wouldn't recognize you," she said, setting two bowls full of chips and pretzels on the coffee table.

"I told your father I would make sure you ate well while they were gone, and this is what you come up with," her grandfather scolded. He pulled out a twenty-dollar bill. "At least order a pizza or something."

"No," I said, putting up my hand. "I'll take care of it."

Clara put the crook of her elbow to her mouth and coughed.

Richard turned to her with concern.

"I'm fine," Clara said with a smile, then she noticed the bloodied handkerchief. "What happened to you?" she asked.

"It's nothing. Just a scratch," I said again. I turned to Richard. "I'll buy the pizza."

He shrugged. "Okay, but just make sure you two get around to eating tonight."

I felt my face flush, and he must have noticed because he gave a satisfied laugh. It was one I remembered—low and gravely, and it shook his entire body. As kids, we would hide in the house, and when he found us, he growled and made us scream. He would laugh as we ran off to find another place to hide. Hearing it again made me smile, but my heart ached at the memory of how much I loved my life when I heard that laugh often. Like everything else at that time, it vanished overnight, and the reasons why still haunted me, like a ghost. A flash of dark cliffs, an overcast sky, and my family crying went through my mind.

A pain shot through my shoulders like a knife, and I winced.

Clara turned to me. "What is it?"

I swallowed and shook my head. "Nothing."

A loud thump came from the washroom, then another, and another. Soon a loud series of slapping noises. We all looked toward the door, and when Richard opened it and turned on the light, he gasped.

"What is it?" asked Clara.

But before Richard could answer, we saw into the room. The four fish had jumped from the bucket and were thrashing around on the floor.

Richard watched for a moment, his face in awe. "I caught those hours ago," he said. He looked over to us and shook his head. "Plus, it's a two-hour drive, and..." he paused in thought. "This can't be. They were dead."

"Doesn't look that way," Clara said with a nervous giggle as she stepped back.

"Let's get them into the sink," I said, moving her to the side and stepping into the room.

"How?" asked Clara.

Richard came into the room with me, and we both started trying to reach down to catch the fish, but they slipped from our hands and continued to flip vigorously around the small room. They were hitting the walls, and the slaps of their slick tails resonated throughout the room. After numerous attempts to grab them, we both stood back and simply watched.

"They've got to stop soon," I said. When I received no reply, I turned to find Richard staring at me strangely. I raised my eyebrows and asked, "What is it?"

It was like I woke him from a stupor. He shook his head. "Nothing," he said. He pointed me out of the room. "Just close the door. I'll take care of it. Take Clara, and you two go." He gave me a side glance with his eyes, and I realized what he was going to do. It was not something he wanted his granddaughter to witness. "Go out to eat," he said.

As I closed the door, Clara stepped beside me. "What's he doing?" she asked.

"Let's go to Scotty's," I said to her.

She looked confused, but agreed.

As we left the house, I saw Richard emerge from the room, holding an aluminum baseball bat. I hustled Clara forward, and just before I closed the door, I took another glance back, and the look he gave me told me that my being there was like a weight on his shoulders. It wasn't a sense of familiar fondness having me back in their life, but rather a grappling dread.

CHAPTER

EIGHTEEN

Milo

"That was so weird," Clara said, looking out the windshield. "The more I think about it, the more it freaks me out. It's like those fish came back to life."

I just nodded. I agreed the situation was odd, but I was more upset it had put a damper on our first time together than with some fish catching a second breath.

We ordered at the drive-up speaker of Scotty's Drive-in, and as we were waiting for the server to bring our food to the truck, we both sat, lost in thought.

"Do you want to go somewhere once we get our food?" I asked her.

She shrugged. "Like where?"

I didn't have an idea. I just wanted to take her mind off the depressing scene that was taking place in her basement washroom. I thought a moment, and when I came up with nothing, I sighed and shrugged myself.

"What about your house?" she asked.

"No." The word came so quickly, she cocked her head in

171

surprise. "We'd have both my mom and grandmother bugging us," I said, trying to keep my horror at the thought of her around them in check. "I want you to myself."

She smiled and leaned into me. I didn't say it as a come-on, but what I said worked, and I enjoyed her reaction.

She put her hand on my chest and snuggled in even closer. This made my heart begin to race, and with it, a sharp twinge shot through my shoulders, and I jerked forward.

She sat up and turned to me. Her brows knitted. "Are you still hurting from the other night when...?"

"No," I said it so forcefully that her eyes went wide. "Just a cramp from lifting stuff at work." I made some side-to-side stretching motions in my seat, and she seemed to buy it, but I felt sweat begin to bead on my neck with the worry of the pain returning.

I was relieved when I saw the girl with our food walking up to the truck window. I paid the girl, and Clara and I unwrapped the different items and began to eat.

I tried to relax as much as I could against the stiff seats. And soon, I found myself again just sitting there smelling her hair and watching her every move. Before I got too consumed by being alone with her, she pointed out two little kids playing on the grass near their car.

As we sat together, I was entranced just watching her smile, react, and giggle as she watched their antics. Everything she did brought me back to what I had loved about her when I was young. I realized those things were why I still loved her even after all those years.

"They remind me of us when we were little," she said sadly.

I was so engrossed in watching her I had forgotten about the children, and when she caught me staring at her, I looked down quickly, embarrassed at how completely entranced I was.

She smiled and looked down shyly.

"Sorry," I said. "It still feels weird. It's been so long."

She shook her head. "Don't be sorry. It *has* been a long time. Too long." Then she looked off in thought and sighed.

"I've missed you so much," I said softly. I didn't mean to say it so intently. It slipped from my mind and out loud before I could reel it back in, and hearing it surprised me almost as much as it did Clara.

She turned back to me with sad eyes. For a moment, we just looked at each other. Then her eyes began to tear, and I knew I couldn't handle the pain of what she was thinking. I started to apologize. Suddenly, I needed to leave and keep myself from breaking down and looking like an emotional idiot. I put the key into the ignition and started the truck, but she grabbed my arm.

"Please, wait," she said. "Let's not go...yet."

I turned off the truck and sat back.

"It's like when I'm with my grandpa," she mused.

I turned to her, confused. "I remind you of your grandpa?"

Her eyes went wide and she laughed. "No! I mean, just sitting in a truck. Every year, he takes me to this place along the canyon, and we watch the sunrise on the morning of my birthday. He brings donuts, and we sit and talk. We've done it every year that I can remember."

I nodded. "I think I remember hearing about you doing that."

She cleared her throat and stifled a cough.

"Do you have a cold?" I asked her.

She looked down and then up at me with sad eyes. "No. I've had problems for years, ever since that day at the cave. Remember when we used to go camping?"

A cold chill went through me. I couldn't believe she wanted to bring that up now—the very thing that had torn us apart. I shook my head, trying to change the tone and keep myself from wanting to bolt.

"You don't remember?" she asked.

I swallowed hard. "Of course, I remember. Which time?"

Our families had gone camping a lot as kids, so I hoped that maybe I could simply act oblivious to turn our thoughts away from the ugly past I wanted to forget.

She raised her eyebrows and nodded. "There were many, but I was thinking about the last time when I almost drowned. We wandered off like we always did, and then we found our cave, remember?"

I sat for a moment. I ran my fingers through my hair. It was the time that had changed my entire life, losing both my grandfather and Clara. Since that time, I had done everything I could to push that terrible incident out of my head, and I wondered why she'd asked me to relive it now.

It started to come back to me. Like water flowing into a dry stream, memories flooded back, filling the gaps and crevices where I had hid so many painful thoughts away.

I saw Clara in my mind, young and spry, her thick dark curls in a sloppy ponytail and her jeans and T-shirt as covered in dirt as mine. We had found our hidden trail leading through a grove of junipers behind our parents' parked trailers, and then up behind a large cluster of boulders. We knew it was out of the range we were allowed to hike and play, but the dark and elusive cave above where the trail led was too much of a lure to refuse.

What I loved most about the camping trips was our freedom to explore the rugged rocky hills and shadowy forests while our families sat around camp playing cards, drinking beer, and talking about old times.

Neither Clara nor I had brothers or sisters, and it was our grandfathers who had initially been friends, so our parents—her dad and my mom—had been linked for decades before we ever came along. We grew up hearing the stories of when Richard and Jorge both moved to Idaho, how their lives always seemed to intersect, and that when Richard's first wife left him, it was Esmeralda who had introduced him to Anita. Richard, who had sworn he never wanted kids, became a father at age forty-two to Mitchell, Clara's father. I had never known my father, and I envied Clara for having one.

Mitchell and my mom were less than a year apart and were like brother and sister. They even went to the same junior college for a year. Mitchell got married; my mom didn't. But when Clara and I were born just two months apart, there were more photos of us together than I expected most twins probably have, but I still never viewed her as a sister.

Clara was my friend and playmate, but as we got older, there was no confusion even then about how I cared for her. To say I felt like I'd suffered a death when she was taken from my life seemed almost trivial compared to how it had actually hurt me. And yet, because of everything else associated with that terrible time, I didn't have a chance to grieve or even contemplate what had caused the rip that separated us.

Now, as I sat with those memories flooding back and filling my head, that awful, ominous feeling of what I didn't want to know came over me.

"There are some things I remember, but so much I don't. Do you remember what happened?" Clara asked again.

I felt a chill down my back as I came out of my stupor. I nodded. But did I really remember? The thought of discussing it with her was daunting.

"I don't just mean when we ran, and I almost drowned." She paused and winced at the thought. "I mean the other thing. Did you see it?"

I didn't because I wasn't there. I left her there alone. I saw red eyes coming at us, and I ran. I heard her scream when I was halfway back to the camp. Whatever happened afterward had shattered our lives. I should have stayed with her and faced what had emerged from the dark. It was my fault that she almost died, and her family needed someone to blame.

But I nodded. I don't know why I lied to her, but I did. I wanted so badly for her to feel we still had that connection, that bond, even if it meant pretending to have seen something I didn't.

She cocked her head and studied me a moment. "You're not just saying that?"

"I saw it. Why would I lie?"

"I don't know. To make me feel better? So I won't feel like a freak or something? No one else will talk about it. And they never believed what I told them." She leaned closer to me and whispered as though someone could overhear. "Sometimes, I feel like I dreamed it. Sometimes, I feel like it's still here with me. I still have nightmares. There were so many times I wanted to talk to you about it, but I wasn't sure if you were mad at me or..."

"Mad at you?" I was stunned. "Why would I be mad at you?"

She bit her lip, and when she looked up at me, her eyes were full and spilling over. "Because that's when everything went wrong. If I hadn't wandered off, you wouldn't have followed me."

My heart fell. She was right. It *was* when everything began to crumble, but it wasn't her fault. "You didn't make me go with you," I said. "I wanted to. I should have...stayed with you."

It was the very conversation I'd dreaded having with her,

and yet, there we were, both buried in the guilt of what had happened to our lives that neither of us could have ever controlled. My world had turned from a child's happiness and innocence to a bitter slap of sadness and the grinding daily horror of remembering what happened. It had taken almost a decade of my life to push it back into the darkest part of my mind.

I shook my head and pulled her to me. I had spent so many years feeling like I had caused all the trouble, and here she was, awash in tears, feeling she was to blame.

"What happened to our families?" she asked. "We all used to be so close. Everything changed after that one day. After that, you were gone, my mom left us, and my dad has never been the same. What did I do that was so bad? No one will tell me. Every time I ask, they tell me to leave it in the past." She coughed. "This is part of it," she said, motioning to her chest. "The water damaged my lungs. I should have listened and never gone up there. None of this would have happened."

I sat up, stunned. It was Clara who had been the victim in all this. She was the one who almost died. I had begged to know what had happened when I was young, but neither my mom nor my grandmother would discuss it. Because we'd lost my grandfather over the events of that day, I knew he'd played some role in what had happened to Clara, and with all the secrets and hushed discussions, I knew he had done something wrong.

This crushed me. Grandfather was my hero. He was kind and funny, and while he was often gone for work, he always made time for me.

My grandma and mother felt he'd been wrongly accused and held their own version of the truth, but the debate and eventual accusations had led to his demise. I don't know if it was guilt or simply shame. However, the details of the story remain a mystery. So, I was curious about what Clara knew and thought. All I remembered about that night was a blur of chaos and feeling like I had done something terrible. Because I was so young, I had only considered my own hurt from that event, yet now, I saw others losing so much more.

The finger-pointing had started with me, and when I told them what I'd seen, the outrage and contention between our families grew. In the end, the blame had landed on my grandfather. It was some of the worst accusations imaginable, but I never believed Clara was the reason my grandfather was gone. We were two little kids caught in the middle of a bunch of adults who had needed someone to blame for their reckless behavior. They should have watched us more closely—that was what I came to believe over the years. And I wasn't about to let their stupid actions years ago get in the way of Clara and me now. It was an accident that had happened years ago. It was over, and it was time to move on. If the rest of them couldn't do it, at least Clara and I would have that chance.

She gave a small shudder and held me closer, and I knew she felt the same way, too.

We didn't realize that the pains in my back and the blood in my veins would eventually have me facing what had caused all the misery in our lives.

CHAPTER

NINETEEN

Milo

It was a week before Halloween, and we met at a forty-acre farm just west of town with a corn maze in the shape of an American flag cut out of the stalks in the immense field. There were hundreds of people, mostly families because it was a Monday night. In Idaho, with the majority of people being Mormon, Monday was the night they did family outings and activities.

When Don and I pulled up, he sighed.

"I know," I said, appreciating him for being my wingman. "I owe you."

"You've said that a lot lately."

This was true. In the two months since Clara and I had reunited, we'd been relentless in our efforts to spend time together. It was as though we were trying to make up for all those years of being apart so we could start again.

We spent hours talking on the phone and texting, and whenever possible, we hung out. I was surprised that Victor rarely bothered us. He seemed to fade from the picture, and

Clara rarely spoke of him. I didn't care either way; I was just glad to be rid of him.

"Why don't you pick her up and bring her yourself? Why do you have to meet her?" Don asked.

Inside, I felt my heart sink. Clara never really came out and said it, but I knew it was her father who was keeping me at bay. What had happened in the past would always make him opposed to having me back in her life.

Since we went to different schools, we spent most of our time together on the weekends. We went to lunch, had bonfires at the lake, or floated down the river, but it was usually with her friends and Don, too. I wanted to ask her why that was, but didn't. I also wanted to know why we never brought up the things that were still unanswered in our past.

After that first night at her house, she never spoke about what had happened in the cave. It frustrated me a bit. I wanted to know more, but I figured things were good with us, and I didn't want to ruin it by dredging up that awful memory.

We arrived at the Haunted Maze in different cars. Many of Clara's friends had brought younger brothers and sisters, so when we finally paid our way in, there were over ten of us. At first, I was irritated with all the little kids bumping into us and getting in the way, but I saw how Clara was with them, following them and laughing. They screamed when the not-so-scary monsters jumped out from amongst the tall dried-out shafts of corn, and I couldn't help but enjoy it all.

I found myself not following the dirt path and narrow corridors of thick stalks, but instead, I was drawn to her. Everything about her made me want to be closer, and the pull she had over me was as if she had a rope tied around my neck.

When the sun began to set, large floodlights suddenly boomed from above, illuminating the entire cornfield and giving the paths of the maze an eerie, shadowy feel. The youngest of the kids insisted their older siblings hold them, and some of Clara's friends decided it was late enough and time to leave.

I saw the dark corners and nooks of the maze as an opportunity to get her alone finally, and knew that time was growing short. When I saw the others turn to the left, I grabbed her arm and pulled her to the right. She uttered a playful squeal, and I quickly found the closest dark corner and wrapped her into it.

Surprised, she looked up at me, and in the dark, her green glow was back. She tucked into my embrace, and before she could question what I was doing, I kissed her. The feel of her soft lips and the warmth of her breath when we parted had me spellbound.

"Hey," I whispered as I looked at her in the moonlight.

She gave a small cough, looking a bit stunned but happy.

"You okay?" I asked.

She smiled at me and nodded. I bent down to kiss her again, but she leaned back. "Are you?" she asked.

Before I could answer, I heard a low and guttural growl. It came from the distance, but I felt the vibration in my chest. I turned quickly, and then the lights above us began to flicker.

"What is it?" Clara asked.

"Did you hear that?"

She looked around as the sounds of the crowd, running and hiding amongst the thick walls of cornstalks, surrounded us. She cocked her head and smiled. "Hear what?" she giggled at the chaos.

I started to explain what I'd heard, but she grabbed my arm and pulled me back into the maze. "Come on!" she called as she began to run through the shadows.

We started along the path, but we came across two girls huddled together when it curved back. They were startled when they saw us.

"Dead end?" I asked, figuring we would need to find another way out.

The oldest girl looked scared. "She's hurt," she said, motioning to the other girl. "Something reached out and cut her."

The other girl's eyes were wide as she stood holding her neck.

Clara went to her. "Are you okay?" she asked.

The girl didn't speak, but shook her head.

She lifted her hand, and in the moonlight, I saw the wound and the blood that dripped from it. I felt my back throb, and I took a step back.

"We need to get help," Clara said. She reached into the small purse slung over her shoulder and pulled out a tissue. "Use this."

My breathing began to seize, and my face was hot and sweating. I felt drawn to the wound, and yet, sick at the sight of it. I turned away and took several deep breaths. Then the low growl returned.

I looked back at Clara, but she was still unaware of the sound and continued to comfort the girl. She took her by the arm to lead her out of the maze. I followed, but soon the path branched off, and we found ourselves lost. We stopped and tried to decide which way to go. Every time I stepped near the injured girl, I could feel her neck pulse and sense the blood on her skin. My head began to spin, and I bent over, afraid I was going to fall.

"Take her," a voice called through the breeze. It thundered in my head, but was a whisper.

The words seemed to swirl around me like the wind, filling the night air that only I could hear. The throbbing in my back was now intense, but my sense of dread was overwhelming.

I could feel a presence coming closer.

"We need to go," I said, trying to move away from the girl who was injured.

"Where?" Clara asked, confused.

I pushed her toward the path and away from the direction from which I felt the presence coming. "Go," I whispered loudly.

As we moved forward, stumbling through the dark, I could feel a waft of something overhead. A chill rushed through me, making my stomach clench. Then I heard screams. Not the fun and excited ones we had heard earlier, but ones of terror. Not the sound of harmless Halloween frights, but horror.

Clara flashed me a look of dismay, and when we stepped out and onto another path, we were immediately knocked into by her friend, Amanda, who was carrying her little brother.

"Run!" she yelled. "It's Victor and some others, and they're shooting stuff." She pushed by us and fled as the little boy cried loudly.

"Shooting stuff?" I asked, but she was gone before we got a reply.

Clara's eyes showed both dread and angst. "Come on," she said, and started to run.

We returned to the path from which we had come, but the crowd of people running past us in the opposite direction grew, so we turned and began to follow.

I heard screams and sounds of what I thought were shots, and with each blast, I could hear a wicked laugh.

It was Victor, giving loud, crazed howls after each bang of the gun.

In the crush of the crowd, Clara tripped and stumbled to the ground. I stopped and pulled her into a cove of cornstalks to keep her from being trampled.

She was already in tears. "Why is he doing this?" she yelled, frustrated and scared.

I helped her up and pulled her close, but she was angry at the situation and pushed me away.

As I watched the stream of people frantically running by, I saw Don. I leaped forward and grabbed his arm, pulling him back to where we were hiding. At first, he tried to fight me, but then he realized who I was. He was breathing hard and had a large red splotch on his neck and chest. Clara gasped at the sight.

"I'm fine," he reassured her, annoyed. Then he turned to me. "The assholes have paint guns. They're on the scaffolds that hold the lights. They're shooting at everyone, even the kids."

He held his composure, but I could tell he was hurt by the way his eyes were wet and pained, and he kept rubbing his neck and shoulder.

"You need to get out of here," he said. "They're calling for Clara."

We ducked back into the dark and waited. Then the shooting stopped, and so did the screams. Once full of laughter and voices, the entire field was now still but for the sounds of children whimpering while everyone hid, wondering what to do.

We heard Victor call out into the night sky. "Clara! Where are you?" he demanded.

"What does he want?" she whispered in despair.

Paintball gun or not, this was no harmless prank. He had caused hundreds of people to stampede and hide, not knowing if the guns were real or a joke. His idea of intimidation had turned from a game to assault. He was using the title of stepbrother as an excuse to stalk her.

She started to step out, but I grabbed her arm. "What are you doing?"

"He's not going to stop until I go out there," she said. "He'll keep shooting at people."

"I'm sure someone's called the cops, so they'll be here soon. Just stay hidden," I told her.

"He'll never let up. He'll just keep following me around, doing stuff like this. And now it's hurting others, too," she said, defeated, looking at Don.

In the distance, we could hear the sirens.

"You're not going out there. I'm not letting him do this," I said.

"If he sees you, it will be even worse."

Victor's constant presence and harassment of Clara were now worse because I was in her life. I was enraged that once again, our being together was a source of pain.

"Clara, don't," I begged her.

"He won't shoot at me if I just get it over with. Then we can all go home." She pulled away from me and ran into the light of the path. "I'm right here!" she called out, loud and annoyed.

I peered up and saw Victor and the others perched high on the scaffolds.

"Too late," he yelled, hearing the sirens. He raised the gun and aimed at her.

As I heard the shot ring out, I was already running to protect her. And as I flung my body across hers, the explosion of the ball hit the center of my back, making me yell out in pain. My body hit hers, and we both landed on the dirt with a heavy thud.

For a moment, I lay there stunned, and when I opened my eyes, it was dark. I looked for Clara, but I found myself alone, and the night had settled over the maze, leaving it still and silent. It was as though it had closed, and everyone had gone home.

I scrambled up to standing, wondering if I had passed out. For a moment, I stood, questioning if it was real.

"Clara?" I called out, and tried to listen in the stillness. I heard nothing. What's happening, I thought, wondering where they had all gone.

I continued to search in the dark for any sign of her—of anyone—but I was alone. The cold air whipped through the path, and I stood motionless as the sound of wind rushing through the corn got closer. I felt the pains in my back begin, and I cringed at the terrible timing of it.

"Clara!" I called out again, frantically. I started to run where I thought they had gone, but the path divided.

"You are mine."

The voice rushed through me. It was chilling, but also familiar. I shivered and turned to try and see who it was, but found only the dark stillness of the field. The low growl returned. I stood, barely breathing, as it seemed to be getting closer. As I searched, blinking to try and push away the darkness, a pair of red eyes appeared in the distance.

My breath caught. I wanted to run, but the terror I felt had me unable to move. I watched, and then a dark cloaked figure emerged. The eyes were still burning, but I couldn't make out a face. I swallowed hard, begging for it not to be real.

"Who are you?" I asked. I began walking backward, keeping the glowing eyes in view. I felt the tall stalks behind me and knew the path had ended. I had nowhere to turn, to flee. "What do you want?" I called out to the eyes. They were coming closer, and my breath began to falter.

Then a hand grabbed my shoulder. My heart leaped, and I yelped in fear. And there at my side was Don. As soon as I recognized him, I gasped in relief.

I turned back toward the eyes, and they were gone. There was nothing but the tall, dried stalks of corn. The darkness began to fade, and the daunting presence lifted as the light of the parking lot came into view. Like coming up from underwater, the noise of the crowd returned.

"Where have you been?" Don asked, annoyed.

I was stunned and confused. What had just happened? "Clara?" I asked.

He shook his head. "She's been looking for you, too. Victor and those guys were shooting the paintball guns, and some girl got really hurt. Her neck was bleeding."

I nodded. "I know. I was there."

Don looked at me oddly. "You were there?"

"Yes," I answered, "I was there with Clara when we found the girl."

"But..." he started to argue, then stopped and just sighed.

As we emerged from the maze and into the scattered glow of the floodlights, I saw Clara standing with the girl. Two police officers were speaking to them. I went to her, and Clara hugged me in relief.

"Where did you go?" she asked, holding me. "We found our way out, and when we turned around, you were gone." Her cough started again, and I put my arm around her.

"Are you okay?" I asked.

She nodded. "Are you? How's your back?" she asked, taking me by the arm and turning me around. "He was aiming for me. I'm sorry."

"Why are you sorry?"

She sighed, and I knew she blamed herself for this, too.

"What about her?" I asked, looking over at the girl. A thick bandage was taped to her neck and she was talking to an officer who was taking notes.

"She says something attacked her and cut her throat. She wasn't hit with the paintballs, but I still think he's to blame. They asked if I saw anything. They may want to talk to you, too."

I was still dazed, but mostly disturbed. What would I tell them? I thought about the voice and the eyes. Red eyes that made my entire body tense at the memory they invoked. I couldn't possibly tell Clara and stir that painful reminiscence in her.

She had her arms around me and squeezed my chest. "Can you give me a ride home?" she asked. "My ride had to leave."

I nodded and then turned to Don.

He rolled his eyes. "I'll catch a ride with Amanda. She lives on my street."

He shook his head and walked off.

Clara and I watched as the officer helped the girl into the police car. She shivered in the chilly night. As the car pulled away, the girl glanced back at us, and just like I'd seen with Clara, her eyes held a shimmer of green. I looked down at Clara, wondering if she saw it, too, and when she peered back at me, I saw the same glow.

"What?" she asked, seeing my query.

"Nothing," I answered.

Word of what had happened traveled quickly. Clara's father called her cell phone while I drove her home. He said he'd heard about the incident and was waiting for us. I was nervous because I hadn't seen Clara's father since that terrible night over eight years ago.

I thought it was odd that in the two months Clara had been back in my life, I hadn't seen her father, and I figured it was her attempt at guarding us all against an awkward encounter with the past. We had continued to avoid talking about what had happened when we were young. It was as if neither one of us wanted to let it out for fear the memory would destroy things again.

We were silent as I pulled to the curb of her house. I waited, wondering if I should even go with her to the door, but she looked at me as though I should. She took my arm as we walked up to the house, but when her father opened the door, she let it go, and I felt my heart sink.

He looked just as I remembered, but a little rounder and more like Clara's grandfather. His face was creased with concern, but when he looked at me, it was a mixture of grapple and burden. It had been so many years, but it was obvious what had happened was still a source of pain.

I tried to smile and greet him, but instead, I felt an overwhelming need to apologize. For what, I'm not sure, and the guilt turned to irritation.

"Mr. Wilson. She's fine," I said, trying to turn his attention back to Clara.

"Thank you," he said quietly. He led us into the house, but stopped in the foyer as though he expected me to remain there.

"Fine?" Clara said, turning to me. "I'm not fine." She started to walk forward, but then realized I wasn't with her and turned back. She looked at me, and then at her father. "Did they tell you what happened?" she asked him.

Clara's father looked tired and also uneasy. "Yes, I heard what Victor did," he said. He put his hand up as though trying to keep her quiet.

"He's gone too far this time. A girl was really hurt, and look," she said, taking my arm. She turned me around to expose the big red splotch on my back. "That was meant for me," she said, annoyed. "Milo kept me safe. And that idiot was shooting all those people, including little kids. They may not be bullets, but they hurt! Who knows what he would have done to me if Milo hadn't been there."

"Mitchell, what's going on down there?" a woman's voice called from upstairs. I assumed it was Clara's stepmother.

Her father's face turned to dread. "It's nothing. Go back to bed!" he called up toward the stairs.

Clara huffed, disgusted. "Nothing? Go up there and tell her what her precious son did this time."

He took a deep exhausted breath. "I'll look into it when I go to work tomorrow," he said. I remembered then that he was a police officer.

"Mitchell?" the voice called again.

"I'll be right there," he answered, then turned back to us. "Please, it's late."

"I should go," I said, feeling awkward and confused. Every time the voice called from upstairs, I felt my body tense. Her father's nervous avoidance and Clara's apparent annoyance with it all made it worse. I started to tell Clara I'd call her tomorrow, but her father stepped in.

"Thank you for what you did," he said, motioning me toward the door.

I nodded, but could tell his appreciation didn't mean I was welcome in their home. He gave Clara a look that told her to wrap it up, and before she could argue, I made it easy for him and reached for the doorknob.

He looked up the stairs and began his ascent. He looked more tired and defeated with every step.

"I'll text you later," I said to Clara.

"You don't have to leave," she snapped.

I looked at her, and then at her father, who now stood at the top of the stairs. His look said it all.

"I really should get home," I conceded, still looking at him.

She shook her head apologetically. "Thank you. I'm sorry about all this."

"I'm just glad you're okay," I said.

She gave me a defeated smile, looked up at her father, and grumbled off toward the kitchen.

As I left and was closing the door, I glanced up to see her father still at the top of the stairs, and the look he gave me was the same one I remembered from all those years ago. The one that has haunted me, forced my family to be sequestered away near the cliffs and left me with confusion about what my grandfather did that had made me a pariah. His eyes locked with mine as I shut the door.

As I drove home in the dark, the pain came again, but I almost welcomed it. For the first time in nine years, I had to face the thoughts, emotions, and reality of what I had pushed away and tried to forget. To be with Clara, I would have to dredge it all up and explore what had happened then and what it meant in my life now. I would have to sift away my grandmother's irrational and emotionally driven stories from what I could coax out of the bitter and jaundiced person the situation had created in my mother.

How would I possibly know what the truth was? And what if Clara's family was right? If my grandfather was a monster, did I deserve to shoulder his legacy?

CHAPTER

TWENTY

Was it the lack of sleep, the early shimmer of the dark morning, or the entire six-pack he drank the night before? Regardless of what had caused it, the sound of something stalking him made Trevor Greene wish he had taken his brother-in-law up on his offer to join him on the short weekend hunting trip.

He had awakened before daylight to hike the ridge and find a place to settle in under the cloak of darkness. There, he planned to wait for deer as they plodded along the thin trail they perpetually followed across the backside of Kinport peak.

He was frantic and panting from trying to run through the dark and rugged terrain, in terror of what was in pursuit. He could hear the rush of wind and scatter of brush, but had no idea what was chasing him. The sound of a human voice called out, making him slow his pace, desperately hoping he was mistaken in thinking his pursuer was a cougar or bear. Did he simply hear another hunter walking in the brush and assume it was something else in the dark early morning hours?

He pulled the rifle up and turned back, facing the direction of where the voice had come. "Hello?" he called out.

As the small slit of the moon shimmered over the hillside, his eyes searched frantically, his gun drawn. The stillness made him shiver, and when he swallowed, he realized he hadn't taken a breath. He took a shallow, quick gasp of the frozen air, burning his lungs, but he held back a cough. The rustle of the brush ceased, and he began to wonder if he had heard anything at all.

He stood, trying to detect a presence in the cold black morning, and found nothing. For several minutes, he let his eyes adjust enough to discern the broad swath of sagebrush and junipers. Even in the light breeze, he could feel the sweat on his face. Nothing moved. He let his shoulders settle back in relief. Then the crunch of dried leaves from behind made him turn, and he saw the glow of red eyes staring back at him.

He let out a startled scream, but before he could gather himself to run again, the thick black of the morn turned even darker.

"It's another head," Derek said, shaking his own. "We're going to have a complete panic on our hands when this gets out."

"Good hell," Lester said under his breath, again wondering why this had happened just weeks before his retirement. He stepped in front of Derek and peered around the blue crime scene tarp at the lopped-off head of the unidentified male hunter.

"Still wearing his orange beanie," Derek remarked. "The rest of him is just behind that juniper. They found his gun, too. No signs of shots fired, but the gun is loaded. And again, hardly any blood." He looked at Lester for emphasis. "It's almost the same as the one in the cemetery. It has to be related, right?"

Lester gave a huff. "Don't get ahead of yourself," he grumbled. And yet, his stomach clenched at what he really thought. He was exhausted just thinking about the amount of uproar this would cause throughout the small town, let alone what he would have to report to the men who had been through the horrid ordeal they all thought had ended decades ago. "Where's his vehicle?"

Derek motioned from behind. "Back at the trailhead where we're setting up the command post."

They had come separately. Lester had hoped to take the morning off. He was a short-timer and took every opportunity he could to escape the job he had done for decades. He would still accompany his long-time comrade on their monthly "outings," but without his connection to law enforcement, they would have to find another avenue to secure what they needed to keep their charge in check.

Because murder in Bannock County was so rare, they immediately called Lester in as the experienced detective. This kept him from a day of puttering and planning and thrust him both physically and emotionally back to a place he'd never wanted to experience again.

"Plates come back to some guy out of Logan, Utah," Derek announced, shaking Lester from his stupor.

"Is there a camp?"

Derek pointed. "A small one. About half a mile over that hill."

"Any signs he was with anyone else?"

Derek shrugged. "Nope. It looks like he was trying to run back to his truck. Like the thing was chasing him."

"The thing?" Lester asked, dreading the clues that this was, in fact, what he feared.

Derek raised his eyebrows. "Still can't imagine what can do this and leave no blood. It's just like the last one. It's clean. There are splatters, and it's disgusting, but there is no pool. Where's all the blood?"

Lester scanned the area and took a long breath of the crisp Idaho air. It was September, and the leaves were gold and red. It was his favorite time of year in the valley, especially up Mink Creek, where he had camped and hunted since he was a child. He hated that this gruesome act would forever taint this gorgeous place.

An older officer approached them. Derek was still holding the tarp.

"The family's been notified. He was up here alone." The officer read the information from a notepad. Ice crystals had begun to form on his white mustache and sparkled in the late morning sun. "Came yesterday for a weekend hunt. Used to live in the area." He looked at Lester. "I hate to drudge up the past, but..."

"Then don't," Lester snapped. "It's the last thing I want to hear or think about right now."

Derek perked up and turned to him. "What?" he asked, dropping the tarp.

Lester rolled his eyes and shot an annoyed glare at the other officer. "Nothing. It's nothing."

Derek turned to the other officer, who had shrugged at Lester's petulance and was walking away.

"Jerry, wait, what is it? Tell me," Derek begged, trailing after him.

"You're the investigator, kid," the officer grumbled, brushing him away. "Figure it out for yourself. This is your case —you figure it out. I'm heading home."

Lester scoffed. "God, Jerry, that'll help. Why don't you just make this into something it isn't," he called out to the officer as he walked off.

The officer gave him an annoyed backward wave with his gloved hand and trudged off.

Derek turned back to Lester, his head cocked, and just waited.

Lester tried to avoid his stare, and then sighed. "It was years ago, decades actually, and this isn't the same thing. We don't have the same thing."

His insistence was so firm, it only piqued Derek's interest more.

"Instead of making me spend hours looking into whatever this big secret is, why don't you just tell me?" Derek asked. His annoyance at being kept out of the loop was evident.

Lester sighed. "Because you'll spend hours making it into something that it isn't. We had some murders years ago that were similar. Not the same," he said forcefully. "Jerry didn't even work the case, so he has no idea what he's talking about. And whoever committed those murders is long gone. This isn't connected."

"You mean they were never caught?"

Lester sighed again, knowing the questions would never cease. "No. But they're gone."

"How do you know?"

Lester gave him an annoyed sigh. "I just know."

Derek refused to let up. "What do you mean by similar? As in, no heads, no blood?"

Lester took a deep breath, dreading the answer, and knowing what he would say would only spur Derek on. Hesitantly, he simply shrugged.

Derek's shoulders sank and his brow knitted. "How many?"

"It doesn't matter. I told you, it's not connected." Lester

rubbed his eyebrow and started to walk toward the command post.

"Why are you so sure?" Derek pressed, following after him.

Lester paused. The fact was, he wasn't sure. He had stewed about it ever since the murder in the cemetery, pondering the possibilities of a connection to the killings years before. Just the thought made him shudder. He wanted to get away from Derek, the questions, and the memories that were bubbling up like bile. Even after almost thirty years, that short stretch of time had forever marred his life and his career as a cop. He wanted to do anything he could to keep it pushed away and forgotten, but there they were, those lifeless, headless, and bloodless bodies, still haunting his mind and now dredged up because he knew it had returned.

CHAPTER

TWENTY-ONE

Milo

We had to learn to be stealthy in seeing each other. Often, it was meeting somewhere, and then taking my truck or going to her house when her parents were at work. They hadn't directly banned her from seeing me, but had made it clear I wasn't welcome. Clara took it as a challenge and pushed their limits, but I still felt the past guilt and found myself avoiding them altogether.

The police never caught Victor, and even though he made himself scarce, I always felt I was on guard. I could tell Clara felt that way, too, yet my desire to be with her only grew.

As the credits began to roll on the movie we were watching, the warmth of her curled into me made me dread leaving. Her parents would be home in less than an hour. She sensed the time, sat up, and then sighed.

In the rosy-hued light of the room, I leaned in and kissed her. The days of building forts, play-dough sculptures, and skateboard jumps were over. In my mind, she was no longer my

199

childhood friend, and as my hands explored the soft bows and bends of her waist, hips, and legs, I pushed those young days back even further.

I wanted all of her, but I hesitated to check and see if she still welcomed my eagerness. Her hands reaching for my face and pulling me back to her were answer enough for me to roll her under my body and feel the entire length of her against me. She hugged me, and I kept hoping and repeating in my mind that she wouldn't feel the growths on my back. *Please don't notice I'm damaged.*

Her mouth searched for me every time I left her lips and kissed her neck. My entire body felt charged by the taste of her, and I reached up and began to unbutton her jeans. Then she stopped me.

"Wait," she said, panting.

"Why?"

"I don't think we should."

We were still kissing in between talking, and I didn't want to stop. I expected her to give me some resistance, so I wasn't discouraged and kept caressing her until she relented and came back to me. However, when I tried again, she gently pushed me back.

"I can't," she whispered.

I gave her a doubtful smile.

"No, really. I don't want this to change things with us."

I sat up. "Change things?" I asked. "What do you mean? How would it change things?"

She tucked a long strand of hair behind her ear. "You've been my friend for so long, and I don't want to ruin that."

I felt my heart sink. We had been friends since we were little kids, and yet, had hardly seen each other in years. Was she really going to use the "friends" thing on me?

I sat up straighter and slid back from her. My feelings must have been evident in my eyes because I saw her face fall.

"Milo, are you mad?" she asked.

"I'm not exactly happy."

She huffed. "Don't you care about us? Doing this could change everything."

"I'm okay with that," I said. "Unless you want to keep playing games and acting like third graders. I'm tired of acting like it's old times. I'm sick of all that shit. I want to move on already." With that, I stood up and lifted the blanket wrapped around us, accidentally rolling her onto the floor.

She gave a little yelp as she landed. It wasn't on purpose, but I'd hurt her feelings nonetheless.

I sighed and reached down to help her up, but she swiped my hand away.

"Don't touch me," she said as she got to her feet and started folding the blanket.

"I'm sorry. I obviously didn't mean to do that."

She ignored me and continued folding another of the blankets.

I shook my head. "Fine. I'll leave." I started to walk up the stairs, and halfway up, she called to me.

"Milo, wait."

I stopped and slowly turned back to her. I was hoping she'd call me back. Pull me into her arms and begin where we had left off. I was already feeling the dull ache in my chest of wanting her and regretting I had hastily decided to leave.

She stood, her face weary and arms hanging at her sides. "I know you want to forget about the past," she said, her eyes beginning to tear. "But I loved that part of our lives, and I don't want to forget that. You left once before, and I don't want to lose you again."

I heard what she said and was stunned. Was she also blaming me for that terrible day?

So many years ago, and I still can feel how cold and dark it was. Like a thick black veil, I couldn't see my hand in front of my face as I swiftly inched my way along, using my fingers to feel my way against the moist, rough walls of the cave. I wanted to call out for her, but I feared the red-eyed monster would find me, and that kept me quiet, even breathing softly when I thought I could hear the shallow puffs of air escape from my mouth.

I had run away, leaving her there to face him alone. I felt her trying to get out, following me as we frantically fled, jumping and running through the many pools of water that had always drawn us into that cavern. But then, I lost her. I heard her scream, but I didn't turn back. How could I not turn back? My shoulders shuddered at the cold dampness and also my cowardice. My fingers throbbed and my toes were numb. Why hadn't I listened when they told us to stay away from the cave?

The air started to warm, and as I felt the wall's curve with my hand, I saw a dim light in the distance. A lightning bolt cracked against the faded blue of the sky. I ran to it frantically. When the sky hit my face, I screamed out for help. Down the rock ledge and along the path, I sprinted. The splatters of rain hit the ground and made dark dots on my jacket. I wanted to look back, but I kept running toward camp. I was crying and screaming, and before I even made it to the third large rock, Clara's grandfather Richard was there, practically clothes-lining me with his arm to stop my flight.

At his heels, the others rushed up, eyes wide, and everyone yelling at me for answers. Clara's father grabbed my shoulders and shook me, wanting to know where his daughter was. I started to talk about what I'd seen, but he just kept screaming,

"Where is she?" Then he noticed the blood on my hand. "What did you do?"

I tried to tell him to warn them all, but there was no listening. The instant I said the word *cave*, they no longer heard anything else I tried to say. There was a chaotic stampede up the hill.

They left me as alone as I had left Clara alone. I sat watching, knowing they wouldn't get to her in time and dreading the anger and words of cruel blame thrown my way when they returned. Only Esmeralda ever listened to what I'd seen that day. The rest never spoke to me about it, and even my mother didn't want to listen to why it had happened.

Our families never talked about it or saw each other again. It was as if we'd died, and in a way, our family had. We retreated to our secluded home near the cliffs, and there, we lived shadowed beneath the place that would forever remind us of what had happened and why we were outcasts.

My grandfather Jorge was the one who found Clara. He was on the backside of the hill, carrying her soaking wet and shivering body when Clara's father saw them.

"Oh, God! Thank God!" he yelled as he ran to them.

She was alive but lethargic, coughing up water. But the most disturbing sight was the blood. It covered her face and neck and soaked into her hair and clothes.

He ripped his daughter from my grandfather's arms, racing her back to the camp and then to the hospital. As thunder rolled across the canyon and spits of rain hit my face, I caught a glimpse of her dangling legs as her parents dashed through in a screaming rampage. Clara's father was wide-eyed with horror as he looked down at his daughter. He cradled her in a blanket and slipped her into her mother's arms as she sat in the back seat of the family car. He went to the driver's side, and as he opened the door, he looked up.

My family stood watching with solemn faces. His face turned to stone as he cast out words like daggers. "Stay away from us."

The dust that was kicked up as they drove off seemed to linger in the air until long after we were quietly packing up our belongings. We drove home in silence, raindrops rolling down the windows like tears, and sat around like ghosts to wait for news.

It was the police who told us Clara had survived. And while my grandfather was the one who had found her, he quickly went from savior to suspect. Tests later revealed that the blood that covered Clara's face wasn't her own.

Richard was the last one we saw before it all fell apart. He came to our house late and asked to speak to my grandfather alone. Even behind the closed door of my grandparents' bedroom, I could hear the conversation clearly through the heat vent of my bedroom, where I pressed my ear.

"Tell me you didn't do it," Richard whispered urgently.

There was silence.

"Please," he asked again.

"She was gone, man. Are you telling me I should have done nothing?" my grandfather pleaded.

"But what now? What will it do to her?" Richard asked. There was a long pause. "What does this mean for you?"

"I don't know," my grandfather said. "All I know is she's alive."

"They're going to arrest you. They know the blood isn't hers. It's only a matter of time before they know it was you."

My heart stopped when I heard this. What could it mean?

I heard the doorknob of my bedroom turn, and I scrambled up so I was sitting.

Esmeralda peeked in and found me on the floor. I played with the shag carpet as though it was a toy. She said nothing but looked around the room as though I was hiding something. When nothing jumped out, she told me to get ready for bed, gave me another questioning stare, and left me, closing the door behind her.

I quickly leaned back to the vent, but the talking had ceased. I went to my door and opened it just in time to see Richard shaking his head and leaving the house. His shoulders hunched and his clothes looked as though he hadn't changed them in days.

The door shut, and my mother and Esmeralda gathered around Jorge, questioning him like hungry chickens pecking after a single piece of grain. He cowered into a chair at the kitchen table.

I didn't understand. He had saved my friend from the red-eyed monster in the cave, from the ice-cold water that had swept her away, and yet, they were all treating him as if he had done something awful.

"Why are you treating him like this?" I yelled at them. "He saved her! She would have died. Leave him alone."

They all stopped their attack on him and turned to me. My mother's eyes turned to stone.

"He wouldn't have had to save her if you would have done what you were told and stayed away from the caves!" she yelled at me. "None of this would have happened if it weren't for you."

"Cassandra, don't!" Esmeralda cried as she grabbed my mother's arm.

But my mother ripped it away. She could hardly look at me as she went to her room and slammed the door.

My grandfather started to cry and left the house. I thought I had stood up for him, but I had only made him feel worse.

I felt the sting of tears hit my eyes as I stood alone in the middle of the room and sank to the floor in a sobbing heap. My grandmother's arms pulled me up and enveloped me. The warmth of her chest and the kindness of her voice was my only solace for months. When my grandfather left us for good, instead of blaming me, it was Clara my grandmother accused of causing his demise.

Clara and I both told the stories about seeing a red-eyed monster in the cave, but they were written off as childhood imagination and dismissed. Clara didn't remember much past that, so the police and everyone else only had the evidence of that day—someone else's blood covering her mouth and neck. Had she spoken up, maybe she could have erased the suspicion, removed the doubt? They all suspected Grandfather of something terrible, even when they couldn't determine what had really happened. He was so ashamed of what people thought they assumed had happened, and nothing could have changed it. It ruined him—it ruined us. And my shame is what has kept me unable to step out from behind the shadow of my family's sullied past.

I could tell from Clara's face that she hadn't tried to hurt me, but the words hit me so hard—"you left me"—that I took a step back. I could hardly breathe. All those years, I had regretted what I'd done, but never realized that she, too, had blamed me. Everything that had happened that horrible day was because I was a coward.

The longer I stood there, the stronger the memories started pouring back into my brain. I began to feel sick from it all. And then, the stabbing truth hit me: I didn't deserve to be in her life. Her father was right to keep me away.

I shook my head as the wave of agony washed over me, and my pain turned to anger. Before I was able to lash out, I lunged up the stairs and out the door.

When I reached my truck, I looked back to see her looking

devastated and confused, but I only glared at her. I felt my eyes burn with anger and my back broiled with pain as I sped from her house.

The closer I got to home, the more the throbbing increased, and by the time I was at my front door, I stumbled into the house and writhed in agony on the sofa.

My mother and grandmother both came to me in worry.

"What is it?" my mother pleaded, but all I had to do was look at my grandmother to know. She knew the pain had been consistently getting worse. I think she'd tried to ignore it, to pretend that I would grow out of it somehow, but I couldn't dismiss the agony I felt.

My shirt wasn't off, but merely pulled up when I heard my mother gasp. She started babbling about going to the hospital. My grandmother tried to object, but was immediately shot down and ended up sitting next to me like a ghost. The silence continued until I wondered if she was still there, and when I rolled slightly to look at her, that was when I saw my future in her face.

The next week my days were filled with screenings, tests, and befuddled ramblings of what it might be. Each doctor who examined me passed me onto several others, and I soon felt like a circus sideshow freak. They kept leaving the exam room and returning with others to poke and stare and pontificate about what they thought.

The pain subsided the first night, but the dull throbbing just below the surface reminded me it was there and ready to boil over. I didn't return to school for days, and I didn't see Clara. I didn't know how I would react or what I would say if I saw her. And this worry intensified when the ache increased just by thinking about the possibility.

I pushed her out of my mind until the throbbing slowly dissipated. Even then, I hardly slept with all the stress of wondering what would happen to me. It didn't help to have my mother wringing her hands and my grandmother skulking around the house the entire week.

They sent my scans and test results somewhere else for study, and when all the advice and opinions came back, they determined I should have the growths on my back removed. They intertwined with my spine, and the medical experts felt this would eventually cripple me if they didn't intervene.

I was nervous about the procedure, but the thought of having the odd ridges removed was a relief. I'd have scars, but that was better than large bulging growths, and even though the pain had not returned, the memory of it was another reason I wanted it done.

The news of my impending surgery had my grandmother despondent and rocking in a corner. My mother hissed at her about how ridiculous she was acting and how uncaring she was about my welfare.

My grandmother ignored her, but she would sneak into my room at night and continue with her foreboding tales. According to her, the throbbing in my back wasn't a health issue, but rather, a destiny.

"Do you remember what I showed you?" she asked. "Do you remember the Cliffs of the Dead and what I told you? That is where your grandfather took his fall. It's how I know about the pain. Only the fall will take it away, and then you'll no longer be in pain and will be free."

"Oh my God." It was my mother's voice. She was standing in my doorway. Neither one of us had heard her come home from work.

I bolted up, knowing what my grandma had just said was sure to set her off.

"What the hell are you talking about?" she demanded. "What are you telling him?"

My grandmother tried to stand her ground, but my mother grabbed her by the arm and pulled her from my room.

"Get out!" she yelled. "I want you out of my house and away from my son."

"Mom!" I said, trying to calm her. "She's just talking shit. It's no big deal. It means nothing. You know that."

My mother turned to me. "She's talking about where my father jumped off the cliff and committed suicide, and she's telling you to do the same thing!"

I felt my heart stop, and I shot my grandmother a pained and shocked look. "Suicide?"

Esmeralda shook her head. "No," she said. "That's not what happened."

"It *is* what happened," my mother continued. "He was a weak, pathetic man who did something horrible. He couldn't take responsibility for it, and he took the easy way out. She's been making up excuses for years, and I'm tired of it."

"That's not true, Cassandra," my grandmother said through tears. "He was a good man. But he had the same thing as Milo."

"Don't you compare this to Milo," my mother raged at her. "Don't you dare. I put up with this for long enough. I'm not going to have you telling him to follow Dad and jump off a cliff. You get out."

"Mom, please," I pleaded with her. I felt it was all my fault for not giving my grandmother her venue to talk. She had lost the only companion she'd had when I grew up and grew out of her stories. She had tried harder, using the spectacle and drama to regain my attention, and now she faced being completely shut out of our lives. Now that I knew the truth about my grandfather, I felt even worse about having her leave us. "They are just stories she's telling. They're not real."

My mother turned and stormed off to her room. "I want you

out," she said to my grandmother again before slamming her bedroom door behind her.

My grandmother looked at the floor, then up at me with solemn eyes.

"She'll cool down in a while," I said as we stood numb and exhausted.

My grandmother shook her head and wiped her cheek with a tissue. We walked to her room, and she sat on the edge of the bed. I took a seat in the same cushioned chair I had sat in as a child.

"I must leave," she said softly.

"Grandma, don't say that."

She put up a hand. "No, I must. The stories I told you are real. Your grandfather didn't kill himself. He loved us. He did what he had to do because of what he was. It is what you are. You'll see."

"Grandma," I groaned, wishing she would stop making it worse.

Seeing I was upset, she raised her eyebrows and nodded. "I know it's hard to believe, but I know you feel it, and it will get stronger. Even if you don't believe me now, promise me one thing?"

I rolled my eyes, knowing I was never going to change her mind.

Her face turned grave. "Promise me, Milo."

Her eyes were so fervent, I couldn't help but nod and ask, "Promise what?"

"Only in darkness. The fall," she emphasized. "It must be at night."

I sighed. "Grandma, I'm not going to jump off a cliff."

"You don't understand things now, but soon you will. Please, just promise me," she said.

I finally relented. "Okay, I promise. But only if you never mention this again."

Her eyes were anguished. She thought for a moment, then she nodded. "Only in the dark," she said again.

"Yes," I answered her. "Only in darkness. Now stop talking about this and go to sleep. You've told me what you wanted, so don't say anything more. In the morning, we can talk to Mom."

But that morning, my grandmother's chair was empty, and so was her room. She was unable to drive, so where she went and how was a mystery.

I could tell my mother was both annoyed and concerned. She wrote it off as my grandmother's dramatic way of protest, and my mother wasn't about to let childish actions divert her attention away from me.

"Why is she so against me getting help for my back?" I asked my mother.

"Because she is crazy and doesn't trust modern medicine. She is an old woman who thinks anything new is wrong. She is doing this to get at me because I won't listen to her silly reasons." She paused in her rant. "Don't let this worry you. She's probably just out on one of her walks. She'll return, and things will be fine."

I nodded at my mother, and she hugged me quickly as I headed off to my room. As I pulled the covers up, I wondered where Esmeralda could have gone. We lived so far out of town, and my grandmother knew no one.

She never went anywhere, except on her walks through the sagebrush and lava fields. I worried about her out there alone. It was after midnight when I heard my mother finally go to bed. It wasn't her words, but rather, the soft shuffle of her footsteps past my door that told me she was worried about Esmeralda.

I took a deep breath and started thinking about my own situation. I wondered what the next few days would hold. I knew I would be asleep for the procedure, but what then? Would I be in pain? Would I have stitches, bandages, wounds? And what if it went wrong? Would I be crippled for the rest of my life? And even though I had never put any weight in her fantastical stories, I couldn't help but contemplate the possibility of my grandmother's omens being real.

I'm not sure how long I had been asleep, but it was my grandma's mournful voice that startled me awake. I began to ask where she'd been, but she hushed me. Her eyes were wide with fear, and I saw a man behind her. He was older, but stood tall. It was all I could make out in the dim light of my room. I sat up, and he stepped toward me. Before I could ask what was happening or yell for my mother, he grabbed the back of my head, put a damp cloth to my face, and held it firmly in place as I struggled to free myself. The odor was strong and sweet, but that was all I remembered.

CHAPTER

TWENTY-TWO

Milo

I woke to the sound of bacon frying. The smell was comforting, but I soon was flooded with memories of what had happened and realized I wasn't at home. Fear of the unknown made me shoot up in the bed.

"Lay back," my grandmother said, putting her hands on my shoulders. "You're fine. I'm here."

"Where's here?" I asked. My head pounded as I tried to keep my eyes open to see my new surroundings. There were whiteboard walls of a long room with a kitchen area and several rows of beds. It had soft light but no windows, and covering the bed were billowing blankets.

"Rest now," she said. "We'll talk later. We'll talk like we used to."

As I began to sink back into sleep, I saw a man enter the room. He was tall, thin, and dark. He was wearing a white coat, looking like a doctor, but I saw a hunch and hobble that struck me as familiar when he moved. Before I could ask who he was, my head spun, and then I saw only black.

. . .

In a dream, I realized who he was. He was the one my grandmother had taken me to visit that dry, dusty day. It was when her fall from grace began.

Years before, we traveled to the middle of the black and craggy landscape surrounding the reservoir and Snake River near American Falls. It was one of the few times I remember my grandmother driving. We took the old truck parked in the shed. It had been my grandfather's, and even though we desperately needed the money, my grandmother refused to sell it. We left on a day when my mother was working late so we could make the trip and be home in plenty of time.

I remember Esmeralda being on edge during the drive, but relieved and almost giddy when she saw the man.

"Esmi," he called her as they embraced. It was a name I had heard her called before, but only by my grandfather. I knew it was short for Esmerelda, and it felt weird to have this stranger be so familiar with her.

My grandmother introduced us, and while I don't remember his name, I thought it was strange that he studied me so closely and kept repeating my full name, Emilio Jorge. While I played amongst the large lava rocks and sagebrush of the rest stop where we met, my grandmother and the man leaned against the car in a huddled discussion about me, but kept away from me.

We weren't there long because I remember still wanting to chase the lizards that darted in and out of the rough and porous lava rocks. It was his walk back to his car I remember most clearly, crutch in hand, hunched, and labored. Even as a child, it looked grueling to me. The walk I'd watched as I stood in the high school parking lot brought it all back in my mind. What seemed like a short and simple car ride with my grandmother would change the course of my life.

"Milo?" I heard a voice call.

I woke up in the same room. My heart was racing, and when I put my hand to my head, I realized I was wet with sweat. The light of the room was dim, and I must have slept for several hours as I was starving. I felt more alert and could sit up without the jarring pain in my head. I looked over to find my grandmother in a chair, watching me.

"How do you feel?" The voice came from my side, and I turned to where a woman stood, holding a vial attached to a thin tube extending from my arm. I began to pull back, but she laid a hand on my arm to hold it in place. "Relax, I'm almost finished."

I shook my head. "What is going on?"

"You need help," my grandmother said. "They're going to help you."

I tried to focus my eyes on her, but her face was blurry.

The woman taking my blood removed the needle, quickly placed a cotton ball, and taped it. She folded my arm. "I'll be back to check on you in a bit." Then she left.

I turned back to my grandmother. "Where are we?"

"This is where you'll learn, and you'll be safe. Listen to what they have to say."

"Who?" I asked. "Safe from what? Is this a hospital? Was that man a doctor? Where'd he go?"

I tried to sit up, but my head still stung. I felt the sickening buzz of nausea wash over me, and I lay back and tried to steady myself. I took deep breaths, concentrating on trying not to vomit, and again, my mind flashed to a figure in the dark and the sickeningly sweet smell of whatever sank me into the dark hole I was now trying to climb out of.

A third time, I woke up in that strange place, and this time, I found myself being stared at through the bars of a cell. It was a boy. He looked to be around twelve years old. He had dark hair and skin, and his eyes were large and light brown.

"He's awake," he said to someone else but kept his eyes on me.

I tried to sit up, but again, I felt the throb of the medicine course through my head. I moaned in pain.

"Don't fight it," I heard a voice call from somewhere in the large room. "It won't do any good. Lay down, keep your eyes closed, and it will go away after a while."

The voice was older, sounding closer to my age. My head throbbed, so I did as he ordered. "Where am I?" I asked with my eyes still closed.

"He lives," said another voice, this one even older than the rest.

I squinted to where the voice came, my head still swimming. He was tall, and his arms were thick. He stood leaning against the bars of his cell with one leg crossed at his ankles. He had on a white cotton shirt and shorts. As I glanced around, I saw others, and they were all wearing the same thing. Like the rest, he, too, had black hair and darker skin, like me.

"What's your name?" he asked.

"Milo," I answered. When my body started to relax, and I began to rise above the haze of drugs and queasiness, it was then I could focus my eyes. I took a deep what-the-hell breath and continued to study the bunker. It was the place I had seen in my dream—the prison I had burst into when I was running through the darkness. Now I was a prisoner there. "Where am I?"

"Good question," he answered. "We don't know."

"Why are we here?"

"Another good question. We've all asked the same thing when we finally came to. One minute, we're walking along, and the next minute we're grabbed and knocked out. Now we're here. That's all we know." He was blunt, but not biting.

"By who? What do they want?"

He chuckled. "I told you: we don't know. We've been here for about two weeks, and we still don't know why or what they plan to do."

A shot of fear washed over me, but I knew my grandmother would never be part of something that would hurt me. She was there when they'd taken me, so she had to know they meant no harm. "Who are you? Where are you from?" I asked desperately.

"You're full of questions for someone who can hardly keep his eyes open," he said. He sighed and took a seat on his cot.

I swallowed and tried to focus.

Tipping his head and studying me, he introduced himself and the others. "I'm Peter, and I'm from Burley. Alex is from Blackfoot. So is Thomas," he said, motioning to the two boys at the far end of the bunker. "And that's my cousin Ivan," he said, gesturing to the youngest boy, who took a seat on his cot, but was still watching me.

I took a deep breath. "I'm Milo. I'm from American Falls," I said, surprised to learn we were all from southeastern Idaho.

Peter nodded.

"What is this place?" I asked as my eyes began to clear. I was able to look around now. The cells were small, and the walls and ceiling were rough black rock. Each cell had a cot, a table with a washbasin and pitcher, and a covered bucket.

I was in a cell at the front of the chamber. Directly across from me was a thin walkway, and then Peter's cell and the cell connecting to my side held Ivan. It was apparent that he was the youngest of the group. He was thin and wiry, and he continued to study me. His face bore the creased brow and sullen eyes of angst.

The two other boys were in cells across the bunker, with a couple of empty cells in between. I couldn't get a clear look at them, but could see enough to know they were about my age. Several strings of lights hanging down the center aisle gave the bunker a dim glow.

Peter shrugged. "We think we're underground, but no one knows for sure. It's cold, and we're surrounded by these rock walls, but that's all we know."

"But why?" I asked. "Why are we here? What are they going to do to us?"

Peter, who up to this point seemed brazen and almost callous, turned troubled.

I watched him and waited for an answer, but I turned to the others when he remained quiet. They all looked perplexed by my question.

Ivan, the younger boy in the cell next to mine, had been quiet and merely listening, but then he spoke up. "If you do what they want, they say you can go home," he said.

I looked at him as he pulled his legs onto the cot and leaned back against the wall.

"That's not what they say," Peter said, correcting him. "They told us if we do what they say, then things will be easier." He turned to me. "Ivan and I were walking home from school. They grabbed us together."

"Who grabbed you?" I asked.

"The two big guys and that so-called doctor," he answered. "What about you?"

I nodded. "It was the doctor and..." I stopped. I didn't want to admit my own grandmother had helped in my kidnapping. "How long have you been here? Have they told you anything?"

Peter lifted his shoulders. "I think it's been about a week.

We don't see the sun, so I'm not sure what day or even what time it is. All they tell us is to be patient and that they're trying to help us."

"I've been here the longest. It's been over two weeks," the boy named Alex called from his cell. "Then Thomas, and then Peter and Ivan. And there were others before me, but they're gone."

I felt a chill go over me. "What do you mean? Where did they go?"

Ivan piped up. "It's the bad ones that go away."

I looked to Peter for clarification. "There have been others?"

"The ones that cause trouble seem to be the ones who conveniently," he used his fingers as quotation marks, "disappear."

"How do you know they aren't just letting them go?" I asked.

Peter gave a huff, then looked at Ivan and tried to compose himself. "I just know," he said.

I waited to hear more, and when he stopped talking, I pressed him. "So, what happened to them?"

"We don't know what happens or even how many have been here for sure," Alex called out. "There were two when I got here that are now..." He paused. "Gone."

Thomas spoke up. "We all just sit here and wait for them to decide what to do with us."

"We're lab rats," Alex piped up. "They keep taking me and doing tests. They scrape the skin on my back, take my blood, and ask me questions about how I feel. They never tell me why, or what they've found."

The others nodded.

"Your back?" I asked, feeling a chill go over me. "Why the skin on your back?"

Peter shot me a look.

"What?" I asked him. "I have this rash or growth thing on my back. I thought that was why I'm here."

Peter shook his head and took a seat on his bed, but continued to look at me.

"What's the growth look like?" Alex pressed. "I have something like that, too."

"So do I," Thomas chimed in. "I think we all do."

"Not all of us," Peter said as I was beginning to describe the ridges along my spine. His eyes darted toward Ivan, who stood, mouth agape and eyebrows furrowed in concern.

We became silent, wondering what it all meant. I had so many questions, but somehow I knew the answers weren't something I wanted to hear.

TWENTY-THREE

Milo

The next morning, a large man dressed in white came with a cart and metal food trays. The smell was heavenly, especially since I hadn't eaten since the morning before. The man had no hair and seemed almost too clean. His shirt strained against his large arms and chest, his eyes gleamed, but his face was void of expression.

"Where are we?" I asked him.

He didn't answer me. "Step away from the door," he said coldly.

I hesitated.

"Fine. Don't eat," he scoffed, and started to turn.

I quickly stepped back as he'd asked, and he unlocked the gate and set the tray on the floor. He closed and locked it again.

"Please, tell me, what's going on here?" I asked again.

He ignored me and simply went about his task of delivering the trays.

"Don't bother," Peter said. "None of these goons that work here does much but order us around."

I studied him with his bright white clothes and massive arms. I picked up my tray, took it to my bed, and dug in. It was scrambled eggs, bacon, and toast slathered in strawberry jam. It was delicious, and I was ravenous.

I was almost finished with the entire tray before the man even left the room, and as he did, I noticed the keyring barely visible in his back pocket. When the door closed, I listened for the sound of a key in the lock but heard nothing.

I sat my tray on the small table in my cell and went to the bars. I looked at the door, and then at Peter. "That door isn't locked," I said, motioning to the main entrance of the bunker.

Peter looked up from his food. "Yeah, so? These doors certainly are." He pointed to the cell gates.

"He keeps the key in his back pocket. If we can distract him, we can take it."

"Then what?" Peter asked, uninterested.

"Then we get away," called Alex from the far end of the bunker. He had overheard us.

"Shh!" I put up a hand to him, worried the guard was still close enough to hear our scheming.

Alex nodded and continued in a whisper. "We escape this place before they kill us or do whatever it is they plan to do."

Peter stood up and shook his head at Alex. He motioned over to Ivan, who was lying on his cot, his hands covering his face. Peter's eyes showed worry for the younger boy.

"Sorry," Alex said. He put up his hands in defense.

Peter sighed and went to his cot.

"Who is that doctor?" I asked.

"His name is Davila. He says he's helping us," Peter said. His voice was low and skeptical.

I thought for a moment, wondering what connection Dr. Davila had to my grandmother. I was sure it was him at that meeting at the mesa all those years ago. "Who else is holding us here? How many are there?" I asked.

Alex was still leaning against the bars of his cell. "I've seen four so far. The two big guys who kidnapped us," he looked over to Ivan, "are the ones who come in with the food. They almost look like twins, and there's a woman who does the cooking and the nurse."

I thought about the nurse taking my blood when I was still groggy. The more I heard, the more I wondered what connection it all had to the pains in my back and my grandmother's odd stories. "The nurse took my blood when I first got here," I told them.

"She takes our blood every day," Thomas said.

"Why?" I asked.

No one answered. They all just shrugged. It wasn't the only question where instead of an answer, there was only more uncertainty.

"There's something wrong with all of them," Thomas said. "They look like they haven't been outside in years, and their skin is..." He paused, searching for the word. "Shiny."

"Shiny?" I asked. I turned to Peter for his take on it.

He nodded. "It's like they're plastic."

Unconsciously, I touched my face. "Plastic?" It was weird and didn't make sense, but almost nothing about where I was or what was happening to me did. "Do you know where we are? Are we still in Idaho?" I asked.

"No idea," Peter said. "We don't go anywhere without Thing One or Thing Two, and there aren't any windows, so we don't ever see outside. We were all knocked out when they kidnapped us until we got here. We could be anywhere."

"Was it the doctor that kidnapped you?" I asked.

"Kind of," Peter answered. "He was there, but it was the two guards who grabbed us."

"The two big dudes got me, too," Alex said.

"Not me," Thomas said. "It was the doctor. I woke up in the middle of the night, and he was in my room. I remember him putting something over my nose, and that was it."

"That's how it happened for me," I said, then I thought for a moment. "Why us?" I asked them all.

They started talking with differing answers. It was so confusing. Everyone stopped, and one by one, we each told our story. Not only how they captured us, but who we were. I became shocked and disturbed to hear our stories were almost identical.

We were all Hispanic, none of us knew our birth fathers, and we all had odd ridges on our backs that had started when we were young. We all told stories about how our mothers had taken us to doctors, tried the different creams, and eventually opted for more drastic measures, and that each of us had undergone a biopsy just before being kidnapped. Peter, Ivan, and Alex were captured right off the street and shoved in a van, then Thomas and me at night while we slept in our bedrooms. All of it was similar, but none of it made sense.

Even though we all lived in the rural areas of southeast Idaho, none of us had ever crossed paths and no one had gone to the same doctor. However, we were all eventually told our ridges were growths taking over our spines that threatened to cripple or even kill us. We all experienced degrees of pain that coincided with specific experiences and seemed to increase the older we got.

The exception to all of this was Ivan. He hadn't experienced any of it. No ridges, no pain, and he was obviously feeling like an outsider.

I thought for a moment and tried to whisper to Peter so Ivan wouldn't overhear. "What are they going to do to us? Why kidnap a bunch of people who have a disease and lock them up?"

Alex piped up. "It's like when people had leprosy. They're afraid we're going to give it to them, so they're getting rid of us. That's what I think."

Peter tried to hush him, but it was too late.

"Stop treating me like a baby," Ivan called to Peter, irritated. "I want to know what's going on, too."

Peter had tried initially to shield him from our discussions, but seeing Ivan's agitation, he stopped coddling him, and the discussion became frank and often troubling. Ivan listened intently, but then became sullen. He eventually went to his cot and turned toward the wall.

Peter noticed and looked troubled, but took a deep breath and kept talking. Being seventeen, he was the oldest of the group. He stood up and removed his shirt, exposing the large growths down each side of his spine. They were far more pronounced than my own, but I knew it wouldn't be long before mine were also distended and unmistakable.

I heard a gasp and looked over to Ivan, who was watching. The sight made Ivan's eyes grow wide with horror, and he turned away.

The rest of us remained in the corners of our cells closest to one another so we could continue to try and learn more. Hours passed, and the more we talked, the more we came to realize we were probably here because of the ridges on our backs.

"Sometimes they ache so badly, I want to rip them out myself," Peter said. "I was scheduled for surgery to have them removed before this happened." He motioned toward the cell bars.

"That's what I thought was going to happen to me, too," I said.

"So, what are they? Is it cancer?" Thomas asked. "I had a test done, but the results didn't come back yet."

"Maybe we're here because we're contagious and they're keeping us away from others. I think they're planning on doing experiments on us," Alex said.

"No," a voice came from the door and surprised us all. It was Dr. Davila. "It is not my intention to torture you," he said.

Startled, we watched in silence as he walked in. "So, you've all been getting to know each other," he said calmly. "And you've realized you have something in common."

"It seems we have a few things in common," I said, annoyed.

"Yes, you do," he agreed. "You will realize very soon, you all are very special. That is why you're here."

"Cut the crap and tell us why you're keeping us all prisoners," Alex piped up.

The doctor took a deep breath and tried to act patient. "Alex, I know you're frustrated, but I'm doing what's best for you."

We all started shouting our disgust and disagreement like the angry caged animals that we were.

"Stop!" he yelled. "I have to do this to keep you safe. To keep all of us safe. When we can go forward without the risk of harm, then..." He paused, and his voice softened. He put his head down and motioned to our cells. "This will change. I promise. But for now, this is the only way."

"What risk is there to you? Are we contagious?" I yelled out. "No doctor treats his patients like this."

The others joined in with loud rants and banging on the bars.

He looked up at me with tired eyes and took a deep breath, annoyed as if he were the one being held captive.

It angered me, and that was when my back began to ache. I bent over in pain. The throbbing intensified the angrier I became. I went to my cot and sat on the edge and felt my head start to spin.

The others' chanting became louder and more intense, and then I heard him shout. "Enough, or I'll call for the shots! Do you hear me?"

At that point, the pain was so severe, I wanted the shots. The idea of being free of the throbbing was worth being drugged out, but then, the shouting died down. I looked up and noticed most of us were exhausted, panting, and in pain.

I then heard a low grumbling noise come from Peter. It sounded inhuman, like a growl. I looked over and saw him reach through the bars. He took a swipe at the doctor and knocked him across the room. Peter's eyes were wide and fixed, and his face seethed. The sound coming from him was so loud, it reverberated, and all of us went silent, except for Ivan, who began to sob.

Hearing the commotion, the two large men in white shirts came racing in and, using a large pole with a syringe, jabbed Peter and pushed him to the floor of his cell. He tried to get up, but the drug quickly took effect and he slumped to the ground.

Dr. Davila was stunned, but soon got to his feet. He smoothed his hair back and took an agitated breath, and went to Peter's cell. He stood looking through the bars, studying him. The agitation in his face turned to sadness and concern, even though Peter had tried to kill him.

"This can't happen," he said, then turned to the rest of us. "These uproars are why you're locked in here. Don't you notice the pain? Don't you feel it rise up when you do things like this? It will only get worse if you don't do what I say and let me help you." His breathing was hard, and he turned to the door. He motioned for the two men to leave, and then he followed, looking even more hobbled than before. He leaned heavily on the cane as he looked back before the door closed.

We all sat silently in our cells for at least an hour. As time passed, the pain subsided, but the ridges on my back remained tender like a bad sunburn. I couldn't lie on my back or even have my light cotton shirt touch the area.

"Peter?" Ivan cried out. "Is he breathing?" he asked me.

I walked to the edge of my cell and studied him. "He is."

The two large men returned. Without acknowledging any of us, they lifted Peter onto his cot. They didn't speak, and as they worked, I saw the odd glistening and flawless smoothness of their skin.

The larger of the two caught me staring and flashed me a glare. I stepped back and looked away, and soon they were gone.

Peter didn't move for the rest of the day. After lunch, I noticed he was awake. I tried to talk to him, but he morosely lay in his cell.

Ivan stayed curled on his bunk and went from sobbing to sniffles, and then to sleep.

As the day went on, we discussed what had happened and tried to ponder what we were facing and what the doctor had planned for us, but Peter simply lay on his cot and stared out, empty.

Later that night, when the others had gone to sleep, I noticed he still hadn't moved in the dim light of a single bulb. "Are you still in pain?" I asked him, trying to get a response.

He shook his head.

"What is it?" I asked. "What's wrong?"

He took a deep breath and swallowed hard. He shot a glance over to his young cousin.

I looked over to Ivan. "He's asleep," I assured Peter.

Peter nodded, and then slowly, painfully propped himself up to a sitting position. He stretched his neck a bit, and I could tell the pain was still there.

"You still sore?" I asked.

"It's not the pain," he answered.

I sat silent, waiting for him to continue.

"You saw it. You saw what I tried to do to him," he said. He looked up at me.

I shrugged. "He's keeping us prisoners," I replied. "You had the right to hit him."

Peter sat up straighter and shook his head. His eyebrows furrowed in thought. "That wasn't me. This thing we have—this thing on our backs that throbs and aches. It's more than that. It's up here, too," he said, pointing a finger to his head.

I cocked my head, confused.

"It's controlling me. It's making me want to do things. It made me try to kill him," he said.

I scoffed. "He's locked us all up. We'd all like to..."

"No," he interrupted. His eyes were urgent and intent. "I'll do it. Eventually, I will kill. He knows that. That's why he has us locked up. He knows that's what's happening to us. This thing we all have is turning us insane. That's what he means by being safe. He knows what we are."

"That's not true," I said. "We're just angry because of this place, because of what he's doing to us."

Peter shut me out then. He shook his head and lay back down on the cot, turning toward the wall.

"Come on, Peter," I urged. I tried again and again to get him back, but it didn't work.

I lay on my cot and thought about what he'd said. I contemplated the pains and the feelings that coincided with them. I realized they occurred with certain events in my life and were more intense with particular stresses, but my thoughts, even when the pain was at its worst, never turned to killing. I looked over at Peter in the dim light of the bunker, and he still hadn't moved. I finally gave up trying to understand what it all meant and went to sleep.

CHAPTER

TWENTY-FOUR

Milo

I think it was morning, but it was still dark. The lights were off. It was Peter's shouts that woke me.

I bolted up in bed and looked over, trying to see what was happening. Only a thin sliver of light came from the door. I saw the two men struggling to carry Peter, and then the door to our chamber slammed shut. It was black again.

"What happened?" I asked into the darkness.

"They took him," Ivan cried. "He's gone like the others."

"I knew it would happen after last night. They always take them after something like that," Alex called out from his cell several sections down.

The lights to our chamber blinked on. The brightness made me squint. We all sat on the edges of our cots, looking confused, worried, and half-asleep.

Just then, there was a loud crash, like metal trays being upended in the hallway, then a piercing shriek so blaring, I felt the inside of my head swell. My ears expanded and exploded in pain.

I grabbed my head and fell to the floor, fearing that the ceiling and walls would come down around me. It was as though waves of noise were crashing over me again and again. I squeezed my eyes shut and cowered there, waiting for the worst. It seemed to go on forever, but then, the noise began to wane. It left me with a dull pounding in my head.

When I was able to look up, I could see the others were also hiding and looking as I did, except Ivan. Instead, he was standing in his cell, horrified. He was yelling something at me, but I couldn't hear him. I could tell he was frantic and confused, but I just stayed on the ground with my ears covered.

When I did try to stand up, my balance was off, and I stumbled. My ears were ringing with pain, and the lights in the bunker seemed bright and glaring. Thomas and Alex were both on all fours and bracing themselves as well, looking as confused and alarmed as I was.

I felt something wet on my chin and touched my face. I looked at my hand and saw blood. I wiped my cheek and realized I was bleeding from my ears. When Alex saw this, he touched his own face and saw that he, too, was bleeding. Thomas was as well. Only Ivan seemed unscathed, and yet, seeing none of us responding to his pleas, he went to his cot and curled up in a ball.

For what seemed like half a day, we all sat in our cells, nursing our sore ears and throbbing heads. Ivan was so confused and kept peppering us with questions, but because we couldn't understand with the ringing in our ears, he became frantic, and then despondent. I wanted to help him, but I could barely function. When I stood up, I became dizzy and had to reach for the cell bars or quickly sit back down.

When the guard came to deliver our lunches, he saw us looking ill and noticed the blood. He abandoned the cart carrying the trays and left the room quickly. Soon, it was Dr.

Davila who rushed in. He looked tired, but when he saw the dry blood in streaks down our faces from our ears, his eyes went wide with worry.

"What happened?" he asked.

I could barely hear him, but could read his lips. I tried to steady myself, but it was useless, so I laid on my cot to answer him as best I could. "It was that noise. It was so loud, I think it ruptured our eardrums."

"What was that noise?" I heard Alex call out in a muffled yell.

Dr. Davila put up his hand when Thomas chimed in and also began to yell for answers.

"What noise?" he asked. His question sounded as though he was asking it underwater.

"The blast," I said. It was the only way I could describe it. "The noise went on and on, and now I can barely hear. And we're all bleeding."

One at a time, each of us was escorted from our cells and taken to be checked. When it was my turn, one of the large men in the white shirts held onto my arm as we walked down a long tunnel-like corridor that was cold and dark. Small light bulbs, strung with hooks, lit the way. It was the first time I was anywhere but my cell and that white room from the first day, so I studied the area as best I could. All signs pointed to an underground bunker.

The walls were black rock, and we passed several doors as we walked. It reminded me of an old mine shaft we'd visited during a high school field trip. Even the smell was that of musty, cold dirt, and when we were away from the lights, going from one room or section to another, the darkness was so complete, it felt like a weight. My eyes hurt from trying to take it all in, and soon I was taken into a room and asked to sit on a bed. I looked around and realized I was in that first white room, and I was sitting on the same bed as when I'd arrived with my grandmother.

Dr. Davila scooted toward the bed on a stool with wheels and reached for my ear with a pointed metal instrument. When he touched me, I flinched back.

"I'm trying to help you, Milo," he said.

His words struck me in a way I hadn't expected, and I let out a burst of frustration and laughter.

"Help me?" I asked. "You've put me in a cage. Where's my grandmother?"

"She went back. She did what was best for you."

"Best for me? Why am I here?"

He took a deep breath and leaned back in his chair. "You're here because you need help, and we're trying to find the best way to do that."

I thought about the doctor's appointment and surgery I was scheduled to have. "Do I have cancer?" The sound of my own voice was strange and garbled.

Dr. Davila lifted his eyebrows, surprised by my question. "No, you don't have cancer."

"Then what is it? Why am I locked up here?"

"Milo, I want to give you answers, and I don't want to have you in those cells, but until I know what we're dealing with and what's best for you, I need to keep you and others safe."

"Keep others safe? Am I contagious?"

Dr. Davila shook his head. "No, but until I know what's best, this has to be."

"What about my mom? She's going to be looking for me. And what did my grandma have to do with all this?"

"Your grandmother did the right thing to bring you here. She wants to help you, too."

I reeled back. "She told me I was part of some ancient tribe and that someday I'd have wings. She's always saying crazy things."

Davila looked at the floor, then he looked up and sighed. "I know this is confusing and unfair, but it's what has to be, at least for a little while longer."

I shook my head, unconvinced.

"Can I take a look at your ears and see if there's any damage?"

I was still annoyed, but I relented. The examination was short, and though he seemed genuinely concerned about my ears, he didn't do anything to treat them.

"It may take some time, but they will heal on their own," was all he said.

"What about Peter?" I asked him as he took me back to my cell. "Where is he? What happened to him?"

He didn't respond, and for days, he didn't return to our chamber. The only person we saw was one of the large guards, and he seemed different than before. Usually purposeful and quick in his duties, he now seemed lumbering, and his white clothes that were usually spotless looked dingy.

We could usually count on seeing each of the men regularly throughout the day, but now, the visits were random, and it was only the smaller of the two large guards who appeared.

One day, after delivering our breakfast trays, the guard left the keys to the cells on the table next to the door. We all saw him do it, and when he left the bunker, we gave each other odd glances as though wondering if it was a test or a trick. We didn't touch them, and he returned later to retrieve them, giving us an inquisitive scan. We wrote it off as his being distracted and confirmed this behavior with his other examples of care-lessness.

At night, I could hear talking through the walls. It was as if the words were just inches away, and I kept wondering where the voices were coming from. At first, I thought it was the other boys in the bunker, but then I noticed Alex and Thomas stirring and awake. I realized they heard the voices, too.

The sounds entered like echoes, sometimes booming, but other times, whispering inside my head. Where I sat and when I woke during the night altered the clarity of what I heard.

Every morning, I talked with Alex and Thomas and compared my night of sounds and voices to what had kept them awake. Our discussions had Ivan feeling even more left out.

At first, he tried to pretend he heard things, too, but soon we all realized it was a ruse. This ailment we had was beginning to make him feel like the one with the disease. And now, without Peter, he felt utterly isolated and alone.

We tried to include Ivan and help him throughout the day, but we were all in a desperate, awful place in life, and there wasn't much we could offer in support, so he often just lay on his cot, staring up vacantly.

We were trying to figure out when this new, odd development had happened, and why. The night of Peter's disappearance had brought on the strange voices. That blaring noise that had exploded our eardrums and made us sick for days now had us hearing even more than before. But not just random sounds; we heard voices and conversations going on in other places.

Each morning, we compared what we'd heard, and we soon realized we were hearing the same things at the exact times during the night.

I was able to distinguish between the voices. I could tune in the guard, the woman who did the cooking, or the nurse who took our blood, but what I waited for was the voice of Dr. Davila. He was the one who held the answers to why we were here and what was going to happen to us. Unfortunately, he rarely spoke at night. We could only overhear the workers who were up past dark.

During these late-night talks, I heard the nurse asking why someone named Patrick was no longer there. She was speaking to the woman who we assumed did the cooking. We didn't see her much, but sometimes, she was with Dr. Davila when we were taken from our cells and brought to the small room where they tested us. She was usually quiet, only answering yes or no as she stood behind Dr. Davila while writing notes on a clipboard.

"With Patrick gone, what do you think George is going to do?" I heard the nurse asking her.

"Are you hearing this?" Thomas called over to me. "They're talking about the guards."

"Yes," Alex and I said at once.

"What is it?" asked Ivan. "What are they saying?"

"Shh," I hushed him. "We'll tell you later."

"I heard Patrick's gone nuts. He saw the whole thing," the nurse said. "That kid turned into one of *them* while he was moving him to the other cell. Seeing that would make you crazy."

Turned into one of them? I repeated the words in my head. Turned into what? Was it Peter they were talking about, and if so, what horrible thing happened to him?

"Do you think George will try to leave? Do you think he'll snitch?" the woman asked.

"And give up the stuff?" the nurse scoffed. "Never. He'll get over it. And I bet Patrick will be back."

The stuff? What were they being given to stay and work at a place like this?

"He better get over it quick. I'm sick of having to do all his work," the woman said. "It was supposed to be only one, but now it's been almost ten of these freaks. How long is this going to last?"

I counted the four of us in the bunker and added the others Alex had said were there, but now gone. We were the freaks they spoke of, but the project that had us here was the big question we all had. It was the reason there was a risk. What could be so dangerous, so precious, that we were ripped from our homes and lives and taken here?

"I think the supply is running out. He'd better find more, or I'll be leaving, too," the nurse said with a huff. "I'm not risking my life for nothing. And how long can he keep that one out?"

"What's going on? What are they saying?" Ivan whined.

"Quiet," I said into the darkness. I settled back and focused on the conversation through the walls.

"With the size of this fortress and the ammo he has, I don't know why he's so worried about that one getting in," the woman said.

"I do. I've seen what they become," the nurse said. "There's one out there that must be even worse than the others."

There was a long silence. I strained to hear more, but the voices faded.

"What one?" Alex pondered to himself as we sat in our cells the next morning, contemplating what we'd all heard the night before.

"One what?" Ivan asked.

We all ignored him, and I heard him give a frustrated huff. We were all sitting in the dark so he didn't even have our expressions or other signs giving him an idea of what we were hearing.

"They said 'that one' was trying to get in. Do you think someone is trying to save us?" Thomas asked.

We all thought for a moment, but no one answered.

"Is someone coming for us?" Ivan was desperate for answers.

"We don't know," I responded sternly. "We're trying to listen."

"She said 'one,'" Alex said again. "What could one guy do? And they made it sound like Davila has an arsenal."

"Sounds to me like we're never getting out of here," I said. If there was such an effort to keep people from finding us, how did we ever think we could escape? "If he has all that to keep one guy out, imagine what he has done to keep us all in."

"I don't know," Thomas said. "It's not like he's got an army. Unless others are here that we don't know about, the only ones we see or hear besides the doctor are the nurse, that other woman, and the guards. I don't think anyone else is around. We only see Davila during the day, and we've never heard him talk at night."

"Maybe there are more of them in another part of this place or another room," Alex said.

I simply shrugged.

I heard sniffles from the cell next to me. I realized then that Ivan had given up with his questions and simply cried in his cell.

It made me feel guilty, and I called over to him. "Hey, Ivan. I'm sorry. It's just that we didn't hear much. If we do, we'll tell you, okay?"

At first, he didn't answer. Just more weeping and sniffles. But then I heard the creak of the springs on his cot and knew he had stood up.

"What's wrong with me? Why can't I hear it, too?" he asked.

Wrong with *him*? I couldn't help but feel the irony in his words. The rest of us heard voices through the rock walls and had ridges growing on our backs, yet he thought he was the odd one.

"If I'm not like you, they'll find out, and then what?" Ivan asked.

I hadn't thought about it that way. He wasn't like us, which meant he didn't have the same traits that were the reason we were being held captive. What made us both peculiar and hunted were the things that made us prized. What would they do to him?

I took a deep breath and wished that Peter was there to watch out for him or try to ease his fears. "I don't know." It was all I could say.

TWENTY-FIVE

Milo

"Milo."

It was Alex's voice that jarred me awake. It was a whisper, but he was urgent. "Do you hear this?" he asked.

"What?" I asked groggily, still half-asleep. I sat up.

"It's Davila. He's talking to someone."

"The other guy is freaking out," Thomas said. He was also awake and hearing the voices.

Now awake, I lay back and tried to focus. When I heard the voices, I stilled my mind and listened.

"It was a hunter, and the others must have turned because it wasn't even five miles from here." The voice was familiar but not immediately one I knew.

"We don't know for certain if the others are part of this." It was Davila. "There have only been two killings outside of the usual place. They hadn't fledged when they escaped. We don't know if they've turned. I still think it was him."

"There have only been two killings so far." The other man

interrupted. "It's not him. He's got no reason to venture out. Look how many years it's been, and he's never left the area or needed anything more. We have to assume the others have turned."

The voice was so familiar, but I still couldn't place it. I wondered if I wasn't just trying to grasp at knowing who it could be. I was so desperate for answers.

"The other three who were here before must have escaped," Alex said. "That's got to be who they're talking about."

I hushed Alex, wanting to hear more.

It was Davila. "I still think it's just him working alone. We don't know if the others have turned."

Turned? I wondered what that meant. I heard Thomas repeat the word, so I knew he had heard it and was pondering it, too. I knew the reason we were caged was that the others had escaped, but the idea they were out there killing people made no sense.

The man whose voice I didn't recognize asked, "What about the other one? Peter? Can you tell anything yet?"

Hearing Peter's name, I perked up. Was he alive? I heard both Alex and Thomas move, so I assumed they were listening closely, too.

"No. Not yet. We're holding him separately," Davila answered.

If they were keeping him somewhere, then he must still be alive, I thought optimistically.

"And what about the boy who came with him? Now that we know he's not one of them," the other man said. "What are we going to do with him?"

They were talking about Ivan. I was relieved to hear the boy softly snoring in the cell next to mine, not awake and asking us what we were hearing. I debated telling him Peter was most likely alive as I didn't want to get his hopes up.

"We just have to keep him here and as safe as possible," Davila said. "When the others fledge, he'll have to be held somewhere else away from them until we know."

"It was those two idiot addicts who screwed that up," the other man said. "We wouldn't be wondering what to do with him if we had gone ourselves."

"I know. I should have tried to retrieve Peter myself or sent you, but there were more than we expected, and we're all too old to be doing this," Davila complained. "These boys are strong, and I can't move like I used to, and neither can you."

"We're lucky we only had the one mistake. We hired these guys because we needed the strength. And even that oversized meathead couldn't handle things when Peter fledged, and look what happened. What's going to happen when the others do? We need to decide and move this along before we lose control of everything," the other man tried to convince him. Every time I heard his voice, it seemed clearer. It was gravelly and brusque.

"I know that, Richard," Davila said.

And with that name, the voice clicked. It was one I had known for years, but hadn't heard until recently. It was the voice of Richard Wilson, Clara's grandfather.

I rolled back onto my cot and gasped.

"What is it?" Alex asked, hearing my exclamation.

"Nothing," I whispered, trying to hush him so I could listen and think. My mind was a whirl of confusion. It couldn't be him. What connection could he possibly have to all this? I knew he and my grandfather had been friends for ages, and I knew Richard was a former police officer, but none of this made sense for why I was held captive. Then thoughts of Clara filled my head, and I wondered if this was an elaborate ploy to keep me away from her.

I tried to refocus on the conversation I heard through the rock walls, but the words were like water, garbled and listing. I was confused and angry about the possibilities of what this could all mean. Would my condition be something that required this type of measure to keep me away from others? Would Richard really go this far to keep me away from Clara? Was he the reason we'd lost touch before?

I sat up and began to contemplate the connection with my grandfather and what role that had played. Did something happen that had created such a rift, they would treat my family like we were the scourge?

"How long before we know if Peter is one of them?" Richard asked.

"No blood was drawn. He didn't even hurt anyone. There's no reason to think he is," Davila answered.

"But he did fledge?" Richard pressed.

"Yes."

I pondered what he'd said. Fledged? I couldn't imagine what that word meant or if I'd even heard it correctly. At that point, I was simply relieved to hear that Peter was alive.

"And what about the others?" Richard asked. "He's got to be out of the stuff, and if they didn't turn, he'd be desperate to find them. It's why Diablo's back."

It was that name again. I knew enough Spanish to know it meant *devil*, but I had no idea who this man they kept talking about was or what history he held with these old men.

"Our supply is also running low. If he's found them, we will have a problem much bigger than we can handle," Davila agreed.

The voices ceased. I moved around, trying to tune them back in, but there was nothing more.

The next morning, I huddled as closely as I could with Alex and Thomas near the corners of our cells to compare our night of voices. They, too, had heard the conversation with Davila and Mr. Wilson, but were unaware of my association with Richard.

They were only interested in the comments made about Peter, Diablo, and the others regarding the killings.

"Who are these others they keep talking about?" I asked.

Alex sighed. "The others were the ones who were here when I came. They are the ones who are gone. It sounds like they're out there killing people. Is that why they keep us locked up? Do they think we'll turn into that?"

I shrugged. The men had kept using the term "turned."

"Why do they think they are killing people?" Thomas asked. "And why are they worried about Peter turning into one of them? What the hell is going on?"

I put my hand up to quiet him, but it was too late. Ivan was already at the bars of his cell, looking nervous after hearing Peter's name. We had become careful not to say much around Ivan. It was clear to us that he was a victim of circumstance and in danger. He was a prisoner with us, but was missing the thing that brought us together and had given us the ability to hear through the walls at night. He was also young, scared, and becoming more anxious with each day Peter was gone.

"We think he's alive and still being held somewhere in here," I told him, seeing his angst and eager to give him some hope.

He didn't say anything, but seemed lighter as he walked back to his cot.

Later that day, when the lone guard came with our lunch trays, Ivan looked odd. He stood at the bars of the cell and just stared out.

The guard didn't notice a difference in him and unlocked the cell and brought in the tray. When he was through the gate, Ivan lunged at him, and even with his small stature, he was able to catch him off guard, shoving him hard enough to knock him off balance. The tray fell and clattered on the floor, and Ivan pushed past him and out of the cell.

The guard turned quickly and tried to grab at Ivan. He was able to snag the back of his pants leg and jerked it hard. Because of Ivan's small size and the guard's strength, this upended Ivan, and he slammed down on the concrete floor, hitting his head so hard, the noise made me sick. We all gasped in horror at the sight of it.

Ivan's eyes rolled up, and then closed as a pool of blood began to spread around his head.

I ran to the bars of my cell. "Ivan!" I cried out.

"Oh my God!" Alex yelled. "Help him!"

"Somebody help!" I screamed toward the door, hoping Dr. Davila would come and save the boy.

The guard scrambled up and ran to Ivan. Frantic, he rolled him over. The gash on the boy's head was gaping, and blood was pouring from it.

"Jesus, no!" I heard Thomas cry out.

The guard pulled off his shirt and pressed it to the wound.

"What did you do?" Alex yelled. "I think you killed him."

The guard was frantic and tried to rouse Ivan, but there was no movement. He bent toward him and put an ear to his mouth. Looking up, I could see his eyes were desperate. He put a finger to Ivan's neck, and after a few seconds, he stared up at us, terrified and frenzied.

"Is he dead?" I demanded.

The guard was breathing hard and looking around the cell in a panic. He stood, and before Thomas could move, he grabbed him by the arm through the cell bars and pulled him hard, knocking him against the steel rods. The guard reached into his pocket and pulled out a pocket knife. He flipped it open.

I saw the blade and screamed at him, "What are you doing?"

Thomas screamed and tried to pull away, but the man was

too strong, He quickly sliced Thomas' arm, and I saw a thin red line emerge. Thomas yelled out in pain.

"Hold still," the man said sternly as he pulled Thomas down to the floor. He then put the bloody cut to Ivan's mouth and held it there while Thomas squirmed and continued to cry.

"What are you doing?" I called out again, but the man ignored me and continued to hold Thomas in place while watching Ivan intently.

When the guard released him, Thomas quickly slid away and looked at his arm. It wasn't a large or deep cut, but the blood was now dripping onto the floor.

"What the hell?!" Thomas bellowed at him.

The man ignored him and kept staring at Ivan. "Come on. Come on," he said urgently.

Ivan lay still with Thomas's blood covering his mouth.

We all were breathing hard. Alex moved away from the bars of his cell, worried the guard might grab for him next. I also backed away.

And then I saw movement. Ivan's eyes began to flutter and then open.

"Ivan?" I said, stunned.

The guard watched as Ivan came to. Slowly and drowsily, the boy began to move and moan. The guard leaned back against the cell bars, exhausted and relieved.

"What did you do?" I asked, stunned.

The guard kept silent and watched. Soon, Ivan pushed himself up to where he was sitting. He looked over at me. The wound on his head was still there, but the blood had stopped.

He took a deep breath and looked around the room at all of us. His face showed confusion. "What's going on?" he asked.

The guard pulled himself to standing and reached for Ivan. "Come on," he said, helping him up. He took Ivan by the arm and started to walk him out of the room.

"Where are we going?" Ivan asked.

The guard was silent.

"Can we go to Peter?" Ivan asked, looking up at the large man.

The guard looked down at him strangely, but stayed quiet and led him from the room.

When the door was closed, I looked over to Alex and Thomas, who were both staring down at Thomas's arm. He lifted it to study the wound closer.

"What just happened?" I asked them.

"He was dead," Thomas whispered.

"He was!" Alex agreed. "We all saw it."

"I can't believe it," Thomas said. "The blood. *My* blood saved him. I saw it."

I shook my head, bewildered.

"It's true," Alex said.

There was a long pause as we all stood, perplexed. As I contemplated what had just happened, something else entered my mind. "The fish," I whispered to myself, remembering what had happened that day at Clara's house. My blood had seemed to bring them back to life as well.

"Fish?" Alex asked, confused.

The more I thought about what had happened back then, and what had just taken place, the more my body shivered. The aching along my spine started slowly, then began to build with my budding awareness of what I was. What we all were.

When the guard brought Ivan back, we all stayed quiet. There was a silent knowledge of what we had witnessed. The guard hesitated, looking as if he was going to speak, but didn't. He was still awash in disbelief and dread.

He handed Thomas a large bandage but didn't speak. Thomas hesitantly took it and said, "Thank you." It struck us all as strange.

After the guard left, I went to the side of my cell, where Ivan stood, looking glum. They had bandaged his forehead, and the blood that had covered his face—both his and Thomas's—was gone. His hair was wet as though it had been washed.

"How do you feel?" I asked him.

He thought for a moment. "Dead..."

Alex, Thomas, and I all shot each other a glance.

"...tired. I'm really tired," Ivan continued.

"Do you remember what happened?" I asked.

"Not really," Ivan said. "I remember trying to go see Peter. Then I was in that room with the nurse. I hurt my head." He put a hand to the bandage. He seemed oblivious to anything else that had happened.

"Is that all you remember?" I continued to pry. We all knew what I was trying to get at, but Ivan didn't seem to remember or understand what had taken place.

He nodded. "They didn't let me see Peter," he said sadly.

"What did Dr. Davila say when he saw your head?" I asked.

Ivan looked over to me and shook his head. "He wasn't there. It was just that nurse lady. She didn't talk to me, only to that guard. She called him George and told him I'd be weird now. Why would she say that?"

I looked at Alex and Thomas, and we all looked confused and baffled.

"Do you feel differently?" I asked hesitantly.

He shrugged. "Not really. Just tired."

He was dead. We'd all seen it. And then, he'd been brought back to life, and all he could remember or feel was that he was tired.

We stood looking at each other, unaware of what to do or say next.

Ivan took a deep breath and looked toward the door of the room. "I'm going to find Peter."

I gave him a small smile. He was still so determined.

"I am," he said again with emphasis. He held up a key. "I'm leaving tonight."

Shocked, we all came as close as we could to Ivan's cell.

"That guard will know you took it and will be back here soon," Thomas whispered.

"Yeah, he'll know it's missing when he tries to open our gates when he brings us dinner," Alex said.

Ivan smiled proudly. "I didn't take it from the guard. I took it from the nurse. It was just lying on a table. When she wasn't looking, I grabbed it."

I looked at him skeptically. "How do you know her key will work? She never comes in here without the guard."

Ivan walked to his cell door, placed the key in the lock, and turned it. It clicked, and he swung the door wide. He grinned at his triumph, then stepped out of his cell for emphasis.

"Get back in and lock it before they come in here and see you," Thomas ordered. "How do you know they don't have cameras in here watching us?"

We all looked around the ceiling of black rock as if we could spot a hidden lens. Ivan stepped back in and locked the gate. He placed the key under his pillow.

"Tonight," he said.

"I want to go, too," Alex said.

I turned to Alex with surprise.

"Me too," Thomas echoed.

I took a deep breath. "I do, too. We all want out of here, but I think it will be too risky. None of us knows the way out. It's like going through a maze in the dark."

"We'll keep going until we find the way out," Thomas said. "We'll be able to hear the voices and know where they are so we can avoid them. We'll be able to tell when they're close,"

We all looked at Ivan, knowing he couldn't hear the same things we did.

"He can follow me," Thomas assured him. "We have to try."

"But what if we end up like the others?" I asked. Even I was surprised by my hesitation. I wanted my freedom, and yet, what I'd heard about what possibly awaited us struck fear in me. It wasn't something I wanted to risk. "We don't know who is waiting for us out there. There's a reason we're in here. What if someone is after us?"

"We can't just wait around and see what Davila has planned," Alex countered.

"I want to find Peter," Ivan said. "He'll know what to do."

I nodded at him. I wanted so badly to get Ivan home and safe. I think I wanted that more than I wanted it for myself. He was only fourteen, and yet, his slight build and innocence made him seem even younger. There was this urge in me to protect him.

TWENTY-SIX

Milo

We should have had a better plan. We should have had *any* plan. Instead, we waited until they thought we were asleep, then Ivan used his stolen key and unlocked each of our gates.

In the darkness, I saw the luminescent green of Ivan's eyes. Why hadn't I noticed it before? Was what was happening to me making me see and hear things differently?

I thought back to Clara and her vivid green eyes. The ones I had always remembered as blue. Was that part of all these odd happenings?

We quietly slipped out of the chamber, and when we were in the hall, it was apparent there were too many of us to make our way covertly through the maze. We had different ideas about where the exit was, and with that, our first few steps had us bumping into each other and into the walls.

Even in the dark, I could see the bend in the halls, and when we were standing still and silent, the swell of voices came from the hollows and paths and directed me where I should go.

I still wasn't sure what I was looking for or what I'd do if I found the way out. I could feel the others following me, and was relieved that if they caught us, at least we would be together.

"You're going too fast," Ivan whined.

I hushed him, but slowed my pace.

"The walls are cutting my hands," he continued, ignoring my hush.

"Keep moving," urged Alex.

I came back to where we were and what we were doing, and without answering, I started again on our journey to freedom while wondering about Ivan and knowing deep inside that his life would never be the same after what had happened tonight. I walked, contemplating how this would affect him and the extreme weight of what this meant. What was it all of us had running through our veins?

Blood. That's what it was, but something more. Our blood had something that could heal or revive. It was why we were locked away and why someone was hunting us out there. My blood had made the fish come back to life and spring from the buckets, and Thomas's blood had resurrected Ivan.

I wasn't sure if we were saviors or monsters.

"They're coming. I can hear them," Thomas said. "They know."

I stood still for a moment and listened. I quickly sensed them as well and heard their frantic voices coming closer. Without speaking, we kept drifting away from the voices, but then the corridor split, and before we could discuss where to go, we all scattered down different tunnels. I found myself with only Ivan.

I went quickly along the corridor, trying to find a way out and listening for the voices to keep from being caught. The hall seemed to curve back toward where we had come, and I felt my heart drop.

The voices were getting closer, and I only hoped the hall we were in didn't lead straight to them. I could hear Ivan's breathing behind me and could tell he was starting to panic. My own heart was racing, and then the familiar ache began in my back. Not now, I thought. I needed all my senses focused.

I kept moving forward, and then felt the floor go from the rough rock and gravel to a smooth, almost slick surface. I saw small lights on the walls, spaced evenly, and when I looked closer, I saw a door. It could either lead somewhere to hide or would have us cornered.

I had no time to weigh my choices. I quickly grabbed the knob and turned it. The door came open, and with Ivan following, I stepped inside.

It was dark, but I could see it was a small room, and I immediately knew it would only have us trapped. I reached back to make sure the door didn't close behind us. I needed a moment to sense where they were and which way we should go from here.

As I tried to focus on where the voices were coming from, I felt something behind me. Through cell bars stood a large figure standing in the corner. It was wrapped in something dark, making it hard to discern more than a shape.

I must have gasped at the sight because Ivan whispered, "What's wrong?"

The figure began to move, to turn. Then it spoke, "Get out."

I reached over to grab Ivan and pull him with me to the door.

"Peter?" Ivan said.

I looked back at the figure and saw a face with eyes that looked like embers. "Peter?" I asked.

The creature lunged forward and grabbed the cell bars, sending Ivan and me stumbling back in shock.

"Get out," he hissed at us again.

"Peter!" Ivan cried.

My breath left me, and I stood staring in horror. "What happened to you?" I asked, both in disbelief and in the hope it wasn't really him. Even in the dark, I could feel a fierceness coming from him.

"Go!" he yelled. "Stay away from me."

"But it's me!" Ivan cried.

Peter was silent, and then he asked, "What have they done to you? Who did it?"

"Did what?" Ivan asked with a whimper.

I could hear him breathing, and as my eyes adjusted even more, I could see his body was heaving.

"I said leave," he urged, turning, and that is when I saw that the covering wasn't a tarp or a blanket, but enormous dark wings protruding from his back. They were made up of thick, leathery skin. I felt my entire body stagger in horror at the sight. "What happened to you?" I asked.

Peter reeled around. "Get out!" It was a roar so loud I was sure my ears would burst again. And then, the voices returned, and I realized they were almost upon us.

I grabbed Ivan and pulled him toward the door. We had to move quickly to avoid them.

"Wait," Ivan said.

"No, we can't," I muttered as I opened the door and continued to pull him to it.

He struggled from my grip and reached into the pocket of his pants. He removed the key and tossed it into Peter's cell.

"We have to go," I said as I pulled him out and closed the

door. We ran down the corridor away from the voices and to wherever I thought an escape might be.

"Stay close!" I called back to Ivan, and when he didn't respond, I stopped and turned around.

He was gone. I started to yell for him, but I heard the voices getting closer. I looked around desperately in the dark, but saw nothing. I wasn't sure if he had gone back to Peter or just in a different direction. I sensed urgent footsteps getting closer, so I continued without him.

As I ran aimlessly through the dim halls of the maze, I felt my soul ache for losing Ivan and not trying to save Peter. I hardly knew Peter and was horrified by what he'd turned into, and yet, I felt I had let him down in some way. My mind was distracted by the pain of my betrayal, and when I turned a corner, I found a door. I quickly opened it, hoping it might be an escape, and when I stepped inside, a strong acrid stench hit me. I winced, and when my eyes adjusted to the dark, I saw a large stone kiln. The smell was that of ashes and soot, but not like the odor of a campfire. It was putrid, and I put my hand over my nose and mouth, quickly stepping back out.

I could hear footsteps getting closer, so I ran down a side hallway that turned abruptly. A rush of cool air hit me and I gasped, both from the chill and the relief of having the odor flushed from me. The dim glow of the moon appeared through a large opening in the ceiling of a massive room.

I stopped just short of falling into an enormous black chasm. I wheeled my arms back, barely catching myself. When I was steady and had backed away several feet from the edge, I fell onto the ground, trying to catch my breath. I heard tiny rocks scattering and tumbling into the blackness.

The footsteps were now behind me. I turned to find Dr. Davila and the guard, both holding guns. Davila looked even more bent and weary than usual, but I was defeated, and my will to run was gone. That, and the gnawing vision of Peter and my guilt for leaving him, had me broken. I put my hand up when the guard reached for me.

"Don't touch me," I growled.

"Leave him," Davila said. His lab coat was askew and he had lost his glasses. He held his cane in one hand and the gun, loaded with a tranquilizer dart, in the other. "Leave us," he ordered the guard, his voice softer. "Find the others."

The guard looked at him skeptically, but Davila nodded him away, so he turned and left us alone in the cold and cavernous room.

Davila tried to straighten his coat and look for his glasses, but didn't find them. He gave up and sighed.

"Where are we?" I asked. "What is this place?"

He sighed again. "Come. Sit." He directed me to an area lit with a string of lights and a smoothed-out space in the rock where he could sit. He kept the gun poised, but settled himself down, looking pained.

"It's the only place we can keep you safe," he said.

I scoffed. "Safe? From what?"

He started to speak, then lowered his head.

"I saw Peter. Is that what's going to happen to me?" I asked.

He looked up.

"Is it?" I demanded.

He didn't speak, but nodded.

I felt defeat set in, and tears began to well up in my eyes. I didn't think he'd admit it. "When will it happen?" I asked, looking out at the dark, bottomless chasm.

"I'm not sure," he said. "That is part of what we're still learning. I know that it's soon. No one we've seen has 'fledged'," he raised his eyebrows at the odd word, "after the age of eighteen or before the age of sixteen."

"Fledged?" I asked. "What does that mean? Do you mean

the wings? He had wings." I felt the burn and ache begin in my back. Wings. That is what the sickening, throbbing pain growing along my spine was. I was truly becoming a monster. "Is that what happens? Is that what we turn into?" I was desperate for answers.

Dr. Davila nodded. "We use the word fledge because it's the first time the wings appear."

"Wings," I repeated wearily. The conversations with my grandmother began to replay in my head. The stories I'd passed off as kooky were now coming back to haunt me. "Will I fly? What does it mean?"

"It's more than just the wings. There are other changes as well."

I shook my head. It couldn't be real. I had to be imagining this entire horrible nightmare. "What's going to happen to me? When?" I asked.

"I'm not sure. Sometimes, it happens like with Peter, when they become angered or upset. That is why we try to keep you contained and safe."

"They?" I asked. "How many?"

"There've been many over the years," he paused. "We know it must have something to do with adrenaline because the murdered boys were thrown off cliffs or buildings or burned to get the reaction to happen."

Hearing the word *burned,* I thought about the room with the large kiln and the horrible stench. Was that what happened there? "Killed by who?" I asked.

"I'm sorry, Milo. I'm not trying to scare you."

I wasn't just scared, I was horrified, and that wasn't all I was feeling. I was stunned, confused, and exhausted. I raised my shoulders, defeated. "You're telling me I'm going to grow wings and people are going to try to kill me."

"It's what happened before. We thought this had all passed,

that it was over. You and the others were a complete surprise to us. When we started hearing and seeing the signs it was back, we did what we could to contain it."

"It sounds like a disease."

He looked at the floor. "We don't know what it is. We saw it years ago, and now it's returned. We brought you here to keep you safe."

"From who?"

"There are people who want to harvest the wings. The wings have a medicinal quality that is very powerful."

"Like a drug?" I asked.

"Yes. A potent one. And some things happen that may have you feeling the urge to do things that aren't good. Things that can affect your psyche."

"Psyche?" I repeated skeptically.

"Yes." He continued. "Giving in to the urges makes you unable to live without the blood of others. Those that have turned can't control it. In that case, there would be no benefit to keeping them alive. That is why we've tried to keep you all in here, not only to keep you safe until you know how the fledge will affect you, but also to keep others safe. It's also important to keep you in darkness."

"In darkness," I repeated his words, and heard my grandmother's voice in my head citing the mantra—*only in darkness*. I took a deep exhausted breath.

"Just like we've learned about how the wings are a source of life, we've also learned what can kill you. The sun can be deadly, especially if your wings are fully out. It's important to stay close to the caves so you can get away from the light. Any sun exposure hardens them and makes the person weak, and exposure while in flight is deadly."

I felt the blood drain from my face. "What about Peter?" I

asked. I remembered my last conversation with him—his talk of killing and his fear of being out of control.

Davila could see my concern and put his hand up. "We're keeping him here and waiting to see."

"When will you know?" I asked.

"I don't know."

TWENTY-SEVEN

Milo

The cavern was massive, and the cauldron was over two hundred feet across and rimmed by a large outcropping. Looking up, I saw where the opening allowed the moon to illuminate the entire breadth of the cavern and inside the large gaping hole. I could see the black rock with its cracks, and the rough bubbled texture was the only element that seemed to make up the entire landscape.

I stood looking out over it all, realizing the vastness of this volcanic area filled with enormous holes, endless caves, infinite maze-like tunnels, and more space than I could ever imagine.

Davila explained that the lava cave's insulating rock had properties that would keep us from being detected. It was our refuge as well as our prison.

"What now?" I asked.

He took a deep, almost painful breath as he thought about his answer. "You remain here until we know it's safe," he said. "That's what we have to do. It's what I promised your grandmother and the rest of those who lost loved ones to the colony."

I looked at the vast chasm, and then back into the corridor from where we'd come. I had so many more questions, but still wanted to escape.

Using his cane, Davila struggled to stand. "Help me find them and bring them back, or I'll have to sedate you."

I shook my head, unconvinced.

Then he raised the gun and pointed it at me. "I can't help you or tell you more until I find the others and bring them back."

I took a step back and stood my ground.

His eyes pleaded with me to relent. "Please..."

Then a roar came from down the corridor. I flinched from the noise, and when I stood back up, the quick slap of footsteps came toward us. We both braced ourselves. My heart was already pounding.

"Oh no," Davila said. He pointed the gun toward the corridor. In a panic, the nurse came around the corner. She was startled when she saw us. Her eyes were wide and frantic.

"There's another one. I tried to get him before it happened," she said to Davila. When she saw me, she flinched away like I was poisonous.

"Which one?" Davila asked, but the nurse ignored his question, looked back at the way she'd come, and kept running around the large cauldron and out another corridor.

Davila put the gun to his shoulder and began to walk toward the source of the noise.

"What are you doing?" I asked.

"Call for them," he said.

"But that roar, what was that?" I asked.

Ignoring my question, he snapped, "If I don't get to them first, they'll be killed. Do it, Milo."

We walked toward the furnace room and out and into the hall. We were heading back toward the cells and the main door

I had tried to reach. Reluctantly, I called out, "Alex! Thomas!" I listened for a moment. "Ivan, where are you?"

My calls were met with silence.

"Keep calling. Tell them to come to you. Tell them they'll get help."

"But..." It was a lie. I would be leading them back to the man who had imprisoned us, yet I wasn't sure what would happen to them if I didn't. And what else was out there?

"Do it," he insisted.

We continued walking down the dark hallway, Davila's hand on my shoulder as I guided him. I kept calling, but there was no answer.

I tried to listen through the walls, and in the stillness, I heard the faint sound of Ivan crying.

I stopped, and Davila whispered, "What is it?"

I turned and whispered back, "I can hear something just ahead. Someone's crying."

He nodded, and we continued forward. When we came around the corner, the crying became louder and more apparent, and soon, in the damp darkness of the cave, I saw Ivan huddled in a corner. I gasped at the odd green glow staring back at me. I started to go to him, but Davila held me back.

"It's Ivan," I argued.

Ivan heard me and stood up.

"How do you know?" Davila asked. He continued to hold me back. "What do you see? Tell me."

"The green. The glow. Don't you see it?" I asked him.

Even in the dark, I could feel Davila's dread.

"Milo?" Ivan asked. Even in the darkness, I could see he was relieved it was me.

"Where are the others?" Davila asked, hearing Ivan's voice. He guided us further into the corridor until a dim light emerged from a distant string of bulbs.

The glow of Ivan's eyes seemed to fade in the light. He was weary, but relieved to see us.

Ivan swallowed and shrugged. "Something bad has happened."

"What? Tell us," I urged him.

"The guard caught me and was taking me back, and then we saw Thomas, but he tried to run away. So, the guard grabbed him and they started to fight, then Thomas..." His lips began to tremble and his face crumpled as he cried. "He turned into this...thing." He put his arms out to describe what he saw.

I looked at Davila, and we both knew what had happened. Thomas had fledged. The excitement from the fight had triggered it, and now he had wings.

"What did you see? Tell me," I asked Ivan. I was desperate to know. Did the booming roar of noise come with the fledging? The wings bursting out through the skin is what I imagined. I shuddered at the thought.

Ivan's face turned pained as he started to answer.

Davila put his hand up to stop the questioning. He asked Ivan, "Which way did Thomas go?"

Ivan pointed down the hall.

"What about Alex? Have you seen him?"

Ivan shook his head.

Davila took Ivan by the arm and put him between us. "You must follow us," he said, leaning heavily on his cane. "Stay close. I'll get you back to where you'll be safe."

"What about Peter?" Ivan asked.

Davila looked anxious. "We have to keep going," was all he said.

Ivan drew next to me. I could feel him trembling as we started again on our way down the corridor. When the hallway widened, I could see the wall of doors, including the one that led to our chamber. We had made our way back to the cells, and I actually felt relief.

Davila opened the door, flipped on the lights, and led Ivan in. He walked him to the cell. "You'll be safe with the cell door locked."

"What about Milo?" Ivan asked, looking at me. "Don't leave me alone."

"We'll come back. I need Milo's help. Stay quiet, and it won't take long." He turned the lights off.

I heard Ivan sniffle, and as we left the room, I looked back at him. In the darkness, all I could see was the gleaming sign of his revival staring back at me.

As the door closed, I contemplated what his future held. Was he one of us now? I wondered what that meant. Who were we, and what was I about to become?

I continued to follow Davila in silence. We were back in a corridor and going toward the area of the nurse's room. I had only been there twice. Once when I'd first arrived at the colony and the second when Davila had examined my ruptured ears. I now knew the rupturing had been due to Peter's fledge.

"Do you hear anything?" Davila asked.

I knew what he wanted me to do, but I refused to acknowledge that I could hear and feel things through the walls. I wondered what else he knew.

I stopped walking and looked at him apprehensively. "Hear what?" I asked, trying to act oblivious.

"Please help me," he said. "You'll help them. Call for them. They'll come to you."

I took a deep breath, but before I could say a word, a scream came from down the corridor. It was one of the guards.

Davila turned toward the noise, the gun drawn. He cautiously started walking toward it.

I followed, but the closer we got, an overwhelming sensation rushed over me. Sounds began to whirl through my head. Were those footsteps, voices? And then I heard it. It started softly, but soon it was pulsating through me. The memory gave me a chill, and I shivered.

I stopped and put a hand on the wall to steady myself. I closed my eyes and continued to listen. It was soothing and alluring, and I'd heard it before. I shook my head and thought, no, it can't be.

"Milo, what do you hear?" Davila asked.

"They're here. They're calling for us." I started moving forward toward the sound. It was the music, and it was pulling me as it had before. It felt warm and comforting, and I wanted to wrap myself in the sweet melodic blanket.

"Wait. Milo, no!" Davila called. He was now following me. I could hear him trying to run, hobbling along with the gun and his cane.

I ignored him and kept going. I knew I'd find the answer when I reached it. I saw a tiny sliver of light coming from the bend ahead and ran toward it.

Davila's voice was urgent. "Milo, wait!"

There was no stopping me, and when I came around the bend and into the light, a large dark figure stood in the middle of the room. I slid to a stop, and Davila bumped into me. We both stood paralyzed by the sight of it.

Peter? He had his back to us. The black leathery wings were slightly open, giving a full view of their magnitude and mass. But when he turned to us, I saw it wasn't Peter, but Thomas. Blood covered his face and tears streaked through the red on his cheeks. On the ground was a guard, his neck and face a bloody pulp, and a crimson pool seeped out from beneath him on the floor.

I backed up at the horrifying sight.

Davila raised the gun, and with a swift strike, one of the

large wings knocked both Davila and the gun backward. Thomas turned to me, and I cringed, waiting for the blow. But it didn't come.

I cautiously glanced up, and Thomas stood still. His shoulders and head were hung low.

I turned toward where Davila had landed. He was dazed but alive and trying to sit up.

"What have I done?" Thomas cried. His face was strained and distraught. He looked down at the body and at me, his eyes pleading. "I just want to go home."

A loud pounding came from the large steel door behind him, startling us both.

Thomas looked over at it. "They made it out. They're calling for us." He motioned for me to come with him.

I was still in awe at what he had become. Large and looming. I was aghast at his size and strength, but then the music began again in my head. It was rich and swaying. It shut out the horror in front of me, and I took a step toward him.

"Milo, no. Don't," Davila said weakly from the ground behind me.

Thomas's face turned sinister and his eyes grew thin. Davila reached back toward the tranquilizer gun, and Thomas lunged forward, his wings spreading so large they knocked bottles and pans off the shelves of the wall.

Then I heard a crack. The sound was so loud it ricocheted in my head, and I cringed back. I saw Thomas flail back and crumple to the floor, wings collapsing around him. I turned to where the shot had come, and behind me stood the nurse. She held a rifle, and it wasn't a tranquilizer gun.

I yelled, ducking away from her.

With the gun still pointed, she pushed by me and walked quickly to where Thomas lay and nervously hovered over him.

Davila pulled himself up and went to Thomas. He tried to

find a pulse, but the massive wings laid flat. Thomas was hardly visible in the inert heap.

I was shaking, and I sank to the floor. I put my face in my hands and tried to remove the scene from my head, and then I realized the pains in my back were so intense I could hardly breathe. I groaned in pain and tried to calm myself to alleviate the throbbing. I felt tears overwhelm me, and then the sting of a needle. The anguish began to let up, and my thoughts went from hazy to black.

It was the same dizzying, sick feeling of when they'd first brought me there. My head throbbed and spun. I moaned, and the sound reverberated in my head, so I lay as still as I could, trying to settle my stomach and mind. My back still ached as the images of what had happened began to flood back, and my heart sank.

Through heavy and painful eyes, I saw I was back in my cell. I rolled onto my side and looked for Ivan. I knew he'd be peppering me soon with questions about what happened, and I didn't want to panic him with what I'd seen. I squinted, trying to see where he was, but even in the small amount of light, I scanned his entire cell and saw nothing. I tried to sit up, and my head reeled. I tried to steady myself as I sat in silence. When my stomach and head had settled, I took another look around the chamber.

I peered over to the cell where Thomas had been, and my gut dropped. I took a low, deep breath and tried to clear my mind of the bloody scene. When I was able to stand, I walked the perimeter of my cell, and when I got to the side that bordered Ivan's, I looked through the bars where we had left him. He had made his bed, and his gate was shut, but then I saw a pile of gray dirt in the middle of the cell.

Since being brought to the colony, I hadn't seen anything but the chamber's rough rock and concrete, so I studied the dirt, wondering where it could have come from. I had to strain to look over Ivan's bed to see it, so I kneeled on the floor of my cell to get a better look from underneath. The pile was less than a foot wide and high. It was so odd and out of place. Had Ivan chipped away at the rock to try and burrow his way out? I saw no holes or signs of damage to the walls or floor.

As I looked closer, I saw a glint of metal sticking from the dirt. I lay on the ground, pushed myself close to the bars, and reached my hand in as far as possible. Using my finger, I fished through the dirt for the object. The soil was light and blew about as I searched. I soon realized it wasn't dirt at all, but ashes. I looked to see if there were signs of fire or anything burnt, but saw nothing.

I strained, using two fingers to grab the object. I had to turn my head away from the bars to allow my body to press into them and extend my reach. I could pinch the end of the item enough to slide it out of the ash, and when it was free of the mound, it fell to the floor with a soft clink.

I looked over and saw what I'd lifted out was a key. It was the one Ivan had stolen from the nurse and thrown to Peter. I pulled it to me and went to my bed to study it. How had Ivan gotten it back?

Ashy grit coated my fingers. The smell was the same as the room with the kiln and the putrid stench. Why were the ashes here?

As I turned the key over in my hand, I wondered if Ivan had lost it or if he had hidden it there. And again, where had the pile of ash come from? Nothing sounded reasonable, but nothing that had happened for days was reasonable or even fathomable.

The main door of the chamber clicked, and I quickly hid the

key under my pillow. The door opened, and the person who walked in was someone I knew.

TWENTY-EIGHT

Milo

"What the hell," I said. "It *is* you."

He walked into the room without looking directly at me. He took a deep labored breath and turned to face me. "Yes, it's me," he said.

I had so many questions, and yet, I stood stunned and speechless. It was Richard Wilson, Clara's grandfather. I thought it was his voice I had heard through the walls, and now I knew it was. I watched him walk in, looking sullen and old, and while I wanted to shake him and demand he tell me what was going on, when I saw him, all I could think about was Clara.

"I'm sorry, Milo," he said, stumbling over his words. "I'm sorry this is happening to you."

"Why are you here?" I asked. "What do you know?"

He looked like he was trying to answer, but instead, he just stood and looked at the floor.

"Get me out of here," I begged him.

"We will, but it's not safe out there yet."

"It's not safe *in here*. They shot Thomas. He turned into this thing. It's going to happen to me, too." I stopped. "It's real. All those stories my grandmother told all those years were true." It was more of a statement than a question, and yet, I wanted answers.

"She was trying to protect you, but she shouldn't have told you..."

"Why not? It's true," I said, cutting him off. "Why not prepare me for all this from the beginning instead of letting me grow up thinking I was normal and trying to be like everyone else?"

"Because we hoped it wasn't so," he said.

The comment stung, and I flinched. I was a pariah. I had the traits of a monster, but I had also stolen Richard's life by his having to follow mine. He had been sentenced to watch over me, the marked offspring, and make sure I didn't blossom into what had brought the evil scourge that started his entire nightmare.

He had been there like a shadow my entire life, watching and waiting to see what might happen to me. He had molded his life to follow mine, and to react if the horror came back. Now here I stood. His nightmare had returned.

"Milo, I want to tell you everything, but all I know is what happened years ago. It all started long before you were born, and I was hoping it would never happen again." He paused. "We all thought it was over."

"So, you know about the wings?" I asked.

He nodded. "But it's more than that."

"More?" I remembered Dr. Davila saying the same thing. "So, I'll have more than wings growing out my back?" I was dumbfounded. What more could there be? "Why won't anyone tell me what's going on?"

"It's why we have to keep you in here. It's for your own safety until we can figure out what to do."

"What to do? If I stay here, they'll kill me. They shot Thomas. I think he's dead."

Richard looked weary and nodded.

"Do you know? Is he dead?"

"I don't know. All I know is that he turned and was a danger. That's what I don't want to happen to you."

"You mean the wings? They'll kill me because of it."

"No, but it's why you're in these cells. We have to control when the wings come open," he explained.

"Why?" I asked.

"Because once you fledge, you'll have cravings, and we need to make sure you don't become like the others."

"What others?" I asked.

He couldn't look me in the eye.

"What aren't you telling me? What do you have to do with all this?"

He finally took a deep breath and sighed. He turned and went toward the door.

"Don't leave," I demanded.

He shook his head. "Not leaving, I just need to sit. I need a chair." He came back with a folding metal chair and sank into it. He began again.

"Milo, I'm part of this because of Jorge."

My grandfather. I knew from the moment I heard Richard's voice that my grandfather was somehow connected, but I didn't want to add sorrow to the already painful past.

I looked up, feeling broken. "My grandfather? He was one of..." I shivered. I couldn't even finish my question.

Richard nodded solemnly.

"How do you know?" I asked.

"I know because I've spent the last ten years helping keep him alive."

A chill rocked me. "He's not alive. He died when I was eight."

Richard looked down.

I shook my head, and a wash of betrayal and sadness flooded me. "He's alive? He's been alive this whole time?"

"I'm sorry, Milo, but we had to keep it from you. We had to keep him away from everyone because he wasn't safe."

"I was told he fell or jumped off a cliff. Does my mom know he's alive?"

"No."

"My grandma?"

Richard paused, then nodded.

"She knew," I said to myself. It was shocking, and yet, unsurprising. Of course she knew. She was in on all of this.

My thoughts turned back to my grandfather. "He was alive this whole time?" I asked. I was confused, and anger was starting to set in. All these years, he was alive, but kept from me. "Where is he now?" I demanded.

"He lives within the caves."

"Like here?" I asked, motioning to my own cave-like home.

"Not here, but yes, like this."

"Where? I want to see him."

Richard looked at the floor.

"I want to see him," I said again. My voice cracked, and I felt the sting of loss rise in my face.

"I don't know exactly where he is. No one does," Richard said.

"But you said you've been keeping him alive." I was beginning to break down into tears.

Richard saw my frustration and pain. "I do, but I don't see him. I just make sure he has what he needs. There's a drop place. He knows where and when. There's a signal I have that he can hear. We decided from the beginning it was better that way."

I was confused, angry, and mostly devastated by this news. I'd been lied to by those I'd trusted, and what they had been hiding would change my life forever.

"Was it because of what he did to Clara?" I asked.

"Yes."

I looked down, crushed. "So what they said was true? He did hurt her?"

Richard shook his head. "He didn't hurt Clara. He saved her."

"What do you mean? I thought they accused him of hurting her."

Richard's face fell. "He was, but that's not what happened."

"Then tell the truth and let him come home."

"Milo, it has nothing to do with that. When Clara drowned in the stream, Jorge saved her."

"Then he's a hero."

Richard paused, his brows furrowing in thought. "Yes."

"Then let him come home," I pleaded again.

"I can't. He's not the same. When that all happened, it changed him. He turned, and it's no longer safe."

"Turned into what, a thing with wings? Why would saving Clara do that?"

Richard sighed and twisted in his chair.

"Tell me what's going on. I deserve to know," I demanded.

A shroud of weariness spread across Richard's face.

"It's my grandfather. Tell me what's wrong with him."

Richard swallowed hard. "He saved her by using his blood to bring her back."

The confusion I felt was evident on my face. If what he was telling me was true, then Clara had actually died that day. I'm not sure why it was hard for me to comprehend, especially with what I had already seen.

Then my mind turned to Ivan. It was true. I had seen it myself. It wasn't like a blood transfusion. Our blood was literally a vehicle to bring someone back from the dead.

"If he saved her, why did he have to leave? You could have shown what he did, proved he hadn't hurt her." I thought about how it had ruined my family and changed my life. And it didn't have to happen. He didn't have to leave if they had explained and proved what he did.

"Milo, I wish that was the case, but it isn't. It doesn't work that way, and you're grandfather knew this. Once they use their blood to save another, they must have the blood of others to survive. That is why he's not safe."

I flinched. "The blood of others? You mean...? No. He wouldn't."

"It's not something he can control."

"Not my grandfather. He'd never do that."

Richard nodded sympathetically. "In most ways, he isn't your grandfather. That man was gone a long time ago."

I shook my head. "Then why do you keep him alive? If he's a killer, why do you help him?" I said it more like an accusation than a question.

"Because of Clara."

Nothing made sense. I gave an aggravated huff. "You keep him alive because he saved her? But he's kept away from us?"

Richard nodded. "I told you he isn't safe. He has to be kept away from everyone because of what he is now. All I knew was I had to keep him alive for Clara's sake. I keep him alive to keep Clara alive."

"What?"

Richard looked tired. "Milo, Clara is tied to Jorge. That is how it works. He used his blood to save her. Now her life is connected to him."

My face showed my confusion.

He took a deep breath. "If Jorge dies, Clara dies," he explained.

"How? Why?" I asked.

"As with all of this, I'm not sure about everything, but I do know that if Jorge dies, so does my granddaughter, and that is the only part I care about. That is why I keep him alive."

"You were friends before all that happened. Did you know what my grandfather was?"

Richard proceeded to tell me of his days as a DEA agent and the horrific way he'd found my grandfather, hiding and scared. He explained why they'd been looking for the drug and the terrible scenes of murdered boys tied to it. Richard was more than my grandfather's friend, he was his protector even back then, and because of what had happened with Clara, it continued to this day.

I felt defeated. "I'm like him. Remember the fish?" I asked, recalling the day at Clara's house when the fish came back to life. "Wings and weird blood. You knew about us. Why did you even allow Clara to be near my family at all?"

He looked at the floor. "I knew what your grandfather carried, but we thought it was over. He was the last of them, or at least we thought. We had never seen a case in girls, so when he and Esmeralda had your mother, we figured it was over."

"What does Clara know?" I asked.

"Nothing. We knew she saw something that day at the cliffs, but with everything else that happened, and with you both being so young, we hoped you would both just forget."

I looked up at him and shook my head. Forget? I could never forget that horrible day. In one quick moment, my world came undone.

"I'm sorry, Milo. We did what we thought was best. For years, there were no signs of it, and then all of a sudden, it was back. We had become complacent, and unfortunately, we didn't see the signs until things got out of our hands, and by that time, Diablo was also aware. Now they're back. We keep you here because they can't get to you."

"Who are they? Who's Diablo?"

Richard was reticent to answer. He looked pained and also frustrated. "He's the one that started all of this. The first one we knew of. We thought we had destroyed him, but now we know that isn't the case."

"What does he want with me? With us?" I asked, motioning to the other cells.

"He knows the power of the blood and the ash. That's what he's after."

"He plans to kill me for it?"

Richard sat up straighter and took a deep breath. "And that's why we brought you here. To protect you."

My head was spinning. I kept asking him questions, but nothing made sense. He finally gave up and went to get Dr. Davila so he could try to explain more. He apologized as he walked from the room.

When he left the chamber, I stared at the empty chair. My mind was spinning with what I now knew and how it all connected in my life. What happened that day near the caves when we were young and how it had changed my life became more evident. My grandmother's stories and her anger toward Clara were beginning to make sense. But it was still unfathomable.

When the door opened again, it was both Richard and Dr. Davila. Richard sat again in the chair, and Davila, leaning on his cane, stood at my cell.

"Thomas?" I asked him, still unaware if he was alive or dead.

Davila just shook his head.

"Dead?" I asked. The murdered guard and Thomas with his monstrous form hovering over him should have been the most disturbing part of what I'd witnessed tonight. Yet, seeing Thomas shot and knowing he was dead left me numb. I could barely stay upright as my thoughts raced. From seeing Peter in his horrifying state to Thomas to hearing my grandfather was still alive and his fateful tie to Clara, I felt my world spinning out of control.

"I'm sorry," Davila said.

I looked up at him, appalled. The words were like sandpaper, harsh and gritty against me. "Sorry?"

Richard sat with his head hung, and my mind went back to what he had said about my grandfather and Clara. My grandfather had saved her with his blood, and to keep Clara alive was to keep my grandfather alive.

The realization of what that meant was like a punch. I turned toward Ivan's cell. Ivan. If Thomas was dead, was Ivan dead, too? I had seen the resurrection of the boy. "Oh, Ivan," I whispered.

Davila looked over to the cell. "Where is he?" he asked. He looked back at me. "Did the nurse come for him?"

My heart began to race, and my eyes stung with tears.

"What is it, Milo?" Richard asked, seeing my distress.

"He saved him," I said, remembering the day Ivan had died and then brought back.

Davila came to me. "Who saved him? Where did he go?"

I shook my head. It couldn't be. Not Ivan, too. "Thomas," I whispered. "Thomas saved Ivan. It was yesterday morning." I explained what had happened with the guard and how he'd used Thomas to bring Ivan back to life.

Davila came to the bars of the cell. His hand clenched the bars as he looked in and saw the pile of ash. "God, no."

"Is that him?" I asked. "Is that what happens?" I looked at Richard, and he knew I was thinking of Clara.

He raised his shoulders slightly. His face looked unsure. Standing up, he walked to Davila. He was silent and bit his bottom lip.

"Yes," Davila answered my question. "They turn to dust."

I couldn't speak. I just stared at the mound in the middle of the floor. I lifted my hand and looked at my ash-covered fingers. I wanted to brush the remains away immediately. "No," I said, feeling sad and sick. I closed my eyes and wept.

Somberly, Davila came back with a box. He knelt, using his cane as a prop, and with a small spade, scooped the ashes and carefully laid them inside.

I sat on my cot and watched. "What now?" I asked when he finished.

"We'll make sure he is buried," Davila tried to assure me.

"But what about his family? Will they ever know?" I asked.

Davila began to speak, but I interrupted him.

"What about all our families? What's happening to them? My grandmother was with you when you brought me here. Where is she now?"

"She is back with your mother," he said.

"What did she say about me? Did she tell my mother?"

"No."

I shook my head, confused. "Does my mother think I just left?"

"Yes. You ran away."

"And I never go back?"

Davila came over to my cell. "I don't know. We've had no time to prepare for this. We thought it was over decades ago. We tried to allow your grandfather to live outside of this, and it didn't work. The draw to turn and become an Oscuros was too great. We don't want the same thing to happen to you."

"Oscuros?" I asked.

He nodded. "That is what they are called when they turn. When they kill is when they turn."

"But my grandpa saved Clara. He didn't kill her," I argued.

"He used his blood to bring her back. Now he will forever need the blood of others."

I lowered my head. "It's a curse."

Richard came back into the room, looking as though he'd aged in that short amount of time.

I thought about my life when I was young and happy before that terrible day. If my grandfather hadn't saved Clara, would he have lived an everyday life? "What if I don't fledge? If I control it from happening..." I tried to argue.

Richard's face turned to sorrow. He had heard that argument before.

"It will eventually happen. There is no stopping it," Davila said.

"What if I make sure it happens when it's dark and never use my blood...I won't turn. I won't become an Oscuros," I pleaded.

"You'll still be hunted, Milo, just like your grandfather," Richard said.

"But my grandfather has been able to stay alive."

Then Richard looked down as though he was ashamed of the part he'd played in allowing my grandfather to live and kill. "Jorge is still alive because he's lived hidden and alone in these lava caves. Diablo didn't detect him, so he thought there were no more. But Diablo is back now, and he knows you and the others are here. We've seen some terrible things. That is how we know Diablo is close."

"Then we should find him and stop him," I said, turning and

pacing in my cell. "He can't keep killing people. Why haven't the police been called?"

Richard gave an exhausted laugh. "This isn't something for the police. They may see the killings, but this isn't something we can let get out. We're trying to find him. We thought we had rid the world of them all, but..."

"But how?" I asked. "If he has lived this long, can he be killed?"

Davila cleared his throat. "Yes, but there are only a few ways that will truly kill the Oscuros."

I thought about Thomas, and my breath caught.

Davila saw my pause but continued to explain. "Many have been killed by fire. For the ashes, for the drug. The fire releases the wings, and it also kills."

"He burns them, not knowing for sure if they're one of us?" I heard the words, but they struck me as so odd, I repeated them to myself. "One of us." Had I really accepted my fate?

Davila nodded. "And Diablo isn't the only one. Others know about the drug. That's how I first learned about Milagro. We thought it was just another drug we had to fight, like heroin or cocaine. It wasn't until later that we found out more. There were so many killed back when this first started. It was a crap-shoot. They came from Mexico and ended up in this area. We think it was because they could hide in the caves and work in the fields. They did migrant farm work, so they were able to blend in."

"But I thought my grandpa was from Nicaragua," I said.

"We found Jorge after he'd been kidnapped," Richard said. "He was on his way here to escape. He was with a group, but the others were killed."

"He was the last of them?"

Richard shook his head. "Eventually, we found others. We kept them here at the colony, but then, they were either caught by Diablo, they died after surgery, or they turned, and we had to..." He looked down.

I knew what had happened. They had to kill them to save others. And now he was faced with me and the choice they would have to make if my fledge turned me into a killer. Thomas had turned, and they couldn't save him. And then, my heart sank as I thought about Peter.

Richard licked his lips. "There were a few of the boys who escaped. We thought maybe we had made a mistake, that they weren't part of it. There was no sign of it returning. Now I think we were wrong. They may be part of what's happening now."

"What about Peter and Alex? Where are they?" I asked.

Davila shook his head. "They've escaped."

"Have they turned?" I asked. Then I remembered Peter's large wings and red glowing eyes. "Will you try to kill them to stop it?"

Both Richard and Davila refused to answer.

I refused to let them stay silent. "What about my grandfather? You're keeping him alive because of Clara. If he dies, so does she," I said, thinking what a cruel turn that was.

Davila gave a weary sigh.

"Who's going to keep my grandfather alive after you're gone?" I asked Richard. "Do you expect Clara's life to end when yours does?"

He lifted an eyebrow, and I knew he had thought this very thing before.

"Someone will have to continue," I said. "If not me, then who?"

TWENTY-NINE

Milo

It was time. I could no longer ignore the pain, nor could I stay and do nothing and allow the people I loved to continue out there alone and in danger. I had no idea what I faced, but I knew the one person I could go to for help—my grandfather. Regardless of what they had told me, he would never harm me, and he knew better than anyone about what I was facing.

I wanted and needed to see him, and not just to prove to myself he was still alive.

My sleep had become disrupted with dreams of what I would turn into. In some dreams, I was soaring above the expansive valleys and craggy cliffs dotted with junipers and sage, skimming the river and feeling the elation and lightness I had missed in my life for so many years.

In others, the visions were dark, and I'm covered in the warm wetness of slaughter. My face, chest, even my hands were soaked in it. I'm sickened, and all I can do is cry out and try to wipe it off me. The idea of it in my mouth made my stomach heave, and I started to wretch. I awakened in the light and expected to see the gory scene, but instead, I saw white sheets, crumpled and damp with sweat.

I planned to go out again and make my way around the cavern—not to escape, but to learn the path, so when I do, I'm prepared. At night, I heard voices and felt the slight presence of those Davila calls the Oscuros, or Dark Ones. They were the ones who had turned. I knew they were out there, waiting. I had no idea what they would try to do to me. Davila said they would want me to join them, to feed off my energy, my blood, and add to their strength. And if I refused, they would try to destroy me and take my wings to burn and produce the drug they call the miracle—Milagro.

I was scared, but the pain coursing through my back and body shrouded the fear of what I faced. It intensified my desire to strike out and take that leap. If I could get to my grandfather, I felt I would be safe, and he would have the answers I was searching for.

For the next two nights, I crept out of the chamber, using the stolen key. I quietly made my way through the dark corridors and took mental notes on what turns to take to get back to that large door leading outside. I still wasn't sure if I would be escaping to a high overlook on a cliff top or would have to climb out of a rocky fissure in the ground.

They told me the location of the cavern was in the desolate desert plains of Massacre Rocks. My own home was only ten minutes from this place, but the expanse of land included in that name was so vast that I could be a hundred miles from where I thought I was.

The first night, I returned to the room where I had seen Thomas killed. That was where I'd find the door to the outside.

The door was large, almost the size of two doors, and I listened through the walls and knew the area was free of voices or movement. The room next to it was the kitchen. I crept into the area and scanned the room for anything that might help me in my escape.

On the counter was a box of Pop-Tarts. The top was open, so I took two. I also found a bag of shelled almonds. I placed it all under my arm, but when I turned to leave, the block of knives caught my eye.

The idea of a weapon gave me pause. I was determined to leave the cavern, but the idea of hurting or possibly killing my captors to achieve my escape was unsettling. Even after seeing Thomas killed during his escape, I was confident I would be able to make my way out without an encounter or need for a knife. Still, I hesitated, which made me wonder if the changes I was experiencing affected more than just the growths on my back.

When I got back to my cell, I felt relieved and exhilarated with my finds. My plan was coming together, and I felt ready to take on my quest.

On the last night before my planned getaway, as I did the final tracing of my escape route, I stopped at the door where I had found Peter. They said he had escaped, but I didn't know if I should believe them. I wanted to see for myself if he was still there.

I stood wondering if he was still inside, should I offer him the means of escape? Even though his transformation was frightening, I still felt guilty for leaving him behind before, even though our attempted getaway had been in vain.

Before I had time to decide, my hand was turning the handle. I took a deep breath and stepped inside. I couldn't see or hear anything, so I called his name, "Peter?"

There was only silence. I knew capture was a risk, but again,

I tried to rouse him. I walked closer to the cell bars and strained to see or feel any sign of him in the darkness. "Peter?" I said again.

As my eyes adjusted, I could decipher a bed, sink, and table in the cell. But nothing else. I felt no other presence with me, so I knew I was alone. I wondered if I was in the right room, but felt confident I had taken the same path. I turned to leave, and when I opened the door, another of my dreams came rushing back.

I was in my cell on my bed and heard the click of the chamber door. I was still groggy from being sedated, but listened to the padding of footsteps creep in and pass my cell. Someone whispered Ivan's name. I felt their presence hovering, waiting, and then the sound of a defeated sigh came past me. When I heard the door handle click to open, I peered up enough to see Peter leaving.

I know now it hadn't been a dream. On his way to freedom, he'd wanted to release Ivan. But when he hadn't found him, he had left behind the key Ivan had given him. He hadn't seen or wouldn't have known that Ivan was already free.

I wondered if Peter had made it out alive. And if so, what had happened after he emerged from the cave with large dark wings and aware of what he was?

I made my way quickly back to the chamber and crawled into bed. As I lay there trying to go to sleep, I wondered if Peter would be my friend or foe in the outside world. Neither Richard nor Davila would tell me what had happened to him or if he had turned, so I didn't know what to expect. I questioned whether or not I would ever see him again.

The dreams were now happening every night. In most, I was frantic and running. My arms, shoulder, even my head were being grabbed and pulled, but I was able to break free and sprint through the dim corridors. I was lost, but following the only light I could see in the hope it would lead me out and away from the darkness.

My feet were bare and the floor was cold stone, just like the walls and ceiling—an endless tunnel through the earth. I saw a door, and when I burst through it, there were prison cells with lost faces looking at me to save them. Their hands were reaching through the bars, and I only backed out of the room and continued my flight. I heard the voices chasing me, calling for me to stop, but I continued to run.

Another door, and again, I opened it to find an enormous pit and the bright sky above. I've found the escape. And then, I saw them. There were others all around me. They were jumping into the pit. Their faces showed terror, and when their wings opened, instead of soaring into the sky, they cried out in pain, and like a match to a moth, they burned in the air and fell from the sky like ashes floating from a campfire.

I watched in horror as one after the other followed, each one seeing the same horrible burning fate until none were left and I was the only one standing at the cliff. It was my turn to jump, and then the voices chasing me were no longer behind me but in my head.

I woke up, and I still couldn't believe where I was and what turns my life had taken.

After what had happened to Thomas and the guard, the nurse or Dr. Davila was now delivering my morning breakfast tray. I never saw the other guard again. I heard him speaking through the walls at night, but even that had become less and less.

On the day of my escape, it was Dr. Davila who came in. He opened the gate, set the tray on the table, and asked me how I felt. I told him I was okay and started to eat because I felt awkward, knowing what I'd planned for that night.

"We've been speaking to some people who may be able to help us. It's gone on too long without getting others involved. We have medical concerns as well as the obvious safety issues, and we need more support."

I looked at him, confused. "What do you mean?"

"I want help in finding and..." he paused, "getting rid of Diablo."

I raised my eyebrows in surprise. "Help from who?"

"There are enough people who already question my research and the crimes that have happened close to here that we need to enlist others. Even the people we've hired here are questioning our mission. We will most likely go to the CID, which is a division within the FBI that investigates the most violent of cases."

"But what about my grandfather?" I asked. "There is no one that will allow that to continue. And who will believe any of this anyway? They'll think you're crazy. I'm right in the middle of it, and I don't believe half the stuff I've seen."

He swallowed hard. "It will take some convincing, just like before. All of us who were involved from the beginning didn't believe it at first. We thought Jorge was the last of them. But that's all changed now. We scrambled when we knew it was back, but this is just a Band-Aid to what we really need to do. What we should have done decades ago."

"If you take out Diablo and the others who have turned..."

"The Oscuros," Davila said with a nod.

"Yes. If you find the help you need to get rid of them, what does that mean for my grandfather? Isn't he one of them?"

Davila tilted his head and pursed his lips in a gesture of not ultimately putting my grandfather in the same bucket.

I wasn't convinced. "What does Mr. Wilson say about this?"

Davila told me Richard was not only aware of the plan, but supportive of it.

I nodded, but still wanted to hear it from Richard himself. "When is this supposed to happen?" I asked.

"Soon. I hope that by doing this, you won't have to stay locked up. We can find the resources needed to keep you safe, as well as others."

Like Peter and Alex? How many others could there be? I put my fork down and sat up from the table. I took a deep breath. "What if my back won't wait? What if it happens before the help arrives?"

"That's why you need to stay calm and be patient. Besides, we need you to prove what possibilities there are. To show this doesn't have to be a bad thing and that something positive can come of it." He smiled, and I shivered inside, realizing I had never seen him smile before. It was forced and awkward.

Good things? Up to this point, I had seen only pain. There was no upside. I looked at Davila, and suddenly felt unsettled and wary. "When is Mr. Wilson supposed to come back?" I asked.

Davila hesitated, but when he saw my concern, he quickly spat out, "He's had some issues he needed to take care of."

"Like what?"

"Nothing to worry about." That smile again. "Just some stuff at home."

"Is it about Clara?" I asked, my heart suddenly racing.

"No," he answered too quickly. "I told you it's nothing for you to worry about. He'll be back soon."

He reassured me again and emphasized the importance of my staying calm as he left the chamber.

I sat stunned. My plans to leave that night were now in

jeopardy. I debated what to do. Could there be a way to make this all work, to live a life outside this cell? I wondered if this new development would allow me to see my family. And Clara.

THIRTY

Milo

I stewed the entire day about what Dr. Davila had said and what it could mean for me. I wanted so badly to believe him, but he'd never assured me they would spare my life if, after my fledge, I turned.

That night, I sat on the edge of my bed and felt the pains resonate in my back. I knew it would be happening soon. There was part of me that wanted to have the comfort of Davila and Richard nearby when it took place. They knew what I was and understood.

As I stilled my mind to ease the pain, I heard Davila's voice. It was odd to hear him since he was usually never there at night. And then another voice spoke that I'd never heard before.

Davila called him Charlie, and his voice was antsy and winded. They spoke about lab tests and the potency of our blood. Davila had been taking my blood regularly since I'd arrived, but I'd just assumed it was to monitor my health. I allowed it because I saw the others sedated when they'd refused.

"You told me there would be more," Charlie said. "Where is it?"

"We don't have it," Davila answered.

I heard Charlie huff. "It's been weeks since we knew they were here. I can't hold off." He paused. "If I go much longer, something will happen."

"I gave you blood," Davila told him. "I have stored what I can. Stay here, and I'll go get it."

"I need the other. You said you'd have it," Charlie pressed.

"We haven't been able to locate it yet."

Charlie huffed. "This is about Richard. He's still standing in the way."

I wasn't sure if Dr. Davila was telling this man the truth, but a chill went through me when he told Charlie that Richard was uncooperative and no longer part of the plan. If it was true, what plan did they have that would exclude the one person involved in all this who I still trusted?

I heard Charlie give an impatient sigh. "You have what you need right here. If you wait, they'll turn and be worthless."

Davila's voice was now loud and urgent. "We can't just burn these boys. You know that."

I gasped. At first, I didn't believe what I'd heard. My mind reeled back to the room with the kiln and the wretched smoky stench. Is that what they planned to do?

"What about before?" I heard Charlie counter. "You were the one who said it was for the good of the whole."

"It was different. We thought those boys were dangerous." It was an urgent but hushed whisper. "It wasn't about the drug."

I thought about Davila's explanation for the wings and the drug they produced. What benefit did Davila have to help me if it wasn't to harvest my wings? I was nothing more than a lab rat, a commodity. Seeing what had happened to the others, I knew my life was in danger. Mr. Wilson wouldn't allow them to hurt me, and I began to wonder if he wasn't merely in the way, desperate to save his granddaughter. Like my grandmother, he probably thought he was protecting me, but instead, I was handed over to be ripened and harvested like livestock.

And now they were coming for me. I had no choice but to flee.

Charlie scoffed. "You told me if I stayed quiet and didn't stray, you would keep me supplied. For over thirty years, I've done what you asked."

"I know that, Charlie. And if I had it, I would give it to you. But I don't."

"I know you have them here. I can sense them."

I heard Davila sigh. "They were here. But they escaped."

"All of them?" Charlie sounded incensed. I could hear the desperation in his voice. Who was he, and what connection did he have to this?

"Yes. All of them."

My stomach tightened. Davila was lying to protect me. I was the only one left.

"I don't believe you," Charlie raged. "Why are you still here if they're all gone? Show me! Take me to the cells."

"I can't do that," Davila said.

I heard Charlie huff. He knew it was a lie. "You will. And you'll do it now."

I heard a click.

"Charlie, we'll figure this out," said Davila. His voice was anxious. "Put that away."

I knew then that the click I'd heard was a gun. Charlie had Davila at gunpoint and would soon be at my cell.

I heard footsteps and knew I needed to hide.

I didn't have time to doubt myself, so I took the items I had pillaged and shoved them into my pillowcase. For a moment, I regretted my decision to leave the knife behind. I was feeling afraid and vulnerable.

I opened my cell using the key and quickly ran to the chamber door. I listened, wondering what path to take once outside the bunker.

My heart pounded as I waited to focus on the sounds and senses of life throughout the cavern. And when the noises were distinct and heading toward me, I knew it was time to make my escape.

I dashed from the bunker and took the path that led away from the voices but circled back toward the main door.

I ran, still trying to hear and sense where they were. I had to make it out before they got to the bunker and saw I wasn't there.

The string of lights ended, and I stopped. I stood in the dark, trying to hear through the walls, but nothing was coming through. While still trying to catch my breath, I stilled my mind. The silence was deafening, so quiet, I wondered if my ability to sense the outside had ended. I had to keep going.

I felt my way through the craggy rock walls toward the room where I'd seen Thomas killed, and then a sound as shrill and as loud as what had pierced my ears before echoed through my head. I knelt, covering my ears in an attempt to buffer them. As it subsided, I quickly continued toward the exit, but then it came again. They must have discovered I was gone.

With my hands over my ears, I stumbled toward the room, and soon the light came into view. I slowed my pace and grimaced with the pain in my ears. When the ringing stopped, I stood and tried to focus on my quest. I could feel a presence, and knew they must be close; however, it wasn't the usual sensations I felt when they were near. This was confusing. I had become adept and aware of the particular sounds and movements of life, and this wasn't it. I became even more anxious to escape.

I moved as quickly as I could, knowing the shrill blast would return. Soon, I arrived at the end of the hall, where the room opened into the large area filled with supplies and a cleared path to the massive metal door. I was alone. It couldn't be that easy, I thought. And I should have trusted my instincts.

I quietly and slowly turned the large handle and pulled it just enough to open a small slice of space for me to squeeze through. The cool air of the night rushed in, making me gasp. I quickly slipped through the opening and out onto the large terrace. I was outside.

The sky was black and cluttered with stars. I looked for a path down, but in the darkness, I could only see the steep edge. The shine of the moon illuminated what looked like a possible trail, but the moment I stepped toward it, I heard a click. I spun toward the noise, and there, I saw red eyes.

They burned like embers in the dark night. My breath caught, and I wanted to run.

The piercing squeal began again. The pain throbbed in my ears and began to radiate throughout me. My back was on fire, and I knew I had one choice and one chance to be free.

"Lay back."

I could hear her voice, but I knew it couldn't be real. The sickening swell of defeat flowed through me. They must have shot me with the tranquilizer and taken me back inside the colony. Again, my head was swimming and my eyes were blurred. I was trapped again, and now must wait in my cell until they take my life. I let a defeated moan escape me.

"You're safe now," I heard the voice again, and it felt like a slap. As if they were playing games with me.

I forced my eyes to focus, and what I saw was her dark weathered face and flowered dress.

"Grandma?" I asked.

She stroked my head and put her hand on my cheek.

I could see she was real, and then I began to sob.

She tried to comfort me, and soon, I was able to speak. "Where am I?" I asked.

"Home," she said.

I struggled to sit up.

"Lay back. You're with us and safe now."

"My mom is here?" I asked.

"No, not that home. This is somewhere else."

I took a deep breath, hoping she didn't mean the colony. Did she still think that was where I should be?

"I've got to get away from them," I said frantically. "They want my wings. They aren't trying to help me."

She put her hands on my face and tried to steady me. "No one will find you here."

The exhaustion set in, and I lay back.

I must have slept for hours, but I wasn't sure. When I awoke, I looked around and saw exactly what I feared. I was in a cave. Jagged rock walls surrounded me, and I lay on a small bed. I was back at the colony, which was all I could figure, but I saw I was not in familiar surroundings when I looked around. An old wood stove sat against the wall, and sparse, simple furniture was scattered around the space. A cord of bulbs gave off a dim light, but there were no cells, no metal bars to hold me in.

When I sat up, I heard my grandmother's voice from behind me. She was telling someone I was awake, and when I turned to where she was, I saw the man I'd missed my whole life. The sight of him was both astounding and devastating.

"Grandfather?"

He stood hesitantly, as though he'd leave again if I made a

scene. I felt my eyes well with tears. He looked at the ground, and then at my grandmother.

"Why?" That was all I could sputter through my tears.

"He had to. It wasn't his choice," my grandmother tried to explain, knowing my sorrow.

I tried to calm myself, surprised that I was more angry than glad to see he really was alive. I put up a hand to silence my grandmother and asked the question directly to him. "Then why are you back now?"

"I'm not back," he said, his voice hoarse and low. It's not what I remembered at all. "I've always been here."

I was confused by this. I looked around the room again. "The colony?" I asked.

"No," they said in unison.

My grandmother spoke again. "This isn't the colony."

"Then where are we?"

"He brought you here. He got to you before they could and brought you back here." Her hands were outstretched as if begging me to believe her. "I didn't know until he brought me to see you. He saved you from them."

"Saved me?" I remembered them coming after me, my narrow escape from the cavern, stuck at the top of a mesa surrounded by sheer cliffs. I remembered trying to climb down the steep side and making it to an outcropping, only to have them trap me with guns aimed down. I remembered the shot, the debilitating faintness, and the same slide into darkness as before. I was drugged.

"Why did you take me there?" I snapped at her. "They planned to kill me."

"I didn't know. I thought they could protect you. Richard did, too. When he learned the truth, he warned me—warned us." She looked over at Jorge.

"Richard?" I asked. My head was spinning as I took it all in.

They both nodded.

"If this isn't the colony, where are we?" I asked.

"This is where your grandfather has been living all these years..."

I interrupted her and turned on him. "I still don't understand why you left us. Richard said you saved Clara. He could have protected you."

He took a deep breath and shook his head slowly.

"You could have stayed with us," I said, the tears beginning to burn my eyes.

Looking up at me, I saw his eyes flicker in the dim light. There was a glow of red, and I shuddered. When he saw my discomfort, he turned to leave. That was when I saw the wings.

"What are we?" I demanded. "How did this happen to us?"

"It wasn't supposed to happen," he lamented. "It wasn't supposed to be in you." He took a step toward me, and I leaned back.

Seeing the uneasiness in my eyes, he stopped. "You should be scared," he said. "And when the sun goes down, no one is safe. That is why I'm not with you."

"Would you really hurt me?" I asked.

He shook his head. "No, but I'll never allow you to see what I've become."

I stood up. "Is this what I'll become?"

His eyes closed tightly in lament.

Esmeralda went to comfort him, but he brushed her aside. He turned, and I called to him. "Don't leave. Please don't leave me again."

CHAPTER

THIRTY-ONE

Milo

My grandmother left when the sun was still bright. She would need to walk the few miles down the hillside trail to get back to the house before my mother returned from work.

It was still hard to believe my grandfather had not only been alive, but had been living this close to us all along. However, it was still a long walk, even if you weren't an older woman.

I remembered as a child seeing Esmeralda's shoes covered in dust and her white stockings dingy when she returned home. I never imagined where her walks had led, and I now knew why she'd never allowed me to follow her.

I went to the opening of the cave when she left. I stood in the sunlight and looked out over the valley. The view was enchanting, yet I hated what I saw because it was the same view I had every day since my family had been forced into isolation at the house at the cliffs. The earthy colors of the rocks and the muted greens and grays of the sagebrush were what I saw

303

every time I'd stepped out of my house. It was what was there when I slammed the front door and looked through angry and resentful tears. And when I'd daydreamed about the way my life was and stared out my bedroom window, this had been my view.

My grandfather had walked my grandmother to just outside the opening, still within the shade. I watched them say their goodbyes as he touched her hand. There were no words, but their faces spoke volumes. I didn't know when she'd return, but she planned to find Richard and ask for help. He would know where to find my grandfather through a high-pitched whistle they used as a signal. I didn't ask what the call meant because I already knew. But there were so many other things I didn't know and wanted to ask. I wondered if my time alone with my grandfather would allow for it.

The idea of being alone with him was unsettling. I didn't fear him, but I felt awkward, and was aware that he felt that way, too. I went back inside before he could see my unease. What would this night bring? The visions I'd had of what I would do if I had the chance to face him again had faded. I was still coming to grips that it was even real, and I sensed he was unsure how to proceed.

"Thank you for saving me," I said when he came back inside.

He paused in the doorway and looked at the ground. He shook his head slowly. I watched, wondering what he was thinking and feeling. Had I angered or upset him?

"Milo, I'd do anything for you." He said it softly, yet with such intensity that I immediately apologized.

It only made things worse. He looked up at me. His eyes were full of angst and tears. "I'm the one who should be sorry, not you."

We both stood in silence for a moment, and then he walked

and took a chair from the table. He directed me to the other chair.

"Is this where you've always lived? I mean since..." I stumbled over my question.

He gave a sad smile. "Yes. I need these walls, this rock. I feel better here."

"What is it about the caves?" I asked, looking around the room. "Is it the darkness?"

"Yes, but it's mainly the stone. The lava is what we were born from."

My face must have shown my confusion because he smiled. "It keeps the light and the noise away. Both can be too much for me sometimes."

"It's like a bat," I said, then swallowed when I realized I'd said it aloud.

His eyes went wide.

"Sorry," I said quickly. Again, I had spoken before thinking. "I didn't mean to call you that. It's just with the wings and the cave."

He gave a big sigh. "The Camazotz. The bat god. Where I come from, they tell stories of what it is. They also call him the death bat."

"Do you believe that? Is that what we are?"

My grandfather shrugged. "I believe it has something to do with it. We aren't the first. There've been many before us."

"Why did you leave Nicaragua? Was it because of this?"

"I didn't choose to leave. However, there are those out there that know what we are, and they know about the Milagro." He pointed to a large stone tomb tucked back against the wall.

"That's it? How did you carry it?" I asked, seeing the immense size of the vault.

He shook his head. "The Milagro is inside. It must be kept in darkness. It is the ashes of those who have passed on. What it can do is miraculous, but can also be evil. That is why we must hide. Those who know of it will hunt us. That is why I was trying to get here. I knew of the colony. Many of us had heard of it and wanted to escape to it. But we were caught before we made it. It was Richard who found and rescued me."

"So he brought you here?"

He smiled. "Kind of."

He told me how he came to Idaho and how he had planned to be at the colony with others like him. Richard had made sure he was safe, but the Oscuros were already here when they arrived, and they, too, wanted the wings.

"Many of the boys like me died. But eventually, the people who knew about us and ran the colony killed the Oscuros and thought they had ended the nightmare. They thought I was the last of them. I tried to live like it wouldn't affect me. I found a place to live near the lava caves, and then I met Esmi." He smiled, thinking about my grandmother.

Esmi, I thought. Then I thought about Davila and how he had called her that. It was the name I remembered my grandfather using, even when I was so young.

"And Richard was a good friend and helped me," he continued. "But then, that day when Clara died. I loved her just like I loved you. I had to save her. I didn't have time to think about what it really meant."

I felt my eyes become wet. "You had no choice. I'm glad you saved her. I love her."

Hearing this, he smiled. "You were so young. I hoped you wouldn't remember what had happened."

I nodded. "Yes, but Clara and I both still remember that day. We talked a little about it. We both saw your eyes, but we thought it was a monster..." I cringed when I heard the word escape my mouth.

He saw my regret. "It's true. I am a monster," he said. He

sat, and his forehead scrunched up in thought. His memories had him torn, and he sighed a bit. "I don't see how you could have seen my eyes because I wasn't in that cave with you. I saw you run out, and that's when I went in. I found her in the water."

"But I saw you," I said. I wasn't accusatory, but I clearly remembered the glow and how it had scared me. "It's why I ran out. It's why I left her. I saw you in the cave, in the dark. I didn't know it was you. I just saw red eyes. We both did. That's why I ran."

He sat up and cocked his head. "You saw red eyes in the dark?"

I nodded.

He shook his head. "I didn't turn and become Oscuros until after I saved Clara."

I thought for a moment, and it didn't make sense. But I knew what I saw, and Clara saw it, too. There was no other explanation. I shrugged. "What do you think it was?"

He thought for a moment. And when he looked up at me again, I saw the worry in his eyes.

A chill went over me. Could it have been Diablo there, waiting for us and watching us all this time? "I've heard that there are others, too."

He nodded sadly.

"Is there any chance for me to live a normal life?" I asked. "Do you think I'll ever see my mom or Clara again?"

He looked at me sadly. "I don't know what normal means anymore."

"Can I live without the wings? Can I keep the fledge from happening?"

He took a deep breath, his brow furrowing with regret. "The wings will come. They are part of you. They tried to remove them from some of us, but it didn't work. Those boys either died or were crippled. You can hide them, but not from everyone."

"What about the caves? Is this where you have to live?"

He nodded. "It's the rock that will give you what you need to survive. Without it, the cravings become almost unbearable."

"Even before you..." I hesitated. "Turned?"

He nodded. "Yes, but it was manageable, but after I turned, there was no question I needed to be here."

"What about me? What about Grandmother? Do you have the urge to kill...?" My question was so horrible, I couldn't finish it.

He shook his head. "Never," he said sternly. "I would never hurt you. I satisfy my urge for blood through other...ways. I keep what I do hidden from her, and I'll do the same with you." He walked to the backroom, motioning for me to stay where I was. When he returned, he handed me a small but heavy wooden dagger. It was rough and solid in my hand, and only the point was sharp.

I shook my head in question.

"This will kill those who have turned. It's one of the only things that will completely end our life."

I looked up at him. "I couldn't."

"To protect yourself, you must. It's all I have to offer you. Use it to save yourself."

I studied it, turning it over in my hands. "A wooden stake?" I asked. Considering what the stake was for, it felt inadequate.

"It's Quebracho. It's one of the hardest woods in the world. The trees grow where we come from. This stake will kill those who want to kill you."

I looked down, reflecting on what I had seen happen at the colony. "I saw one of the others, his name was Thomas. It was a gun that killed him."

My grandfather lowered his head, sad at what I had

witnessed. "Yes. A bullet through the heart will also work." He sighed heavily. "There are other ways, too, but to truly kill an Oscuros, they must be burned. Fire or the light of the sun on our wings. That's why it's important to cover up or simply stay in the dark."

"The sun?"

He nodded. "It robs us of energy, and flying in daylight...we'll turn to ash."

The image made me cringe. I thought of Ivan and the pile of dust on the floor of his cell. "I've seen the dust, but he wasn't one of us. Thomas's blood saved him. And when Thomas died, Ivan died, too."

He frowned. "Yes," he said, and sighed. "There are so many risks."

I sat silently, thinking. Then another wave of sorrow crashed over me. "You didn't have a choice to leave." It wasn't a question as much as a realization.

His eyes were wet and his face creased with grief. "I would have rather died than leave you, but when I did what I did, I knew I had no choice. I'm sorry, Milo."

This man who I had loved and lost gave up his life so Clara could live. He sacrificed all he had and now lived a life of isolation and carnage. As I studied him, I didn't see the dark wings or morose expression, nor did I see a discreet and brutal killer; instead, I saw my grandfather.

I cried with him. For what he had sacrificed, and for the years we had both been robbed.

He wiped his tears, patted me on the shoulder, walked to the back of the cave, and began to make dinner. It was a normal thing to do, yet it seemed odd in this bizarre and unimaginable new state of life.

I walked to the cave entrance and watched as the sun dipped and thinned into the black pool of the horizon. I wanted to go home, to resume my old life, but I knew that would be unlikely. I also didn't want to leave him. He was back in my life, and I never wanted to lose him again. I still held the stake, and with a deep and weary sigh, I placed it through the belt of my pants, resolved with what I might have to do.

As I turned to walk back into the cavern, a shrill piercing noise came from the valley. I put my hands over my ears and went to my grandfather. I found him, hands-on-ears, standing and studying a calendar on the wall. When the noise stopped, I asked him what it was.

He shook his head and continued to look at the dates. He seemed confused as he counted the numbers again.

"What are you doing?" I asked.

"It's my signal, but it's early."

I realized what signal he was talking about. It was the whistle Richard used to call him to the prey. I watched and saw his distress over the calendar. The high-pitched peal came again, and I flinched. I had been told what he had to do, and had thought I'd reconciled it in my mind, but I felt a sickening awareness now that it was happening.

"I need to go," he said, relenting to the signal. He put the knife on the table and left the half-sliced carrots in a bowl.

I started to follow him, but he stopped me. "Stay here," he demanded.

"But—"

"No. You can't go with me. I don't want you ever to see this."

I didn't argue. I felt the dread of what he had to do. "When will you be back?"

"Soon," he said. "Stay inside and keep the stake close."

"Do you have to go?" I asked. I wasn't really asking him to stay because I knew the necessity of his obligation and life. It was the timing. I had just begun to believe he was back in my life. There was so much I wanted to know and tell him.

"Yes, I have to go," he said.

Before he'd said a word, I'd known he would go, but wanted so badly to be with him. I went to the cave's opening and watched as he walked to the rim. He turned back as if wishing I wasn't there to see, but I needed to witness it. Then he fell from the cliff and disappeared into the blackness below.

It felt as if I was witnessing the same event that had taken him before. I went to the edge and looked out over the valley, but all I could see was darkness.

Only in darkness, I thought, hearing my grandmother's voice. She knew what it meant, but I wondered if she really knew the grave consequences.

Reluctantly, I pulled my sweatshirt close around me to block the wind and walked back inside the cave. There was the bowl of carrots and the knife where he'd left them. I went to where he had been standing and looked up at the calendar. A circle marked the date, but that was not the one he had pointed at when he'd heard the signal. I stood staring at the number as a horrible shudder went over me. The number he had pointed to was November 15th. If that was today, then nothing about the signal could be right. If Richard was the only one who would beckon him to the kill, then it was someone else who had given the signal that night. November 16th was Clara's birthday, so there was no chance that Richard would be anywhere else on the night before but on that overlook, waiting for the sun to rise.

I tried to rationalize that it was still early in the night, and Richard may have planned to do this and then celebrate Clara's birthday. But the more I stewed and contemplated the possibilities, the more I knew it had to be a trick.

It was a ploy to lure Jorge and destroy him.

THIRTY-TWO

Milo

It was dark, but I knew what was below and beyond this towering perch. I didn't have to see it to know the vast depth of it. I could hear the rush of the river and the echo of the canyon winds, and now I stood at the edge, knowing it was time for me to step off and into it.

The pain had become so intense, it called for me to release it and become what is inevitable. The anxiousness and anticipation were pushing me forward, and the urgency for what I must do for my grandfather had removed the fear.

The throbbing in my back intensified still. My urge for release was so overwhelming, I paced like an animal in a cage. My breathing was now like a train trying to climb a hill—I was chugging and ready to explode. No more waiting or wondering as I inhaled the Idaho breeze and became one with it.

Then I took that leap. I immediately felt the massive lurch of my stomach as I free-fell. The rush of air was frigid, and I gasped from both the cold and panic.

And then, just as the regret and terror started to overtake me, I felt my back burst open. There was pain, but also satisfaction, like a terrible itch you scratch until it bleeds. And then the jarring hit of the wind stopped my fall and sent me soaring upward.

The fear was still there, but I was also completely in awe of what was happening. It was real. I was alight. I had wings, and I was flying.

I couldn't see a thing, but I felt the space and objects around me and used my wings to veer away from what I might hit. The air rushing by me let me know how quickly I was traveling.

The wings were a part of me. I felt their movement and heard their beat. I sensed the warmth and energy of the small creatures of the desert. I was drawn to their heartbeats and coursing blood. Through these abilities, I hoped I could feel my grandfather's presence and find him.

The longer I flew, the easier it was for me to focus and detect my grandpa. I could tell where I was going. It gave me angst, yet I was pleased that my ability to navigate was already adept. A warmth rose in my chest when I wondered if my grandfather would be proud of my maiden flight.

The longer I went, the more I wished this was happening in the daylight. The idea of soaring over the immense canyon carved through the lava rock and limestone, and skimming above the mighty Snake River lined with juniper, sage, and pine was incredible. And yet, I knew the consequences exposure to the sun would bring.

I felt a swell in the earth below and rose to follow it. When I reached the bluff, I sensed life. I knew he was near.

I stayed close to the ground, and the feeling became more intense. When I came up above another rise in the landscape, I felt others were there as well, and that was when I began to panic. My heart raced with my instinct that this was a trap. I decided to land, using my senses to feel if he was near.

And then, I saw him. High in the night, I saw the red glow of his eyes. I wanted to call out to him, to warn him, but before I could, a glaring light came out of the distance and fell on me. I crouched down to avoid it, but they saw me. I heard rustles in the dry grass, and the movement was coming toward me.

I ran from the light and into the safety of the darkness. Looking back, I could see the silhouettes of two men, both holding guns. The guns weren't pointed at me, but rather, to the sky.

I yelled to warn my grandfather, but I heard the shots. They drowned out my calls as the blasts exposed the fire flare from the guns.

My warning was too late. I watched him get hit and begin to fall. As I ran to him, a loud shriek echoed across the desert, and in the dim light of the moon, I saw an ominous form pounce down upon the men with the guns. Their screams pierced the night, and the noises that followed sounded like an animal taking its prey. I cringed at what I knew were their dying pleas but continued forward, hoping that by some miracle, my grandfather had survived.

As I got closer, I could still feel his body's warmth. But I saw no movement, just a lifeless form and a mass of broken wings.

I called to him frantically, "Grandfather!" When I reached him, I shook his shoulders, trying to rouse him. He was slack and still, and when I turned him over, I saw the blood and the wound in his chest.

It couldn't be. After all this time away, to finally have him back, but for only a day. I felt my rage boil over, and I wanted to fly off and kill them all.

"There are more, and they'll be here soon."

I jumped at hearing the voice. When I turned, I saw Peter.

"You need to leave now," he urged.

I motioned to my grandfather. "He's dying. He needs help."

Peter looked at me with a mixture of frustration and sadness. "There's no time."

"No. Not without him."

"It's too late," he said with a growl.

When I looked up at him, I saw the red glow of his eyes, and now I knew what he had become. My heart dropped, and he realized I knew he was lost.

"He's still breathing," I yelled at him, unwilling to give up.

Frantically, he looked around and tried to push me away. "I stopped the two, but more will be here soon. I won't be able to stop them all. You need to go."

I ignored him. Even with what he'd done to save me, I couldn't leave my grandfather behind. I stooped and reached under his limp arms. I lifted his lifeless form and began to walk as I carried him. My anger surged with every step, and my need to rise grew stronger. I felt my wings expand, and with just a few strong beats, we were airborne. I was clumsy and slow with the extra weight, but I was able to get him back to the cliff and up the steep incline to the cave.

His body was still warm, and I was pleading through tears that my worst fear hadn't become real. I couldn't bear to lose him again.

I lay him on the bed. His eyes were slightly open, but there was no life in them. I touched his neck as my fingers trembled to try to find a pulse, but I soon realized there was nothing. He was already beginning to turn cold. I couldn't feel his force or even a weak pulsing of blood through his veins. I found no life.

"Grandfather," I whispered. "Please don't go. Please don't leave me again."

But I knew he was already gone. I'd lost him, and this time, I would never get him back.

I felt the low and guttural sob begin in my chest, and when I looked up, I saw the carrots in the bowl and the knife where he'd left them.

Then I saw the calendar, and what I thought couldn't get worse completely wrecked my world.

My grandfather was gone, and so was Clara.

THIRTY-THREE

Milo

All that I'd fought for and desired was gone. Without those I loved in my life, the threat of Diablo was meaningless. What did I have to lose? I was unsure what path my life would take, and now all roads led to empty fields.

For several hours, I sat with my grandfather's body. I wrapped him in a blanket but left his face exposed. I wanted to see him for as long as I could. I spoke to him as though he could still hear me, the way I'd dreamt for so many years. The way we did when life had seemed so right. And I cried because I couldn't save him. It was so unfair that what I had running through my veins couldn't save the people for whom I would have gladly given my life.

My heart sank when I thought of Clara and where she may have been when her end came. Then I thought about Richard and how his loss was as significant as mine. An enormous urge to be with him came over me.

The overlook, I thought. I groaned in sorrow when I realized he was probably there and had possibly witnessed the horrible event. And right there, during their special occasion. I took a deep breath and knew I needed to go to him.

It would still be dark for several hours, so I walked to where I had taken my first fall and the last time I had seen my grandfather alive. When he had looked back at me before he left, the vision of his face was that of sorrow and regret. That was how I felt at that moment. I didn't know what I could have done to save him, but the guilt weighed heavily on me as I leaped into the night to find Richard and express my sorrow.

The canyon's complete black slowly became dotted with lights as I followed the river, and it gradually opened up to the valley. I was high above and undetectable from the living beings below. Their energy played chaos on my senses, and the higher I was, the less it seemed to affect me. The area I was looking for was easy to find, even though I had never imagined it from this view.

The sun's orange glow would soon highlight the desolate mesa's beauty as it peeked out to announce the dawn. It's why he was there, to celebrate yet again the life that had changed his own. I thought of the last time I was with Clara, and my heart broke again, knowing I would be seeing and feeling everything about her as soon as I arrived.

I don't know if I was sad or relieved to see Richard's truck parked exactly where Clara had told me he had every year on that date. I knew he would be there, but wasn't sure if he'd stay after witnessing Clara's horrifying demise.

The lights were off, but I felt the warm pulsating beat of life rising from where the truck sat. He would be devastated and in shock with the mound of ashes that was once his beloved granddaughter. What would I possibly say to him? There was nothing I would be able to do, but I needed to be there.

I landed behind the truck and brought my wings in as close

to me as possible. I walked up to the driver's side. I didn't want to startle him, so I came up slowly to the window. The closer I got, the more I felt something was amiss. But of course, it was. She was gone.

Then I peered into the truck and realized it was empty. I put my face to the window and tried to see if anything was inside, and even in the dark, I could tell it was bare. I stood back, wondering where the sensation of life had come from.

Then I saw him. He was sitting at the edge of the overlook and staring out over the valley. Even in the dark, I could see he was disheveled and worn.

"Mr. Wilson?" I called to him softly.

He was startled, and when he saw me coming toward him, he put his hands up to block his face and winced back.

"It's me, Milo," I told him. I realized the darkness and the changes in my body since I had fledged had hidden who I was.

He slowly lowered his arms and tried to study me in the dark. When he spoke, his voice was low and broken. "She's gone," he said.

A frigid chill rushed over me. "I know. I'm so sorry."

"You need to save her."

I straightened, wondering what he meant and if he was in his right mind. I started to apologize for not keeping the awful tragedy from happening, but he stood and looked at me with urgency.

He pointed off to the east. "The cave. It's where she is."

I shook my head, confused. Had he lost his mind? I wondered if he wasn't mistaking the terrible loss he'd just experienced with that first awful time that Clara was lost. "I can't. She's already gone," I said sadly.

Again, he pleaded with me. "You need to save her. The cave. It's where he found her before."

"He?" I shook my head, then I realized what cave he was describing.

"Diablo," he said, defeated. "It's where you'll find them both."

When I reached the cave, I hesitated, unsure what awaited me, but more than that, I was haunted by my memories of the past. Just standing there after following the path up and through the ragged sage and black lava boulders had my heart racing, and the sweat began to pool above my lip. Knowing what I had to do made being back after all these years no less disturbing.

It looked the same as when we would sneak inside and breathe in the stark coolness of the dark hollow. So many times, we had made up scary tales while in our shadowy hideout, but it was no ghost story that had sent us running that day. Even now, I felt the fear as I stood at that cusp.

"Come inside, Emilio."

The voice was his. It was like I'd known it my entire life. It was Diablo. I felt his presence even before I heard him speak.

The mist had turned wet on my skin and made my skin prickle. The stories I had heard from my grandmother and those at the colony about the Winged Devil were no longer just in my imagination. He was real. The glow of the cavern entrance was inviting, even though I knew a sinister force awaited me inside.

A sickening dread flooded through me, and a rush of wind came up from the valley floor as though driving me forward. Pebbles crackled under my shoes with each step, and even with the orange glimmer of a flame coming from within, it seemed to get colder the deeper I went inside.

"Closer," he called to me. His voice was surprisingly lucid. I had expected it to sound old and inhuman, but instead, it was clear and almost calming.

I shuddered with a sense of familiarity as if I'd been with him before. I wanted to see him, and oddly, the horrors I had envisioned—bloodthirsty, ravenous, with glowing red eyes— were slowly falling away with every word he spoke.

There was a small flame lit in a crevice, and as I turned the corner of the dark and porous wall, there he stood, half shadowed, with the light flickering off his black clothes. He hid his face, but I could see his hand as he leaned against the cave wall. It was bony, and the veins were bulging and blue.

"All this time, they thought it was Jorge who saved her when it was actually me," he said.

This statement shook me, and I stopped and took a deep breath. "It was you that day in the cave. It was you we saw." My voice cracked, and I tried to clear my throat, but it was dry.

He laughed, and I caught a slight glimpse of his eyes as they shone from the dimness. The red glow I had remembered all too well.

"Come," he said as he stepped back into the maze of lava tunnels.

I knew nothing good would come of this, but something much more powerful than I could control was pulling me. I began to step forward when I heard a familiar, muffled cough.

My breath caught, but my instincts were to be wary. It couldn't be her. I knew she was dead, but then I heard it again. With abandon, I rushed forward and into the darkness. I had to know.

"Clara?" I called out.

"Milo," a voice returned.

My chest seized. I knew the voice was hers.

I ran, calling her name, almost in tears as the possibility of her being alive hit me. In the distance, I saw another flickering light coming from around a corner. There was no other path, both in the cave and my life, so I ran to it. I felt the pain begin in my back as the anxious fury began to build. I kept my wings tucked in close. I wasn't willing to expose what I'd become.

"Milo," she called again, and I felt her presence surge through me. Could it really be her, or was it a trap? I didn't care.

I came around the corner, and there she was, sitting by a small fire, her back toward me. She had on a black velvet gown, and her curls were darker than before. Even in the dim light, her shoulders and arms looked pale.

"Clara?" I called. My heart was racing. But when she turned back toward me, I saw a face I didn't expect, but knew.

"It's you," I blurted out. It was the woman I had seen at the school with the violin. She was wearing the same dress, and I recoiled in shock.

"Where's Clara?" I asked, then I scanned the large room, wondering where Diablo could be. The ploy to pull me farther into the cave had worked. "Where is she? I heard her."

The woman slowly stood up. The fire burned softly in a small metal cauldron on the floor. Her face, while still beautiful, now looked almost like ceramic, as if it would crack. And her eyes were the glowing green I'd seen before.

"Who are you?" I asked.

At first, she seemed somber. She studied me, and then her eyes widened and a small smile crept across her lips. "Huna?" she asked.

I flinched again. It was the name she had called me when I'd first seen her at the school.

"You are one of ours. You are of Huna. And I'm here," she said, reaching out to me.

"What?" I asked. "Why do you call me that?"

She looked at me, her expression fervent and elated. "You've returned to us. You've come back." She spoke as though I wasn't there, as if she was looking through me, into me, and searching for someone.

I backed away from her—the realization of danger and capture set in. My back began to throb, and I frantically scanned the room for an exit.

"Did you bring it?" she pleaded. "Huna, please."

Her voice and that name haunted me. They had tricked me into thinking Clara was there, and now I wanted to flee.

I turned toward the opening of the room and started toward it. Into the dark maze, I ran blindly, feeling my way with my hands against the sharp and rugged rock walls, just as I had as a child when I ran from the red-eyed monster before. My fingers began to bleed as I searched for a way out. My throat caught, thinking about the effect he'd had on me my entire life. When was I going to stop running from him, from it all?

The light of the full moon directed me to the cave's entrance. I took a deep breath, and when I emerged, that was when he appeared. Large and dark, his face still hidden by the shadows of the night, he moved and blocked my escape.

My heart and breath both heaved. I stepped back, and when he came toward me, the light of the moon exposed his grotesque face. The sight was so horrifying, I stood paralyzed, convinced it wasn't real.

The skin of his neck and face hung in listless folds, and when he parted his lips to speak, I saw rotted and fang-like teeth. But as I looked at him, I saw what I should have seen all along. When I stared into those smoldering eyes that were festering on the verge of death, I saw Victor.

"It's you," I gasped. "You're Diablo."

He raised an eyebrow, unaffected, then he sighed. "I am not the one they call Diablo. But he is my savior. And I am theirs," he said, spreading his arms toward the other Oscuros. "We all came from the two who were born of fire."

THIRTY-FOUR

Nicaragua, 120, BC
Xbalan

J ust as Masaya was beginning to shoot enormous bursts of lava, his rise began. The village people had scattered and gone back to hide in the jungle, having seen the Winged Devil, and now their god was threatening them. Even the sentries had fled when the ground began to shake beneath them.

His rise went unnoticed. His dark wings and ominous roar echoed out, but because the threat of Masaya's anger was so loud, no one knew that the twin of the Great One had also come alive.

They were of pure Camazotz blood, and now Xbalan was eager to begin his wrath over those who had dismissed him before. He knew what he carried, and now desired what he'd been denied and needed to thrive.

As the molten rain covered the valley below, he moved to the area above the palace, where he waited and watched the one he once called father carry out the killings of those who were like him. The precious miracle dust that followed is what the Camazotz carried and would cause them to turn on themselves eventually. But before these formidable and fearsome hunters turned, they found themselves as prey.

The exodus of the Winged Ones from the valley of Masaya and into the adjoining lands caused fear. Even those who had shunned the desire for blood found themselves persecuted. Soon, the Camazotz learned that to survive meant fading into the masses and assimilating into the world, keeping their deadly desires at bay as best they could. Those who turned were tied to the night to continue their scourge and hunt for the miracle.

Many lost their fight and perished. Their numbers diminished, along with the Milagro, but the attraction was so strong, so keen, the Camazotz who were left could sense it and made the pilgrimage regardless of risk or the atrocities they had to commit in attaining it.

Those who did may have held the miracle, but they never found peace in their quest to keep it.

CHAPTER

THIRTY-FIVE

Milo

"Those who follow me call me Salvador. I am their savior." Victor licked his lips and smiled. "You have the Milagro. I know the power it holds. I know how it can save, and only I know how to use it. Join me, and you, too, can be called Salvador."

He could feel my urge to kill him.

"It won't serve you well, this anger toward me. Kill me, and you kill her," he said, stepping aside to reveal Clara sitting on the ground behind his large black wings. Her eyes were wet and weary.

My entire body seized when I saw her. "Clara!" I called out, but then I hesitated, knowing Victor had tricked me before. I blinked to clear my mind and my eyes. Was this real? And if so, how could it be? I had witnessed my grandfather's death and, with that, believed she was gone, too. Was this a mirage, a vision to somehow trap me?

She looked up, and when she saw me, she cried out weakly, "Milo."

I instinctively stepped toward her, but Victor blocked me, and I realized what I now faced. I was stunned and frantic. It couldn't be true, and while I was desperate and angered, I also felt my hope restored. She was alive and here. I could see her, and more importantly, I could feel her force within me.

"How could it be?" Victor said, knowing my thoughts. He smiled. "It is the glory of first blood. You all may have thought it was Jorge, but alas, you were wrong." A sickening smile spread across his face. "I got to her first."

I felt the rage boil up into my face.

My anger only spurred Victor. "All that time, they kept him alive, and for naught. Even he thought he was the one who had saved her, but now we all know that isn't true."

I flinched at what he said. My grandfather had told me he hadn't turned until after saving Clara. I felt my body deflate. If what he was saying was true, it wasn't my grandfather's red eyes we'd seen in the cave, but Victor's. He was Diablo and lying in wait, hoping to claim his next victim. My grandfather may have rescued her from the water, but he hadn't saved her from death.

With that, my elation in seeing Clara alive sank. If Victor indeed was her first blood, not only was Clara forever connected to him, but it also meant that my grandfather's act had been pointless. I shook my head as the anger made my eyes burn. Nothing mattered now. I'd lost my grandfather again, and Clara was now Victor's.

"Why so glum?" he asked. "All is not lost. You're already part of us. You are a descendant, just like Jorge. But you can have more. You don't have to live this life alone and hidden away. You can still be with her and have all that we have."

He spread his arms out to the others who stood behind him. Dozens stood, wings rising from their backs and their eyes glowing red. "Join us. Unlike them, you'll be like me.

You'll lead the others because you, Emilio, come from the first tribe."

I cringed as he used my real name. I stood distraught, staring at Clara. I was still stunned that she was alive, yet devastated at what that meant. Again, I had failed to save her.

"Live for eternity and rid yourself of the burden you carry," he said. "Do this, and you'll be with her forever. The Milagro will bring her eternal life."

I looked back at him, defeated. Join him and be with Clara. Or what? I thought. What would I do? What would my life be like now? I could spend my life fighting him and the other Oscuros, but for what? What was I fighting for now? All I could think was that Clara was alive and tied to him.

"You've been told lies about me. We are of one blood," Victor said. "We may have come from different lines, but we both want the same things."

I shook my head.

"What is the difference in our motives?" he continued. "We both want to live and to thrive. Isn't that what everyone wants? Even animals have the same intent. They are no more evil than we are."

"I won't spend my life killing."

Victor huffed. "Every living thing must kill to survive. And every living thing must eventually die. It's a part of life. Even when you pluck a tomato from the vine, it dies."

I listened to what he said, but my eyes returned to Clara.

"The time has come for you to choose. You have the blood. You can't deny who you are. Join us, or you'll live your life alone."

I squared myself and felt the disgust of what he was saying sink in. "If you're so proud of what you do and who you are, why do you hide in the dark? What is so hideous about you that I can't see? Are you afraid to show me what I'll become?"

I wanted to draw him closer, knowing what I held in my belt.

He balked and stepped back. "I have nothing to hide, and neither should you. You want to be with her. It's what will make you happy. The only way to achieve that is to join us and live forever."

I scoffed. "I'll never become like you."

"But Milo, you already are like me. Why do you fight it? Why do you listen to them? They caged you and took you away from everything you loved. *They* killed Jorge, not me. They'll destroy you too because they don't understand. Eventually, they will fear you and kill you for what you possess. Why not accept who you are?"

"I'm not a killer."

He gave a laborious sigh. "Why is that the only thing you choose to see? It's not killing—it's survival. Your grandfather chose this path."

I shook my head. "He didn't choose it. He thought he was saving Clara."

He smiled wickedly. "Pity all that time she actually belonged to me."

I felt my face flush with anger. He saw it, and it seemed to spur him on.

"Join us, or you'll eventually die alone. You can't ignore what you are."

The rage continued to fill me because what he said was true. Regardless of what I did, I would never have a normal life. I carried with me the mark of my kind. It wasn't something I could change. Why did I think I was any different? I knew that my grandfather, Richard, and even Dr. Davila were trying to help me. They wanted a better life for me than what they had seen the others endure, but they could never really change what I was.

"We have everything you want to be happy. Endless food, endless sex." Victor smiled. "An eternity of pleasure. And with the Milagro, Clara can also live forever."

I realized then the value of the ash. That is what would keep her alive, long after her life should naturally end. It's what made the drug so precious and sought after. It was the miracle of eternal life. It's what I saw in the woman. Alive, but dead. Is that what Clara would face?

"I want to talk to Clara. I want to be able to touch her and know that it is her," I said.

With that, Clara looked up, confused. I tried to see her face, but she still looked away.

Victor sighed. "We have no time."

"I thought you had endless time," I said, lifting my chin to confront him. "I won't choose until I know."

Victor stood and contemplated my demand. After a moment, he relented and motioned for her to come forward.

She walked sullenly toward me.

"Don't be foolish and think you can take her away," he smirked. "Remember, she is tied to me forever."

I heard him, but kept my eyes on her. When she stepped close to me, I reached out and took both of her hands. "Is it you?" I asked, keeping my voice low.

She nodded, but refused to look up at me.

I bent down, trying to catch her eye, but she hesitated. A gentle roll of thunder echoed across the valley. I looked at her hands in mine. They were so thin and small. They were stark against my dirt-covered and bleeding hands, and it was the sight of the tips of my fingers dotted with blood that evoked something in me. But it wasn't the desire to kill.

They told me the commencement of my wings would create a need for blood, and through that, I would reap eternal life. But as I stood holding Clara's hands in mine, my only thoughts were to save her.

"The time is now," Victor called. "Come with us, or lose everything."

I looked over at him. The dark tips of his wings flicked in the breeze. I wondered how many years he had spent hiding what he was just to continue a death-filled life.

I turned back to Clara. "I'd rather die than live forever like this," I whispered.

That is when she lifted her head and looked at me. My heart seized, and an incredible rush of awareness shot through me—the realization of what I saw in our hands. It made my head spin and my mind play back the shuttered memories of the day I had tried for so long to forget—a storm, a dark cave, and the childhood ritual of a forever bond.

Victor wasn't her first blood—I was. It was what we were doing when the red eyes had come upon us in the cave. We had no idea the gravity of what our childhood ritual had meant. We'd seen the small cuts in our fingers and the smear of red when we placed them together as merely signifying our forever friendship. Just as we never realized the love we would later feel for each other, neither of us could have ever considered what our little act of alliance would mean.

I was so young when that awful tragedy at the cave happened, but I still harbored the shame for allowing the monster to run me off. The regret I felt in leaving Clara had never left me. The red glowing eyes were what had made me flee from our childhood hideout, and now that I knew who those eyes belonged to, I refused to let him run me off again.

My grandfather thought he was saving us all by leaving. However, he didn't know that I carried the same bane and eventually faced the same path.

A crack of lightning broke my reverie. My consciousness returned, and with it, the reality of what my birthright meant.

I rubbed the soft pad of Clara's finger with purpose. I yearned for her to understand what I'd come to realize.

She looked confused, but held my gaze, and then I heard her voice inside my head. She knew. Her eyes widened and her brows raised in the knowledge—a burning shot through my back. I caught my breath and held my composure to keep the urge from overwhelming me. My breathing became rhythmic but intense. I dropped her hands and looked over to Victor.

He was impatient, but raised his face to me as though he was confident of what I had decided. He knew nothing of what Clara and I had just shared. He still thought she was his.

I stepped in front of Clara. Standing tall, I allowed my wings to release. Again, thunder broke the silence. The storm was getting closer. I saw several of the other Oscuros recoil and look nervously toward the sky. The sunlight would send them back into the black abyss of the caverns, where forces of the lava would shelter and rejuvenate them.

Victor wasn't sure if my stance was a sign of defiance or surrender.

He leaned toward me, his voice gruff and anxious. "Come with us now." He went to grab my arm, and I instinctively backed away, and with all my force, I lunged and shoved him hard.

Startled, he stumbled backward. Then he saw the wooden stake in my hand.

"You fool," Victor scoffed, challenging me. "Kill me, and she dies, too."

I heard Clara behind me release a halted gasp, but I kept my focus on him.

He sneered with confidence, then spread his wings and

offered me his chest, knowing I would never put Clara in danger. If he died, so would she, he thought.

"He is of Huna," I heard the voice, and there stood the woman in black, her eyes as bright green as Clara's.

"Go back inside," Victor snarled at her.

And with his attention diverted, using my wings for force, I lunged toward him and plunged my grandfather's Quebracho spike into his heart.

His eyes wide with shock, Victor stumbled forward and stared to where the stake protruded. He looked up at me, unable to believe I would take his life, and Clara's life.

"You weren't her first blood—I was," I hissed at him. "You were right. It wasn't my grandfather's blood that saved her, and it wasn't yours. It was mine. That day you found us in the cave, we had made a pact. It was a blood pact." I held up my hand. "I still have the scar, and so does she."

His face went wild as life began to leave him. He turned to Clara, and instead of seeing her weak and gasping for life, she stood looking at her hand as awareness spread over her face.

A shriek rose out over the canyon as the Oscuros began to dive into the darkness. They felt their end had begun along with their savior's demise, and they were drawn to the lava caverns, trying to escape Victor's fate.

Still grasping at the impaled stake, Victor hobbled to the rim of the cliff, trying to flee with the others. With his last bit of strength, he yanked the stake out of his chest and flung it aside. With a glare of haughty satisfaction, he spread his wings and dove off the side.

I gasped in defeat, feeling what I had done wasn't enough. He would still live.

But as I watched him begin to soar, a slit of light peeled across the darkness, and the sun broke through. Then bit by bit, as daylight ignited, a shriek roared across the canyon as his demise began. It started with the tips of his outstretched wings and slowly spread over him. Like a moth lit by flame, he began to glisten and turn to dust.

Clara's face went from horror to a knitted forehead, showing her uncertainty of what it meant. There was relief in her expression, but also doubt.

The ashes shimmered and flickered in the sunlight. They whirled in the breeze and began to flutter over the canyon. A low growl followed, slowly succumbing to a dull moan, and then silence. Soon, all that was left was a wisp of dust drifting with the current of the early morning breeze.

Clara and I stood watching it together. I waited, giving her time to let the vision and Victor's end sink in.

She looked at me. "Is it over?" she asked, her voice cracking and her eyes filling with tears.

I took a deep breath. "Yes," I said, because for Victor, it was.

She closed her eyes in absolution as tears spilled down her cheeks. She leaned back and let the sun spread over her face. She felt free now. Her demon was now gone. As I watched her relief and joy, I wanted to join in her reverie, but knew this lull would be short-lived.

I looked out over the canyon and took in the view. I wondered if I could love it as I had before. The pain of what that place represented now seemed so long ago, and was slowly dissolving. Just like Victor, it had disintegrated into dust. I felt the warmth of the morning as if it was the first new day in years. As if it was the first day of my new life.

My wings were tucked back and hidden, but things would never be like they were before. My eyes were now open to what I was and what that meant. The shame and fear I'd felt for so long had been replaced with awareness and also a purpose.

I was now the keeper of the Milagro. It would be my role to protect that gift from those who would be after it, and after me.

I know its power and frailty if exposed to the light, but I also know its potential. It was up to me to hold it close and protect it.

There are those out there who wander the night, searching for a savior. When the twilight returns, they will expect me to surrender to it, relent to the desires, and be their shepherd in death. This day, I was saved by the light, but each night, when that ominous black shroud covers the valley, I will be waiting for what comes only in darkness.

Acknowledgments

I would like to acknowledge and thank the people who made this novel possible. My agent, Donna Eastman, whose generous guidance and support will always be appreciated. Beverly Wadman, my proofreader, friend, and mother. For David, whose devotion and support are why I'm able to do what I love. To Andrea von Kampen for her song "Tomorrow," which was part of my writing playlist and the muse for this novel. And for anyone who has taken the time to read my stories, I thank you. There is no greater gift for me as a writer.

BOOKS BY BRENDA STANLEY

FICTION:

The Treasure of Cedar Creek

The Still Small Voice

Only In Darkness

The Color of Snow

Like Ravens in Winter

I Am Nuchu

ABOUT THE AUTHOR

Brenda Stanley is a former television news anchor and investigative reporter for the NBC affiliate in Eastern Idaho. She has been recognized for her writing by the Scripps Howard Foundation, the Hearst Journalism Awards, The Idaho Press Club, and the Society for Professional Journalists. She is a graduate of Utah Tech University and the University of Utah in Salt Lake City. She is the mother of 5 children, including two sets of twins. Brenda and her husband, Dave, a veterinarian, live on a small ranch near the Snake River with their horses and dogs. You can reach her at her website: brendastanleybooks.com

www.ingramcontent.com/pod-product-compliance
Lightning Source LLC
Chambersburg PA
CBHW050514110726
47899CB00005B/1456